BEGIN ANEW

C.J. Roark

For J and A for seeing me through this insanity.

CONTENTS

CHAPTER ONE

"...Pinch your nipple... Twist it... Tweak it..." the seductive voice instructed. Hands drifted up to her chest on their own volition, but before the order could be carried out her eyelids fluttered open. Wide green eyes gazed back at her reflected in the floor length mirror. No sign of steel grey curls or the dark glare of The Magician loomed over her shoulder. Giving her head a shake, she ignored the faint flutter in her belly and smoothed her hand over her shirt.

"It's all in your head as usual," she muttered, reminding herself yet again that Kennett Shariq was *not* going to miraculously appear. For one thing, he didn't exist. There was also no Void, no frozen Terra Anglia, and she was certainly no Tempest Vega. She was, however, the creator of all those things.

Tucking a long strand of red hair behind her ear, she barely refrained from breaking out into her happy dance at the thought. She did, however, grin, her eyes sparkling brightly. Today was the day. The day she would embark on an adventure which would, fingers crossed, bring the characters and worlds she had slaved over for so long to life. The grin slid away as a grim face appeared beside her own in the mirror's reflection.

"Keep calm. You've got this," Carraig's voice instructed in her head and Clemency struggled to paste a smile on her face as she turned to face her husband.

"I just talked to mother. She's on her way over to watch Lucy while I drive you to the airport," Elliott informed her, his eyes focused on a spot just over her shoulder. She sighed and wondered, not for the first time why her husband wouldn't *look* at her... *see* her. She was *happy*. Her dreams were coming true. Once upon a time he would have shared in her joy. Hell, early on, when she had first embarked on this crazy quest to become a writer, he had been a huge support. Now she realized that it was only because their sex life had gone under a kind of renaissance during that time. Writing erotic fiction can have that effect on a marriage... Nowadays, the success of *Tempest* had brought only tension to their marriage. When talk about turning her novel into a film began and it appeared likely to be optioned to a studio in London, she tried to imagine a new start. Her, Elliott and their eleven-year-old daughter cozily ensconced in an English country cottage. She eventually gave up. Even her imagination wasn't that good.

She was the first to turn away, moving to examine the contents of her suitcase one final time. She felt her muscles tense as Elliott strode toward the window. She waited, blindly gazing at the luggage tag she was clutching. Was he finally going to say something? Did he really think he could talk her out of doing this now? She glanced up at him and instantly regretted it. He looked quite lost. He opened his mouth, only to shut it again before turning toward the door.

"I'll be waiting downstairs," he muttered, quietly closing the door behind him as he departed.

She let out a breath that she hadn't realized that she had been holding and unclenched her fist. The plastic tag slowly unfurled in her hand to show the name CEE CEE OLIVER. Her eyes narrowed and she reached for her trusty backpack. Digging through her pencil case, she withdrew a marker and in no time flat had replaced offending name with CLEMENCY JAMES. It may be her pseudonym, but for the next month she was determined to embrace it as her identity.

"Good girl," she imagined Carraig cheering as she hoisted her backpack onto her shoulder and reached for her suitcase. At the threshold of the room, she paused to glance back at the bed she had shared with her husband for the past eighteen years. She closed her eyes, but instead of recalling happy memories of times spent between the sheets with Elliott, she was met with

Kennett's hard gaze. He quirked one ferocious eyebrow while his lips twitched up into a semblance of a smile. Shaking her head to dislodge the image, she turned to make her way down the stairs.

She was met by a commotion as her mother-in-law barreled through the front door followed by her sister-in-law and her gaggle of children. Clemency understood that it was Thanksgiving weekend and Elliott's family was important to him, but she would have preferred to bid farewell to her daughter in a less exuberant environment. In the end, she was able to remind Lucy that she would call her every day and they would be together again by Christmas.

A light snow was beginning to fall as they drove toward the city. Watching her husband's hands grip the steering wheel, she wondered when she had stopped being aroused by the sight of his long, slender fingers. She tried to recall the way they were able to reach all the right places in all the right ways. A smile touched her lips at the thought. Maybe there was still a chance for a new beginning here. After all, didn't absence make the heart grow fonder?

"Elliott, do you think that---" she began only to be interrupted by him slamming on the brakes to avoid a family of deer darting across the road. He glared in her direction as if to blame her, and she silently turned away to watch the scenery pass by. All thoughts of trying to placate him had vanished. Instead, she passed the miles trying to imagine the adventure that lay ahead.

"Am I supposed to turn right or left?" Elliott's voice broke into her thoughts. She sat up straighter, realizing that they were approaching the airport, the city skyline glowing in the distance.

"What did the phone say?" she asked, glancing down at the screen held firmly in her hand.

"I don't know. That's why I'm asking you!" he snapped.

"Well it's not like you ever listen to me either," she retorted before biting her tongue and turning her attention to her phone. She really didn't want to leave this way. "Turn left, then stay in the right lane. That will take you straight thru to the terminal drop-off."

"You don't want me to go in with you?" he asked, glancing at her as he flicked the turn signal.

"This will be easier," she replied.

She grabbed her backpack and began double checking that everything she needed was quickly accessible as Elliott pulled up to the curb.

"Look Cee," he began, using his nickname for her. "There's something I wanted to discuss before you--"

"You're not going to talk me out of this now, E," she said with a sigh.

"That's not what I'm trying to do. You made it clear that this is your dream and you're going after it," he stated. He was focusing on his hands where they still lay on the steering wheel so she could only see his profile, but she sensed the anger in his voice. She waited as he tried to collect himself but found herself becoming impatient.

"Elliott?" she asked, laying a hand on his arm only to have him shrug it off.

"I want to take this opportunity..." he began before faltering. "What I would like, is to... Okay..."

"What do you want, Elliott?" she asked, glancing down at her phone to check the time.

"I want a break," he said, turning to face her for the first time.

"You want a... a what?" she asked meeting his eye.

"A separation," he clarified. "A trial separation. While you are away, you're free to do whatever you want, and I can--"

"You can what?" she interrupted, horrified at what she was hearing. "Is there someone else?" He averted his gaze, but there was a subtle nod as he turned to gaze back down to the steering wheel.

"Whitney?" she guessed, latching on to the name of a new co-worker who had been popping up in conversation more frequently. She struggled to keep her voice under control as he nodded again. "So, I'm off to London to work for the next month while you stay here and fuck Whitney. Is that the plan? Do you plan on screwing her in our bed, Elliott?"

His silence was all the reply she needed. Grabbing her backpack, she leapt from the car and raced into the terminal. It wasn't until she was handing her license over to the dour TSA officer that she realized she had left her luggage behind. Taking her place in line, she closed her eyes and tried to calm down.

"Oh Sweetness, no worries... we've got this," Carraig soothed. *"No need to panic. We just need to come up with a plan. I'll get Benjamin. He's good with plans. Have I mentioned that you look fabulous?"*

She let out a manic laugh, causing the woman ahead of her to turn back with a frown.

"Don't mind me," Clemency muttered under her breath. "Just dealing with the voices in my head."

She tried to ignore them as she made her way through security. Benjamin and Carraig were arguing over the best course of action.

"You have your phone and laptop. You're good to go," Benjamin stated. *"Go online and order a new wardrobe. It can be delivered tomorrow."*

"Yes!" Carraig agreed. *"New clothes. Something posh. None of this jeans and t-shirt business."*

Clemency glanced down at herself as she made the trek to her gate. Her jeans were comfortable, but the idea of something more 'posh' did make her smile. While the chatter continued, Carraig and Benjamin staunchly avoided the elephant in the room. It wasn't until she dropped into a seat overlooking the runway that Clemency risked closing her eyes. There behind her lids she found The Magician's dark gaze glaring back at her.

"He wants a break," Kennett said, his voice silky and full of speculation.

"He wants a break," she murmured resting her head against the cool glass of the window. She closed her eyes as a lone tear trickled down her cheek. The voices ceased and she imagined her boys, Carraig, Benjamin and Kennett surrounding her. Wrapping her in their embrace.

She wasn't crazy. At least, she was fairly certain that she wasn't. She imagined all writers lived with the voices of their favorite characters constantly running through their head. She had been hesitant to ask any of the number of fellow authors she had encountered at conferences and conventions in recent years. To be honest, she wasn't quite sure she really wanted to know. She was happy with her imaginary friends.

Benjamin was her fixer. If she had a problem, a conversation with him was guaranteed to come up with a solution. If she needed solace and comforting, Carraig was a shoulder to cry on, and he never failed to bolster her ego by telling her how great she looked. Then there was Kennett... She felt herself flush at the thought of her dark Magician. No, she couldn't imagine calling any of her friends for advice in this time of need. Her boys would see her through, she thought with a smile as a chirp from her bag brought her back to reality.

Have a safe flight! I'm looking forward to finally meeting you tomorrow.

Clemency smiled at the message that greeted her. Georgie was her studio liaison. They had been communicating via text and email for several weeks and in that time a friendship had been forged. Glancing at the clock, she thumbed in a reply, deciding to tackle the minor problem of her luggage first.

Thanks! Any chance you can recommend any clothing stores that deliver?

She squeezed her phone willing a response to appear. If she could focus on this, she could ignore the major catastrophe of her entire life unraveling. She jumped as the phone chimed again.

Dozens. Is everything okay?

She settled back into her seat and stared at her phone. Was everything okay? Eighteen years was a long time. Was she willing to just toss it aside without a fight? Was Elliott? Especially over a young piece of ass? She felt her eyes well up and imagined Carraig's arm slide around her shoulder in comfort, only to shrug it off and sit up when her phone chimed once more.

Don't worry, whatever it is, we'll handle it. I'll email you a list and see you in the morning.

Clemency couldn't help but smile. Georgie's text sounded exactly like something Carraig would say. Moments later an email alert popped up containing the promised list. She spent the remaining time before her flight perusing websites and filling virtual carts. Heeding Carraig's demand for *'posh, posh, and lord girl, you'll absolutely rock that!'* she ignored the more casual jeans and t-shirts, and instead chose leggings and tunics, dresses and blouses. She grinned when the selection of sexy bras and panties she chose were met with his declaration of *'FABULOUS!'*

She completed her transactions as she boarded the plane and was directed toward the first-class section. Settling into her seat, she was on the verge of placing her phone into airplane mode when a message from Elliott appeared.

I still love you...

Dropping her phone onto her lap, she rested her head against the window, watching the snow fall outside. As the tears began to fall, she pushed Carraig and Benjamin and their attempts at consoling aside. Scrunching her eyes shut, she sought out Kennett, wanting nothing more than to be embraced by his darkness.

"What do I do, Magician?" she murmured.

"You know you're going to have to be punished," a voice said, and Clemency let out a squeak of surprise when she opened her eyes to find Kennett Shariq, her dark Magician in the flesh, glaring down at her.

CHAPTER TWO

"You know that there are consequences to your actions, Gracie. We will discuss this more in the morning when I get home," Peter declared, adding a quick 'I love you,' before whipping off his headset and storing it along with his bag in the overhead compartment.

He spared a glance at the woman gaping up at him as he ran his fingers through his grey curls, making them stand on end. She recognized him. Of course... Having a peaceful flight home was just too much to ask for after the hellish weekend he had just endured. Whatever had possessed him to agree to a meet and greet over the holiday weekend? If anything, the fans were more obsessive and boorish than usual.

Lowering himself into his seat and focusing on adjusting his seatbelt, he reminded himself that it was the last event of the year. He just had to make it through the flight with the woman who was apparently on the verge of gushing over how she was his biggest fan... Glancing out of the corner of his eye, he noted that she had a phone in her hand. Oh God, not the surreptitious selfies, he thought. No... she was texting... He found himself absorbed in watching her thumbs fly across the screen. Her long mane of red hair obscured her face, but he imagined that she was in a ferocious temper as he saw the word 'fuck' appear more than once on the screen. So, it appeared that she wasn't a fan after all...

Reaching for his glasses, he wondered what he had done to cause her ire. He was leaning close, trying to make out her rant when the flight attendant gently informed them that they were about to depart. Peter was squirming in his seat after reading a fairly descriptive suggestion as to what someone named Elliott could do with a certain part of his anatomy. Absorbed with imagining such a feat, he failed to cover his intrusion into her personal space and found himself staring into bright, teary green eyes. They widened in surprise, and Peter, quite taken by their beauty froze. He gave her a sheepish grin and was rewarded with a glare before she hit the send button with more force than necessary. He struggled to find the words to apologize, but she had turned her back on him. As the Manhattan skyline receded in the distance outside the window, Peter settled into his seat. He had a feeling that it would be a long flight.

Several hours in and his prediction was proving to be valid. Peter was struggling. His tablet rested on his lap; the work he had hoped to get done forgotten. Instead he continued to be distracted by his seatmate. She was asleep. Only now she had shifted. Her head rested on his shoulder, her long hair falling onto the shared armrest, tickling the inside of his wrist. More than once he had found himself examining a lock of hair, marveling at the gentle spiral of the curl. He wondered if it was natural, or if, like Vanessa, she had to spend hours in front of the vanity primping to get it just right.

Vanessa... He had nearly managed to go the entire weekend without thinking about her. Amazing since today had been the one-year anniversary of her cancer diagnosis. Her demise had been swift, but in all honesty their marriage had died long before she had. His wife had been keen to point out that she had ceased to be the love of his life when she had produced their daughter, Grace, nearly twelve years ago. Thankfully, Gracie had never sensed the resentment her mother felt towards her. Instead, she mourned her mother's loss bitterly and it hurt Peter to see his daughter in such pain.

He caught himself twirling another red curl around his finger as he wondered if it would help Gracie if he moved on. Found someone who would be a strong, supporting female presence in his daughter's life. Hell, he would love to find someone who would be a strong presence in his bed, he thought with a grin. He felt a slight tug on his finger and looked up to find the woman glaring at him once again. He muttered an apology and offered her a smile as he relinquished the lock of hair, then quickly leapt to his feet when she made it clear that she wanted out.

Bloody fucking hell, he thought, already picturing the tabloid headlines - PETER BENNETT ASSAULTS INNOCENT WOMAN ON PLANE. The last thing he needed right now was to be embroiled in the whole Me Too Movement. He watched her disappear into the lavatory, and several minutes later was on his feet again as she emerged. However, she must have still been dazed from her nap, as she continued down the aisle, walking straight into him. His arms instinctively came up around her to keep her from falling and he breathed deeply as he held her close. Citrus. She smelled of citrus. Not orange or lemon, but something sweeter. He felt her breath on his neck as she sighed and he swore she called him her 'Magician,' before she pulled out of his arms with a quickly murmured apology.

He saw that she had been crying again. Returning to his seat, he motioned to the flight attendant and requested a pair of pillows. Handing one to her, he placed the other behind his own head as he reclined his seat. He didn't typically sleep on flights, but he figured it was the safest option for him now.

Sleep, however, proved to be the harbinger of dreams. And for someone who hadn't gotten laid since Tony Blair was Prime Minister, Peter was mortified to discover that his dreams on this particular occasion were quite graphic. He lay on a bed of orange blossoms while the woman rode his prick, her red hair falling around them in a silky curtain as she leaned down to claim his lips.

"Fuck," he breathed, as he slammed his cock into her before opening his eyes to find the passengers around him bustling to right their seats.

"It's just a little turbulence," the woman explained as she shifted to refasten her seatbelt. Moving to mirror her actions, he realized that a certain aspect of his dream had manifested itself in reality.

"Fuck," he repeated, flipping his tray table down to hide the evidence of his discomfort. Think of Vanessa, think of Vanessa, he chanted to himself.

"Sir, we need you to please secure your table at this time," a flight attendant chastised, and he quickly moved his pillow onto his lap and leaned forward, his elbows on his thighs.

"It will be okay," the woman soothed. "We should be landing soon." Her hand gently patting his was not helping the situation. He jerked away from her as he felt his cock twitch at her touch. He was trying to figure out what had come over him. Sure, he could understand this happening were he a young man, but for God's sake, he was fifty years old!

Clemency glanced at the agitated man sitting beside her and wondered what she had done to offend him. His head was bowed, and his fingers wove into the salt and pepper curls atop his head, making them stand on end. She felt her fingers twitch, itching to reach out to see if his hair was really as soft as it appeared. Elliott had begun balding soon after they married.

She sighed at the thought of her husband. When she had opened her eyes to see what she had initially thought was Kennett Shariq standing before her, she took it as a sign. She had immediately messaged Elliott, telling him exactly what he could do with his sad excuse of a dick. Now, hours later she wondered if she had been a little too hasty. Of course, the man sitting beside her wasn't her Magician. For one thing, he was casually dressed in jeans and a faded blue t-shirt. Kennett wouldn't be caught dead in any color other than black. Then there were his eyes. They were every bit as bright as her Magicians were dark. She would have gotten lost in their blue depths had she not been distracted by his impish smile. Kennett rarely smiled, unless you counted the suggestive twitch of his lips a smile. Then of course there was the fact that Kennett was a fictional character. Not real. Someday she would get that through her thick skull.

She shifted to look out the window at the foreign landscape peeking through the clouds as her thoughts turned to his touch. It had been disconcerting to awaken to find him playing with a lock of her hair. She had been contemplating requesting a change of seats when she had walked straight into his arms. The electric jolt she felt as he embraced her was exactly how she imagined Kennett's touch to be. It certainly made her feel more alive than Elliott ever had. Although, surely at some point, early on in their relationship she had experienced a thrill from her husband...

They had met during her final semester in college and quickly engaged in what they both had thought would be a short-term fling. He still had another year of school left, while she was determined to move to the city.

Fate, however, had other plans. A week before graduation her parents and younger brothers were killed by a drunk driver. Suddenly she found herself alone in the world. Elliott had been her rock during that time, pledging to stay by her side for as long as she needed him. She remained in the small New York town she had always called home and slipped into a comfortable relationship which eventually led to marriage. That had been nearly two decades now. Did Elliott feel that she no longer needed him?

The plane dipped again, and she swiped at another tear as a disembodied voice came over the cabin speaker.

"Ladies and Gentlemen, we will be landing shortly. The local time is 11:32. The temperature is 12 degrees. Please stow away any electronic devices at this time. Welcome to London."

She smiled as the last of the clouds parted and she got her first glimpse of her new home. Her heart leapt at the thought. Home. It felt... right. "It doesn't look that cold though," she murmured, thinking that there should be snow on the ground if the temperature was as low as reported.

"Celsius, love," the man beside her offered. "That makes it a balmy 53 degrees Fahrenheit. We're in the midst of an unexpected heat wave. It's supposed to be quite warm all week.

Lovely weather for your visit."

Smiling her thanks, she turned to watch their approach, trying not to show how his calling her 'love' had affected her. Damn the British and their sexy accents, she thought as the wheels of the plane touched down. As they taxied toward the terminal the cabin resounded with a multitude of bleeps and chimes as the passengers around them woke their dormant phones. Reaching into her bag, Clemency noted that the man beside her was glowering and muttering a few choice words down at whatever messages he had missed during their flight. He looked more like Kennett than ever. What was more, he looked vaguely familiar. Her own phone buzzed, and she saw a stream of messages from Elliott pop up. Ignoring them, she pulled up the instructions Georgie had emailed her and determined that she was to meet her driver in the baggage claim area. Then, because she imagined some catastrophe involving the safety of her daughter, she quickly perused Elliott's texts. Her eyes burned with unshed tears of anger this time as she skimmed over his paltry excuses. By the time she finished the plane had come to a halt and passengers were disembarking. She emerged into the terminal in time to see the familiar grey curls of her seatmate quickly disappearing into the crowd. Hoisting her bag onto her shoulder, she joined the stream of people. Half an hour later, the ink not yet dry on her freshly stamped passport, she made her way to the baggage claim. To her dismay she found a sea of men in black suits holding placards with names upon them.

Clemency stemmed the rising panic as she scanned the signs once, and then a second time. There was no 'Oliver' among them. Suddenly the crowd parted, and a woman appeared. While she, too, wore a hat similar to the surrounding chauffeurs, the hot pink hair sticking out from under it and the lemon-yellow pantsuit she wore set her apart from the others. In her hands she carried a colorful sign embellished with glittery stars and boasting the name 'James.' The woman grinned as Clemency stepped forward, but Clemency froze in her tracks, feeling the blood drain from her face.

"Oh my God, you're Georgianna Sutton."

CHAPTER THREE

The woman's laughter was melodious, and Clemency soon found herself wrapped in a warm embrace.

"And you are Clemency James," Georgie declared. "Although, I shouldn't say that too loud. You are quite the celebrity here. We don't want to incite a mob."

Clemency sputtered a protest, suddenly feeling very much like a star struck young girl. She mentally kicked herself for gushing, but when she closed her eyes to try and reign herself in, Carraig's high pitched squeal of delight brought a smile to her lips.

"I'm a huge fan of your work," she proclaimed and opened her eyes to find the woman watching her thoughtfully.

"The feeling is mutual," Georgie declared, wrapping an arm around Clemency's waist and directing her toward a clean-cut young man who was obviously waiting patiently for them. "This is my driver, Roger. Isn't he dreamy?" Georgie asked, handing over the hat which had been concealing her bright pixie cut. The man flushed and muttered a quiet 'good day,' before requesting her baggage claim tickets.

"No luggage," Clemency replied sheepishly, and at Georgie's startled look mumbled something about it being a long story.

"Well, color me intrigued," Georgie declared, guiding Clemency out of the terminal toward a waiting car. "There will be plenty of time for explanation on the way home, but first, tell me... did you really not realize it was me you were communicating with all this time? How is that possible?"

Clemency was wondering the same thing. Settling into the backseat, she tried to mentally go over the multitude of messages that had passed between them nearly daily for the past several weeks. In that time a friendship had been forged based on mutual likes and dislikes. She wracked her brain trying to recall any particularly embarrassing confessions she might have made. As they pulled into traffic, she blushed as she felt the woman's eyes assessing her. Georgianna Sutton was one of England's biggest stars. She had begun acting as a child and had done it all - stage and screen, both big and small. Now, pushing fifty, she had been at the helm of her own small studio for nearly a decade making a name for herself behind the camera. Clemency had known that Georgianna Sutton's 3S Studio had bought the rights to *Tempest*, she just never imagined that Georgianna, herself, had been the one to take an interest in the work. Focusing on her hands, clasped in her lap, she found herself at a loss for words. It didn't help that Carraig was still excitedly dancing around inside her head, ignoring Benjamin's pleas to calm the fuck down. Closing her eyes, she tried to conjure Kennett, only to be met by the more serene, blue eyed gaze of the man from the plane. She shook her head to dislodge the image, looking up when the woman beside her let out a chuckle.

"You look even more lost than the first time we met," Georgie said.

"We've met before?" Clemency asked, unable to refrain from smiling at the sound of Georgie's laugh.

"I don't expect you to remember me. I was one of a mob of people who attended one of your book signings this past summer. You looked like a frightened little deer, ready to bolt at any moment."

Clemency grimaced at the description. "I'm not accustomed to being the center of attention. It can get quite overwhelming." She immediately bit her tongue, appalled that she was saying this to Georgianna Sutton of all people, but Georgie merely threw her head back and laughed.

"No, don't apologize," Georgie protested. "I know exactly what you mean. Now, tell me, how do you plan on surviving our wild weather patterns here for the next year without an extensive wardrobe?"

Clemency opened her mouth to explain about the delivery she was expecting, but something else in Georgie's question caught her attention. "Year? I thought I was only scheduled to be here for three weeks?" she asked.

"The first three weeks are a trial. We want to see if you can comfortably transition into script writing. But my films are highly collaborative. I want as much input from you as possible. You will be involved in every aspect of this project, from casting to costuming. Is that going to be a problem?"

Clemency thought of Elliott and wondered what his response to this news would be. Immediately, tears sprang to her eyes. He would probably love it. A year of freedom to fuck Whitney, she thought turning to look blindly out of the window.

"Homesick or heartbreak?" Georgie's gentle voice broke into her thoughts.

"Both," Clemency whispered, turning to meet the sympathetic gaze of the older woman. Georgie, however, merely patted her hand before reaching for her phone. Turning back to the passing scenery, Clemency focused on pulling herself together. Her heart leapt as she caught glimpses of familiar landmarks.

"That's right," Benjamin's voice soothed. "No need to be homesick when *this* is home now. Everything will work out. Your new clothes are due to be delivered tomorrow, we'll *focus* on that which we can handle, and worry about the rest later."

Leaning back into the plush seat, Clemency closed her eyes and focused on conversing with Benjamin. Together they plotted a strategy for keeping as busy as possible in order to keep her thoughts from drifting back to home and Elliott. Her eyes shot open at the sound of Georgie's voice.

"Yes, Frankie, all of them, just like my message stated... There wasn't anything too major was there? I know Peter's due back in town today, see if he's up for meeting with Jack about his project..." Georgie gave Clemency an apologetic smile. "Yes, tomorrow... no, not morning, I'm not certain how the rest of the day will go, better make it noonish. Okay love, see you then."

Pulling off her headset, Georgie gestured out the window. "*This* is your home now, Clemency. At least for the next year if you wish to work with me."

Clemency noted how they had since left the bustle of the city and were slowing down to crawl down a narrow retail district that ended with a small park. There was a pleasant looking cafe followed by a line of charming, identical walk-up houses. Presently, Roger pulled to the curb, and Clemency was out of the car and onto the sidewalk before the driver could open her door for her. Looking up at the two-story house before her, Clemency's heart swelled. This *was* home. Behind her she heard Georgie and the young man conversing, the older woman explaining that there had been a change of plans.

"You want all of this?" Roger asked, the astonishment in his tone caused Clemency to turn. "Oh, Ms. Sutton, no. You remember what happened the last time you had three bottles..."

Georgie chuckled and patted the young man's arm. "Never you mind that, this time will be different. Just fetch the items on the list and then you can enjoy a free afternoon. Now, let's get you, um... unpacked and settled," Georgie declared, turning to Clemency.

She followed Georgie up the steps and into a small foyer. There were three doors, one on either side of the hall and a third at the top of a staircase. As soon as the front door closed behind them, the doors on either side of her opened and Clemency was taken aback as two identical heads popped out. Angry eyes glared across the entryway at one another before their owners toddle out to greet Clemency with a smile.

"Clem, this is Abigail and Amelia Norris," Georgie said with a smile to the two little old ladies before raising her voice several decibels. "Ladies, this is Clemency, your new neighbor."

"Nice to meet you, Nancy," the first woman said, giving her hand a squeeze.

"It's Clemmie," Clemency corrected, smiling down at the withered old face.

"Yes, you daft old woman. I told you your hearing needed

checked," the second woman berated her sister as she claimed Clemency's hand. "It's so nice to meet you, Emily. I hope you enjoy your time here."

"I'm sure I will," Clemency replied with a grin before following Georgie up the stairs.

Her contract had mentioned the use of a studio owned apartment, and Clemency had expected something bare bones. Instead, the door Georgie ushered her into opened to a homey little flat. There were curtains on the windows, bookshelves full of knickknacks, and even an old guitar perched in the corner of the living room.

"The studio has let this place out for decades, and everyone who has lived here has left a little bit of themselves behind for posterity," Georgie explained, running her finger over a small metal figure of the Eiffel Tower sitting on a shelf. "The towels and bedding are new, but if you find you need anything else, just ask."

"It's perfect," Clemency declared, returning from examining the bedroom and small attached bath. She set her backpack on top of the corner desk and grinned as she imagined Benjamin leaning back in the wooden desk chair.

"This is it... This is where it will happen. There's plenty of natural light from the window here, plus the desk lamp for those long nights of work..."

Clemency turned her back on him to find Georgie watching her intently. Avoiding her gaze, she moved to inspect the small kitchenette.

"You miss Lucy," the older woman observed. Clemency looked up from where she had been examining the contents of the fridge and gave a curt nod. She did miss her daughter, but Luce, despite being eleven years old and completely immersed in an 'it's all about me' phase, had been surprisingly supportive of Clemency's plan. Now she wondered how she would handle explaining this new turn of events to her daughter. She glanced to Benjamin, but the imaginary man could only shrug his shoulders as he spun around in the desk chair.

"I can relate, actually," Georgie said, moving to sit on the sofa. "When she was sixteen, my middle daughter, Alex, woke up one morning and declared that she wanted to go live with her father in California. That was ten years ago now, and she has yet to set foot back in England. I see her as often as our schedules allow, but..." her voice trailed off, before she pasted a smile on her face. "You must have Lucy over. We'll be filming come summer, it would make a splendid holiday to see the behind the scenes action of a movi-- oh, wait... Is Lucy even aware of *Tempest* and what it's about?"

Clemency was shaking her head and struggling to suppress a grin at the look on Georgie's face. "It's okay, though," she said. "It will still be great to have Lucy visit."

"So that covers the homesickness... now, tell me about the heartbreak," Georgie instructed. Clemency flushed and turned away, making a show of examining the cabinets and their contents. "Let me guess, you found out that your husband is cheating on you and you feel as though the world around you is falling apart..."

"How did you know?" Clemency whispered.

"Been there, done that, bought the t-shirt," Georgie said and Clemency found that the woman had silently crossed the room to join her, taking a hold of her hand. "Plus, you have been unconsciously rubbing the spot here where, until quite recently I'm guessing a wedding band sat."

Before Clemency could reply, there was a knock at the door. Roger strode in bearing two large pizza boxes which he deposited on the counter along with a bag before he was out the door again. He returned momentarily bearing a box.

"Everything you asked for, Ms. Sutton," the man said with a tip of his cap. "Do me a favor, and if it's as bad as last time, *don't* call me in the morning."

Georgie laughed and swatted him out the door before turning to face Clemency.

"What is all of this?" she asked, poking her nose into the box. There were several bottles of wine along with an assortment of liquor.

"This is my remedy for a broken heart," Georgie explained. Pushing away from the door, she moved into the kitchen and lifted the lid to the top pizza box and swiped a slice of pepperoni. "We're going to get shitfaced, girlfriend. You're going to drown your sorrows in alcohol and the greasiest food the neighborhood has to offer. It won't necessarily solve all your problems and come morning we will most likely see all of this floating in the loo, but it will help get you through the worst of it."

Clemency looked skeptical, but an hour later she drained her third glass before picking up the chopsticks which were becoming increasingly more difficult to use. She stabbed at the container of fried rice while Georgie digested all the information Clemency had related.

"You've been married for eighteen years and out of the blue Elliott the Prick has decided to start shagging one of his coworkers?"

"I don't know if they're shagging yet, but I now know that he wants to be," Clemency said, looking up to see Georgie frowning at her.

"Eighteen years?" she asked. "Were you twelve when you got married?"

"No, twenty-two," Clemency replied and fell into a fit of giggles as Georgie sputtered on the drink she had been taking.

"There is no bloody way that you are..." Georgie paused, holding up her fingers to do the math before giving up. "You can't be that old. You don't look a day over thirty."

Clemency tripped over her feet, rising to retrieve her backpack from the desk. Digging through her wallet, she found what she was looking for and tossed her driver's license onto Georgie's lap.

"Proof," she declared.

"Lord love a duck, is that really your name?" Georgie asked, examining the small plastic card. "I can see why you go by Cee Cee. I take it Clemency is your middle name?"

Clemency grimaced and nodded. "I'm named after the two grandmothers and great grandmother that were alive when I was born."

"Well, I still find it hard to believe that you are forty. You're way too hot. We're going to have such fun finding you a man. That's step two of my heartbreak cure - getting a young stud in your bed," Georgie said, raising her glass in a toast. "Just avoid the mistake of getting knocked up and marrying them like I did."

Clemency smothered a yawn, but not before Georgie noticed and declared that perhaps it was time for bed. Squinting at the clock, Clemency protested that it was still early, but her friend insisted, assisting her as she stumbled toward the bedroom.

"You aren't by any chance hitting on me, Ms. Sutton? Trying to get me into bed and all..." Clemency asked.

Georgie let out a sultry laugh. "Oh, sweetie, I have yet to play that field, but even if I were tempted, now that I know your age, I can honestly say that you're too old for me."

Clemency threw back her head and joined her new friend in laughter before collapsing onto the bed.

CHAPTER FOUR

Peter did nothing to hide his yawn. If anything, he embellished it, leaning back in his chair and stretching his arms above his head in the hope that the young kid sitting across from him would finally get the hint. But no... Jack kept right on rambling about his 'vision.' This was not how Peter had envisioned his day going, but the fates had been against him from the beginning.

While the plane had landed on time and traffic had been blessedly light, allowing him to arrive home earlier than he had anticipated, he was greeted by a silent, empty house. He knew that his housekeeper, Mrs. Bea typically did the shopping on Monday morning, but he had thought that he had made it clear to Gracie that he had intended to discuss her recent actions. Instead, he found a hastily written note waiting for him.

Went back to school early. Evening activities scheduled all week, so I'll be staying on campus. I'll try to come home for the weekend... Love Grace.

It didn't take a genius to realize that his daughter was avoiding him, and it wasn't just because she anticipated being punished for skipping class. No, this had been going on for eight months now, ever since Vanessa's death. Peter couldn't wrap his head around why. He and Gracie used to be so close. He could only assume that she was still grieving her mother's death. He had tried to give her space, but he now realized that something had to be done. Exhausted after a long weekend, he hoped that pushing off that particular confrontation until the following morning didn't make him a bad father. His eyes were closed before his head even hit the pillow on the leather couch in his office.

He was dreaming about the woman from the plane again when he was roused from sleep. This time it was his phone, more specifically Georgie's assistant calling to ask if he was willing to take a meeting that she had scheduled but was unable to attend. He wondered if he would have been so inclined to assist if he had known that it was with an aspiring director who required mentoring.

"Look Jack," he finally broke into the long-winded description of what the man planned to achieve. "I see where you are going, and admire your drive, but you need more than merely a 'vision' to achieve your goal. Let's meet again in a few days. In that time, I want you to assemble a team. People you trust to rein you in, because you're going to be so focused on every tiny little detail that you'll lose sight of the big picture." Peter went on to explain in detail what kind of people should comprise his core group of assistants, before rising from the table to make his getaway. He had one final stop before he could head home.

Walking down the carpeted halls of the studio's main office annex, he realized that it felt good to be back. Of course, he had made customary appearances at meetings and events during the past year, but today, despite being so bloody tired, he felt engaged for the first time in ages. Perhaps this chance to mentor young Jack was just what he needed to get him back in the game. He wouldn't put it past Georgie to have orchestrated the whole thing in the first place. They had dined together recently, and she had asked about his plans for the future.

Entering a suite that held his and Georgie's offices, he found Frankie at her desk packing up for the day. He noted that the desk belonging to his own assistant was vacant.

"Erika got reassigned," Frankie said apologetically. "Is there anything I can assist you with, Mr. Bennett?"

Peter suppressed a grin. He had known Frankie Sutton forever... Hell, he had changed the girl's diapers. Yet, here at the studio, she insisted on formalities. She had been working as her mother's assistant for nearly two years now, but Peter knew that she longed for something more.

"Did Georgie ever make it in?" he asked, plopping down onto one of the vivid, leather chairs that lined the wall.

"No, she canceled everything for the day," Frankie explained.

"Is she ill?" Peter asked, sitting up. It was unlike Georgie to neglect work.

"No, no. The author of her new project arrived today and Mum... I mean, Ms. Sutton, decided to spend the day with her."

"The needy type? It's not like your mother to be a hand holder," Peter said, rising to his feet.

"Oh, no. She's not... The author is Clemency James," Frankie declared breathlessly. When Peter just looked at her curiously, she went on, explaining as though she were talking to a clueless child. "You know... the author of *Tempest*... Have you been living under a rock this past ye-- Oh. I'm so sorry Mr. Bennett, I didn't mean--"

"It's okay, Frankie," Peter replied, moving toward the door to his office. "Some days it does feel as though I've been doing just that. Can you let your mother know that I'll handle Jack and his project? He'll probably be in contact with you to schedule a meeting later this week. Just forward the information to my calendar please."

Entering his office, he closed the door on Frankie's repeated apologies. Leaning his head against the door, he wondered how long he would have to put up with people stumbling over themselves in an attempt to placate him and his feelings. Closing his eyes, he tried to imagine what would happen if the next person who told him that they were sorry for his loss was greeted with the response of 'I'm not.' And he wasn't. Pushing away from the wall, he threw himself onto the nearby sofa that faced his desk, coughing at the cloud of dust that flew into the air above him. Now, if someone told him they were sorry that his wife had been a cheating, manipulative bitch, he would whole heartedly accept that sympathy. With that thought, he closed his eyes and slept.

When he woke, weak sunlight was streaming through the window highlighting the dust motes circling his head as he shifted. Spending the night at the office wasn't unusual, but it certainly wasn't something he had done in a while and Peter was feeling it in his bones. This couch was certainly not as comfortable as the one he tended to sleep on at home.

Checking his watch, he saw that it was early. Bracing himself for the confrontation ahead, he moved to the adjoining bathroom for a shower and a change of clothes. Less than an hour later he had braved the halls of Crestwood Academy and found himself sitting before Gracie's dour faced headmistress. She had just concluded outlining all his daughter's misdemeanors and Peter struggled to keep a suitably concerned expression on his face. So, Gracie had skipped a few phys ed classes and was found hiding in a stairwell reading. Her grades, otherwise, were quite excellent. He was more concerned over the fact that his daughter had somehow left the school over the weekend without his permission and managed to make her way home, navigating the London city streets all by herself.

The headmistress brushed his argument aside. They were an open campus and could not be expected to be able to keep tabs on *every single* student, especially those such as Gracie who split their time living both on campus and at home. She was anxious to hear how he intended to deal with Gracie's truancy.

"Well, I'd like to discuss that with my daughter. Would you be so kind as to have her fetched?" he inquired.

"Now?" the headmistress asked, frowning.

"Now," Peter replied, leaning back in his chair and gazing lazily at the woman who reluctantly reached for her intercom.

"Would you summon Grace Bennett to the office please," she instructed, before adding with a grimace, "she should be in the gymnasium. She has phys ed this period."

Half an hour later, Peter watched his daughter out of the corner of his eye as they crossed the street. Other than the initial awkward greeting where Gracie had tensed at his embrace, she had remained silent. Now, making their way toward a once favored spot under the large oak tree in the park situated a block away from their home, Peter wondered how he was going to be able to get her to string more than two words together.

"So, Ms. Truchbull back there seems awfully concerned over you missing out on phys ed," Peter finally began, nudging his daughter good naturedly with his shoulder. They sat atop a picnic table, watching a group of toddlers fight over a pail in a nearby sandbox. "Do you want to tell me about it?"

Peter waited, refusing to take her shoulder shrug as an answer. Finally, he was rewarded.

"I hate it," Gracie cried. "Can't you do something so I don't have to take phys ed?"

"I doubt it," Peter replied, making a mental note to look into her schedule and what options were available. "I'm sure it is seen as an integral part of your education. Something everyone has to suffer through. It doesn't concern me nearly as much as your leaving school this weekend did. You had me worried sick," his voice became more soothing as the child beside him dissolved into tears. "Do you want to talk about it?" They were back to square one as Grace firmly shook her head, her mouth clamped shut. Frustrated, Peter counted to ten and took a swig of his coffee. "Okay, maybe you will feel more like talking when you return home this weekend."

"But I don't wa---" Gracie began.

"It doesn't matter what you want, Gracie. You will be returning home this weekend, and every weekend for the remainder of the year," he declared. "We will consider it your punishment."

CHAPTER FIVE

On the other side of the large oak tree, Clemency let out a snicker. Punishment always conjured up thoughts of Kennett and his dark methods of training Tempest. A screaming child ran by and she immediately scrunched her eyes shut and dropped her head into her hands.

"Drunkenness is nothing but voluntary madness," Benjamin sagely quoted from a dark corner of her mind.

"Yeah, yeah, yeah," Clemency muttered. "I know I did this to myself."

She took another swig of coffee, hoping its restorative powers would soon take effect. She imagined that she looked about as bad as she felt, and only the quest for caffeine persuaded her to leave the flat that morning. She couldn't recall how late she and Georgie had stayed up. She only knew that her friend looked decidedly none the worse for wear come morning when she brightly woke her up with the news that her phone was ringing. Clemency had sat up and hit answer, only to be hit with a wave of nausea as her husband's voice came across the line. She immediately dropped the phone and bolted for the bathroom. A few minutes later she felt gentle hands pulling her hair back as she hovered over the toilet. She sighed in relief as a cool washcloth was placed on the nape of her neck.

Sitting on the edge of the tub, Georgie informed her that she took the liberty of telling Elliott to fuck off, before instructing her to take the day off. "Get some coffee, get some fresh clothes, and be prepared to get to work tomorrow bright and early," she said cheerfully, before leaving Clemency.

Clothing was easy as she found herself pulled from her

shower by a knock on the door. Dripping wet and wrapped in a towel, she greeted a deliveryman who speechlessly dropped a large box at her feet. She conveniently found coffee a block away at a small cafe and had crossed to sit in the small park. She had her phone in hand, debating whether to call home now before Lucy left for school when she found herself eavesdropping on a conversation between a father and his distraught daughter. She could totally understand the young girls desire to avoid gym class. She was guessing that she was about the same age as Lucy, and while her daughter was very outgoing and had no qualms about changing in a locker room full of other girls, Clemency was guessing that this was where the majority of dislike for the subject of phys ed stemmed from. On the other hand, she gave the father points for his concern over the child traipsing all over the city on her own. Living in a small town, Clemency worried when Lucy biked to the local library on her own. She shuddered at the thought of her child alone in the city.

Even before she had begun writing, Clemency had enjoyed eavesdropping on conversations and making up stories to go along with the snippets of overheard dialogue. She usually preferred to keep the speakers anonymous so she could develop her own characters. However, this time, as the man and his daughter departed, she couldn't help but glance up as they passed by her table. She let out a gasp as she recognized him as the man from the plane. What was more, he recognized her as well and appeared none to pleased to see her if the glare he sent in her direction was any indication.

"Damn, that man has a fine ass," Carraig piped up as Clemency watched the pair exit the park. She couldn't help but agree, and she felt the effects of her hangover fade as she suddenly got the inspiration to do a little writing.

Several hours later, the light beginning to fade and her laptop battery giving her a warning, Clemency packed up and took a stroll around the neighborhood. She found it quite charming, everything she needed within walking distance to her flat. Picking up some Indian takeout, she returned home. She nodded a greeting to the Norris sisters who had poked their heads out of their doors on her return.

"I tell you, she's one of those lesbian people," one of the women whispered not very quietly across the hall, nearly causing Clemency to trip on the stairs. "I saw Georgie leaving early this morning. She must finally be over young Donnie and is experimenting."

"Oh, pish posh," came the reply. "Georgie will never stop loving Donnie, no matter how pretty Emmie is."

Clemency felt her cheeks burn and thought of how the Cee Cee Oliver of old would have slunk away, pretending not to overhear such comments. Instead, as she reached the top step, she glanced over her shoulder and gave the sisters a broad wink before disappearing into her apartment.

Later that evening, Clemency finally bit the bullet and picked up her phone. There had been an array of messages from Elliott throughout the day, but she had ignored them. Now, calculating the time difference, she hoped that she could safely call home and get Lucy, fresh from school and not have to deal with Elliott the Prick. She shook her head, realizing that she shouldn't refer to him as such, but Georgie's nickname had stuck.

Luck was not on her side though as Elliot's voice came over the line before the phone had barely rung.

"Cee, please. We need to talk about this," he implored.

"Talk about what, E?" she replied. "You made it clear what your plans are. I called to speak to my daughter. Can you please--"

"Our daughter," Elliott interrupted, his terse tone indicating that he was not pleased with her brushing him off.

"I stand corrected," Clemency replied calmly. "As such, you can bear the responsibility of explaining to her how her parents split because you couldn't help fucking some young piece of as----"

"It's not like that," Elliott snapped. "I'm sorry, it's not like I planned for this to happen."

"Is that Mom?" Clemency heard her daughter's voice in the background.

"We'll talk about this when you return," Elliott continued. "You're home at Christmas, right?"

"Yes, but only long enough to see Lucy and pack," Clemency agreed. "I'm moving here permanently, Elliott. Now let me talk to my... our daughter."

She spent several minutes listening to Lucy ramble on about school and her friends. She promised to video chat next time so her daughter could see where she lived. By the time she pressed end call and settled back onto the couch, Clemency felt drained. Had she just told her husband that she was moving to England permanently? Was that even a possibility? After all, after only one day she felt completely at home here. Somehow the idea didn't terrify her as much as it should have.

Clemency was bright eyed, and bushy tailed the following morning as she waited on the stoop for her ride. When Roger pulled up, she greeted him with a smile and a cup of coffee. She handed a bemused Georgie a cup as she climbed in back beside her.

"I know I said that stage two of my heartbreak remedy is finding a young stud to warm your bed," Georgie said in a stage whisper. "And while I agree that Roger is young and quite handsome, he is also deeply devoted to his partner."

Clemency blushed and began to stammer, only to be rescued by the driver who caught her eye in the rear-view mirror and winked.

"Don't fret, Ms. James. Ms. Sutton is all talk--"

"Roger! Such insubordination. I should have you sacked," Georgie declared, her smile belied the affection she had for her young driver.

"I'd like to see you get around without me," Clemency heard the man mutter before pulling into traffic. Georgie's sultry laugh let her know she had also heard the comment, but she chose to ignore it, turning to ask her how her day had been instead.

Clemency spent the drive regaling her friend with the tale of shocking the delivery man and leading the Norris sisters to believe that they were lovers. She found herself hesitant to mention the man in the park. A part of her acknowledging guiltily that it was because she found him attractive.

Georgie threw her head back and laughed. "It sounds like you have your own method for attracting young studs."

"Please," Clemency implored, completely serious. "I don't need a man to make me happy. I came here to work."

Georgie sobered and reached for Clemency's hand. "I will pause phase two of my heartbreak remedy for now, but you need to be honest with yourself, sweetie. You're here to start a new life. If that includes love, you are not to turn your back on it, agreed?"

Clemency nodded vaguely and turned to look at the passing scenery. They were on the outskirts of the city and before long they passed under an archway bearing the logo for 3S STUDIOS. Several hours later, Clemency's head was spinning. Georgie had led her on a whirlwind tour of what she had affectionately dubbed 'her fourth child.'

"Most of the initial prep work will be done here," Georgie explained. "Casting, set design, costuming, et cetera. But come summer we will shoot on over to Wales for most of the filming. We have a sister studio in Cardiff that is much more convenient for outdoor work. By the time we're done there, everyone should be well acquainted which will make filming the more intimate scenes less daunting."

They were walking down a hall towards Georgie's office when Clemency stepped aside to let a group of gentlemen hurry past. A young man was talking animatedly to the group, but it was the familiar grey curls of the quiet man at the back that caught her attention. She glanced over her shoulder to, once again, admire his retreating back only to catch him watching her. His fierce eyebrows knit into a frown and Clemency stumbled. Only Georgie's arms catching her prevented her from tumbling to the ground.

"Not interested in a stud, huh? I know Jack there is quite easy on the eyes, but unfortunately he also plays for the other team," Georgie explained, turning to open the door leading to her office.

Clemency felt Carraig perk up as she followed her friend. "He doesn't look like a Jack though," his voice complained. "He looks more like a..."

"Kennett," Clemency muttered, shaking her head and plastering on a smile to cover the sudden disappointment she felt as Georgie glanced back at her questioningly.

"My office is just through here," Georgie said, indicating a door behind a clutter filled desk. The room she stepped into was totally Georgie. It appeared as though a rainbow had exploded. She had no sooner been seated in a bright orange armchair when a young girl with curly black hair and glasses that took up her entire face tripped through the door after them.

"Ah yes, Clemmie, this is Frankie, my right hand... everything," Georgie said by way of introduction. "Frankie, meet Clemency James." The girl froze and gawked at Clemency who offered her a shy smile. Georgie, looking up from a sheath of memos laughed. "Stop goggling at the famous author, love and get us some coffee. Then be prepared to take some notes. I'm sure Ms. James will be happy to sign your copy of *Tempest* later." Georgie sat down and swiveled toward Clemency as the girl stumbled backwards out of the office. "Frankie is also my eldest daughter. She has dreams of working in the industry, but we're still struggling to see where exactly she'll fit best."

Frankie returned bearing a tray of coffee and biscuits and retreated to sit on the sofa behind Clemency. For the next two hours they discussed *Tempest* and Georgie's vision for transitioning it from page to screen. Clemency began to realize that she had signed onto something much bigger than she had initially expected and she had a newfound respect for the woman sitting before her. Georgie was a true collaborator; it was part of what made her so successful. She was well known for making accurate adaptations of much-loved novels, and it was because she sought the author's input every step of the way.

Finally, setting down the pen she had been toying with, Georgie leaned back in her chair and gazed at the ceiling. "I have one final question, and it's strictly hypothetical... If you could cast one character, who would it be and who would be your number one pick for that role?"

Clemency blushed. If pressed, she could probably list off who she would choose to play every character in her novel. Narrowing it down to one was harder. Stalling, she rose to refill her coffee cup and moved to stare out the window. There was a small courtyard below, a lovely green space where people could relax in the center of the bustling studio. She knew that Kennett would have to be her choice. Initially he had begun as a minor character who she had planned to kill off, but he had struck a chord and quickly became her favorite. Ignoring Carraig's enthusiastic demand of 'pick me!' and Benjamin's quiet smile, Clemency turned to inform Georgie of her choice.

Her friend leaned forward, her elbows resting atop her desk, and Clemency could tell that she had the woman's full attention. "...as for who I would cast to play him... Peter Bennett."

The bark of laughter from Georgie was not the reaction Clemency expected. Even Frankie, who had been sitting quietly through the whole meeting, let out an audible snicker.

"Oh, love, that would never do," Georgie exclaimed, wiping the tears from her eyes. "Peter Bennett unequivocally does not do romance. Have you ever seen him kiss on screen? Hell, I played his wife once and the closest I got was a chaste peck on the cheek."

Clemency was beet red and turned back to the window muttering that she wasn't familiar with the man's full body of work. To be honest, she had only ever seen him once in some show or movie Elliott had been watching. She had been writing *Tempest* at the time and had glanced up in time to see the face of a man who had become the embodiment of the character of Kennett. She couldn't see anyone else in the role.

"Frankie, love, go type up those notes. I'm going to see Clemmie home," Georgie instructed her daughter.

Sliding into the back seat of the SUV, Clemency's thoughts were still on Kennett. She was dismayed to realize that she couldn't seem to conjure up his image anymore. His dark gaze continued to be replaced by the bright blue eyes of the man from the plane. Feeling her friend's eyes on her, she turned to find Georgie looking at her inquisitively.

"I asked if there had been any word from Elliott the Prick," Georgie repeated as the car pulled out of the gate.

"I may have impulsively told him that I was moving here permanently," Clemency admitted to a squeal of delight from her friend.

"Has the d-word come up?" Georgie asked.

Clemency shook her head. Divorce. No, they hadn't spoken the word... yet. Clemency hesitated to even think it. It screamed of permanence and she wasn't quite certain that she was ready to give up completely. As they turned onto the now familiar street where she lived, Clemency turned back to her friend.

"Georgie, about Peter Bennett... I could easily make the character of Kennett more distant and less romantic; do you think he would consider the role?"

"This means a lot to you, doesn't it?" Georgie asked. "You can try. The worst that can happen is he says no. However, I must ask, would it still be *your* story? Don't lose sight of the big picture here."

Clemency nodded before opening the door and stepping out onto the sidewalk. She hadn't realized that Georgie had followed until she felt her hands on her shoulders. "Don't fret, sweetie. We're still weeks away from casting. Your job is to focus on the script. Write two of them if that will make you feel better. I'm going to be out of town for the next several days but promise me that you won't spend the entire time holed up in your flat. Get out and enjoy the city a little, okay?"

"Okay, mom," Clemency replied with a grin.

"Very funny," Georgie grinned back. "Now, I spy with my little eye a pair of old ladies watching us from behind closed curtains. Shall we give them a little something to talk about?"

Clemency laughed as she embraced her friend, but the smile slid off her face as a small black sports car slowed down as it drove by. While the driver's eyes were obscured by a pair of sunglasses, she was certain that, once again, it was the man from the plane watching her.

CHAPTER SIX

The blasted woman was haunting him. Peter was certain of that. She was everywhere he turned. His nose flared as he walked down the hall to his office. It had been nearly a week since he had spied her talking to Georgie Sutton in this very corridor, and yet he swore he could still smell a trace of her citrus scent in the air. It was Monday morning and Peter was surprised to find the outer office empty, before recalling that Georgie wasn't due back until later that day. No Georgie meant no Frankie, and no Frankie meant no coffee. With a groan of dismay, Peter entered his office, closing and locking the door behind him. The last thing he needed this morning was to be corralled by Jack. He wasn't avoiding the kid, exactly... Okay, he was avoiding him, but only until he was sufficiently caffeinated.

His desk was as orderly as usual with only two new items in his in-box. The first was the script to Jack's project with a note - *Feel free to make any changes you see fit ~J.*

When did he become script editor, Peter wondered as he crammed the papers into his bag. The second item was a message, neatly typed, presumably by Frankie.

Ms. Sutton is happy to hear that you have resumed your role here at 3S Studios and kindly requests a meeting at your earliest convenience. The following dates and times are available. Please select one and message me. ~Francesca Sutton.

Peter chuckled as he lowered himself into the desk chair. Frankie was ever the diplomat. He was certain that the carefully worded memo was translated from Georgie's 'well, it's about fucking time he was back. Tell him to get his ass in here asap so we can discuss our game plan.'

3S Studios was Georgie's baby. She had purchased it fair and square from Ephraim Foster when he had decided to retire nearly ten years ago now. He joked that Georgie kept him around as a silent partner in order to make sure he kept silent about the details of the negotiations, including the poker game that determined the final asking price, something that Ephraim's widow still seethed over. However, he and Georgie made a good team. They had been friends for decades, and together they built the small, no-name studio into something respectable.

He felt a twinge of guilt over abandoning his friend for the past several months. It was clear after this weekend that he could no longer use the excuse of wanting to be there for Gracie as a way of avoiding work. His daughter had returned home as he had demanded. However, she had spent the majority of the weekend holed up in her room. When they did meet for meals, he had been hard pressed to get her to string more than two words together. Instead, she hunched over her plate, picking at the food on it until she was excused.

Although, he had finally seen her elusive smile and got to hear her laugh towards the end of their visit. Sunday had been yet another unseasonably warm afternoon and donning a pair of sneakers, Peter had insisted that Gracie join him for an afternoon jog before he return her to school. The promise of a pint of ice cream clinched the deal. They had just turned the corner into the small commercial district when he spied the redhead. She was across the street at the florist, bending over to examine a bouquet. The next thing he knew, Peter was sprawled on the sidewalk, the Norris sisters' angry glares sent shivers down his spine as their groceries scattered from the overturned wagon he had tripped over.

"Now look what you did," Abigail Norris said, waving a dented can in his face. "You and your running about hither and yon. What are you trying to accomplish? Hmmmmm. Why can't you watch where you're going, instead of mowing innocent old ladies down?"

"I think he had his eye on young Emmie," Amelia Norris quietly declared, and Peter felt his face flush as his eyes darted across to the flower shop. Thankfully the street was empty. Moving as quickly as his battered body would allow, he got to his feet, gathering up bruised tomatoes, and crushed aubergines and placing them back into the sister's wagon with the promise of replacing their damaged items as soon as possible. Ignoring their grumbles, he turned away in search of his daughter, finding her sitting on a bench under the oak tree in the park. As he approached her, he could see that she was struggling to stifle her laughter.

"I'm sorry, Daddy," she said with a giggle as he joined her on the bench. "The Norris sisters scare me. Are you alright?"

Peter nodded, stretching his leg out to examine a minor scrape. "Don't worry, they scare me too," he admitted. "Are you still up for ice cream?" His heart leapt when she responded with a smile and a nod. However, halfway down the block, she became serious as she turned to him.

"Daddy, were you really checking out that woman like Ms. Norris said?" she asked, nearly causing him to collide with the pavement for the second time in as many blocks. Before he could reply, she continued. "Because it's okay if you were. I think it's time you got out and met someone, don't you?"

She grinned at him, but rather than wait for a reply she darted through the door to the ice cream parlor.

Perhaps it was time to get out there and meet someone new, Peter thought, sitting behind his desk toying with a pen. But it certainly wasn't going to happen if he stayed holed up in his office, and he definitely wasn't going to be getting any coffee here... Grabbing his bag he made a hasty exit, keeping his head down as he darted down the hall, ignoring the young man's voice calling after him.

A storm bearing a much desired cold front broke as he sped across town. Luck was on his side as a parking spot opened directly in front of the coffee shop, and he managed to dodge the sporadic raindrops of the passing shower on his way through the door. He had been far luckier than the woman in line ahead of him if drenched auburn tresses were any indication. The rain did nothing to quell her scent, however, and Peter felt a pull in his groin as he was enveloped in citrus. Not for the first time the thought crossed his mind that she was stalking him. Frustrated at the idea, he leaned close to make it clear that he did not appreciate her attention.

"If you have made stalking me your life goal, you can stop now," he growled into her ear. "I don't play into those kinds of games."

He was immediately confronted by a pair of vivid green eyes. How had he forgotten their beauty, he wondered, completely missing the spark of anger they held.

"I don't know who the hell you think you are. If anyone is doing any stalking, it's you. You're nothing but a... a... menace!" she forcefully declared.

Peter refrained from comment, merely nodded toward the counter where the barista was impatiently awaiting his next customer. She would be referring to the unspoken battle they had undertaken over the coveted picnic table in the nearby park. It had long been a ritual for Peter to take his morning jog, pausing at the table for half an hour to peruse the morning headlines before heading home to start his day. This past week, however, saw his plans disrupted as several days he would reach the park to find her already camped out under the oak tree, a laptop and papers spread all over the table. It had become a game, trying to get to the coveted spot before she did. Glancing out the window at the icy rain, he realized sadly that mother nature, in the end, had won that particular war.

They stood, silently fuming and awaiting their orders before the woman, claiming hers stomped across the room to claim a seat by the window. Eyes narrowed, Peter contemplated leaving her in peace, but he had been looking forward to his coffee, damn it, so he was going to sit and enjoy it while it was still hot. Taking a sip from the cup handed to him, he nearly spit the contents out. Instead, he stormed across the room to where the woman was sitting. Slamming down his mug, he removed hers from her hand.

"They mixed up our orders," he grumbled before crossing to an empty table on the other side of the room. He pulled out Jack's script and began the futile effort of making heads or tails of the young man's vision. It was a short film, intended to be admitted to the yearly festival the following autumn. Jack was already getting a late start, and Peter's inability to concentrate wasn't going to help him catch up.

He slammed the papers down after reading the same line for the fifth time. It was all her fault, he thought childishly, instantly regretting it when he glanced over to watch her surreptitiously wipe away a tear. Oh, great, now he had made her cry. He didn't know what had possessed him to lash out at her. His initial thought, when he had caught her listening in on his conversation with Gracie was that she worked for the tabloids. He nixed that idea when he saw how cozy she was with Georgie. There were two things Georgianna Sutton didn't suffer - fools and the press.

Thinking about his friend being cozy with this woman made him recall the embrace he witnessed them sharing. That image had haunted his dreams that night. Come to think of it, the woman had featured quite prominently in his dreams most every night. He didn't always recall the details, but he always woke to the fleeting scent of orange blossoms and the feel of silky hair brushing across his skin. Maybe she had been right. Maybe, subconsciously, at the very least, he was the one stalking her. He caught himself staring. She had a lovely smile, he thought as he watched her press a message into her phone. She met his eye and he glanced away from her glare before picking up the script again.

He managed a good ten to fifteen minutes of solid concentration before his attention was once again drawn to the table across the room. This time it was her slamming her phone down in anger that made him look up. He was halfway across the cafe when the door opened and Georgie breezed in. The woman rose and threw herself into Georgie's waiting arms and Peter veered away to stand before the counter. He feigned interest in the menu on the wall while listening in on the conversation happening behind him.

"Oh, sweetie, Elliot the Prick again?" Georgie soothed. "What did he do this time? I thought we were done shedding tears over that man."

"I'm not crying over Elliott," the woman sobbed. "I'm crying because I killed Ziggy the Dwarf. I'm fucking pissed at Elliott the Prick!"

Ziggy the Dwarf? Elliott the Prick? What kind of life did this woman lead? Sensing the barista becoming impatient, Peter placed an order for a second coffee and added a sandwich. Not wanting to risk getting cornered by Georgie, he belatedly requested them to go and managed to escape with a brief wave to his friend.

He dreamt of the woman again that night. This time a midget and a man in a cock costume danced around them as he fucked her senseless. Upon awakening Peter realized that he would soon need to seek professional help if these dreams continued.

CHAPTER SEVEN

I have betrayed our wedding vows and understand should you wish for a divorce ~E.

It had been over a week since Clemency had received the text from her husband and she was still fuming. *He* understood if she wanted a divorce? Of course, he was going to manipulate things so she came out looking like the bad guy. She imagined him telling his family and their friends that *she* had requested a divorce, all the while conveniently neglecting the fact that it was because he couldn't keep his prick in his pants.

Georgie had arrived at the cafe just in time and immediately asked her what she wanted to do. Clemency outlined a highly descriptive plan that brought peals of laughter from her friend. However, while they had discovered kindred spirits in one another, their friendship wasn't quite at the 'I'll help you bury the body' stage just yet.

"What do you typically do when Elliott pisses you off?" Georgie had asked and it hadn't gone unnoticed that her friend had offered a wave of acknowledgment to the man who had proved to be quite the menace since her arrival in London. "Clemmie?" Georgie prodded, drawing her attention away from watching the man's ass as he departed.

"I usually cut off my hair," Clemency muttered in reply, her mind still on the menace. He did have a fine ass. It was a shame he had to act like one too, she thought. Seeing her friends confused look, she went on to explain how her husband had derived pleasure from her silky mane caressing his naked body. In the past she had cut it off to punish him. Now, however, it seemed petty and futile.

Still, Georgie jumped at the chance at a makeover. It was Wednesday, and Clemency was scheduled to return home at the end of the week. It was hard to believe how quickly the weeks had sped by. She hadn't replied to Elliott's message, figuring it would be better to do so face to face. The plan was to return home and sort out the mess that was Cee Cee Oliver's life before returning to London and her new life as Clemency James.

But first things first. She was on her way to meet Georgie and her daughters for a girl's day. She was pleasantly surprised to learn that her friend lived a mere two blocks away. Turning down the street, she noted that the houses here were larger, but every bit as charming as the walk-ups in her street. Each door was painted a different vibrant color. Head down, examining her phone in search of the house number Georgie had texted her, Clemency neglected to hear a nearby door slam and a moment later she had careened into a man, sending him sprawling onto the icy pavement.

"Oh, I'm so sorr----" she began, before looking down to see who she had accidentally assaulted. "Oh, fuck."

"We meet yet again, my little menace," the man said with a grin. "It's been over a week. I had begun to think that the fates had given up on us."

Clemency, taken aback by his friendlier demeanor pulled back the hand she had been offering him. "I swear I'm not following you," she was quick to protest. "I'm here to meet--"

She was interrupted by Georgie who had poked her head out of a bright purple door. Seeing an escape, Clemency bound up the steps and into the house.

"Peter, is everything all right? Why in heavens name are you on the ground?" Georgie asked, leaning against the door frame.

"I'm on the ground because that friend of yours is a pain in the ass who has been making my life a living hell for the past month," Peter declared emphatically, rising to brush himself off. Shit, the seat of his trousers was all wet. Now he would have to go change and he was already running late for his meeting with Gracie's headmistress. His attention was soon drawn to the fact that the seat of his trousers was the least of his worries. He had known his attacker's identity the moment she had run into him. He immediately became aroused as his senses came under assault by the scent of orange blossoms.

The look on his neighbor's face let him know that she was quite aware of his predicament. She smirked as she watched him hobble up the steps to his door.

"Such passion, Peter. Good to see you getting back on your feet... Both literally and figuratively," she said with a consoling smile. "By the way, Donovan will be down to visit Frankie this weekend. Would you like to come over for drinks?"

Peter acknowledged the invitation with a wave of his hand before disappearing into his house.

A few days later he found himself waiting on Georgie's stoop with her first husband listening to the doorbell echo. Only it wasn't Georgie who greeted them, but the redhead, her newly shorn locks a curly riot framing her face. She smiled at Donovan as the man stepped aside for her to pass.

"You cut your hair," Peter said, sounding so despondent that Donovan paused, one foot in the door to watch him. The woman nodded, absentmindedly brushing a shoulder length curl behind one ear. "I don't like it."

She threw her arms up in the air in reply. "And here I was, trying to anticipate your every desire." She saluted him with a rude gesture before turning to storm off down the street. Turning, Peter found both Donovan and Georgie struggling to hold back peals of laughter.

"Who was that enchanting young woman?" Donovan McDougal asked as he greeted Georgie with a quick kiss on the cheek.

"Down boy, I do believe our Peter has his eye on her," Georgie replied, holding the door open for them to enter and ignoring the profanity laced growl Peter sent in her direction.

"As always, I only have eyes for you, my love," Donovan declared before turning to his friend. "As for you, I know it has been quite a long time since you tried to woo a woman, but you're supposed to *complement* their appearance."

Peter had a few colorful words for his longtime friend as well, joining them at the kitchen counter. What the hell was wrong with him? Every time he encountered that woman, he either assaulted her... or threatened her... now he was insulting her appearance...

He half listened as Georgie and Donovan chatted. As usual they were flirting shamelessly with one another. He and Donovan had been friends since their school days, and he had been responsible for introducing the two. After a whirlwind courtship, Peter had stood beside Donovan as they wed, and then had been a shoulder for Georgie to cry on a year later when his friend had foolishly cheated and destroyed their marriage. That was all water under the bridge now. The three shared a strong friendship and took advantage of any time they could get together. Of course, it would be better if he didn't sometimes feel like a third leg, he thought as he watched Georgie blush over something Donovan had whispered in her ear. Vanessa couldn't stand Georgie, so that had never been an option, but he could easily imagine the redhead sitting alongside them, laughing at some witty comment he whispered in her ear, their eyes meeting over glasses of wine as they anticipated parting company with their friends and moving over to his place for a more intimate party...

"Peter?" he looked up to see Georgie watching him expectantly. "I asked if you had anything lined up for next year? Other than mentoring Jack of course, I haven't had a chance to thank you for taking him off my hands."

He shook his head. "I'm going to keep it slow. I want to make sure I'm available for Gracie should she need me."

"How's my goddaughter doing?" Donovan asked.

"Rebelling as only Gracie can. Skipping phys ed and being discovered hiding in a stairwell reading," Peter replied with a wry smile.

"That's my girl," Donovan chuckled.

"To be honest, she's handled Vanessa's death better than I expected. This evening when I dropped her off at school she asked if I was dating anyone. She seems to think that I need to get out more."

"I can't say that I disagree with her," Georgie ventured.

"Same here," Donovan agreed. "Tell me more about this charming redhead who very eloquently told you to fuck off."

Peter just shook his head and changed the subject, asking Donovan about the medical practice he oversaw in Edinburgh. He realized as he listened to his friend talk that there was absolutely nothing to tell. After all, he didn't even know the woman's name, and she had made it quite clear how she felt about him... Still, as the evening progressed and the three of them made their way through a second bottle of wine, his thoughts continued to drift back to her. He could always ask Georgie for information, but the bemused expression on his friends face every time he caught her watching him made him hesitate.

When Frankie came to claim her father for their dinner date, Peter tried to take the opportunity to make an escape, only to be cornered by Georgie.

"This is my next project," she said, handing him a book. "If you're up for a little work in front of the camera, I think you may be a good fit for one of the characters. Read it and let me know what you think."

Peter examined the plain black dust jacket with the word *Tempest* emblazoned across the front. Shrugging into his coat, he tucked the book under his arm before braving the cold night air for the brief trip to his neighboring house. The night was young, and the house was empty. Plopping down on the couch in his office he opened to the first page.

CHAPTER EIGHT

She was late. She took another quick sip of her still too hot coffee, thankful that she hadn't sloshed any onto her as she tried to navigate the halls of the studio. Only days until Christmas and the staff had gone into full party mode. But not Clemency. She had been up all night... all weekend, for that matter, completing not just one, but two scripts.

Juggling her coffee and backpack, she tried to shrug out of her coat as she skirted another group of revelers. She tugged on the hem of her cardigan as she entered the outer office and froze as she heard a voice raised in anger. It was coming from the office opposite Georgie's. She had often wondered who it belonged to but had never gotten the opportunity to ask.

"Tell your mother that I don't know what the hell she was thinking when she gave me this rubbish to read. The idea that I would be interested in playing *any* of these characters is utterly preposterous," the voice proclaimed as Clemency poked her head around the door just in time to see her book slammed onto a desk. Frankie stood facing her and had a deer caught in the headlights look on her face as Clemency entered the room. However, before she could open her mouth to berate this man for his rude unfounded attack on her friend's daughter, Clemency found herself drenched in coffee as the man had swung around to leave.

"Shit, fuck, and God damn it," she cursed as she tried to pull the hot, wet fabric of her sweater away from her skin.

"Bloody hell, I'm so sorry," the man apologized. "Here, let me help."

Clemency froze, finally recognizing her assailant's identity.

It took her longer than it should have to realize that he was unbuttoning her cardigan, and still longer before she recalled that she wore nothing underneath the sweater. Coming to her senses, she smacked his hands away and clutched her sweater to her chest.

He stepped back, gaping at her. Yep, she had given him an eyeful. She couldn't help the fact that she had been too busy to do laundry. Hence, she was going commando today. She didn't think it would matter. She was due to be on a plane home in a few short hours and she had plenty of clean clothes there. She closed her eyes and counted to ten.

"Keep calm, sweetness. You've got this," Carraig's voice soothed.

"First of all, this young woman deserves an apology," she calmly stated, ignoring the shocked look on the man's face as she straightened her sweater and began refastening the buttons. "She has done nothing to provoke your anger and yelling at her was completely unacceptable. I'm sorry if my book is not your cup of tea. Personally, I have no clue why Georgie recommended it to you in the first place. I can assure you that you are the last person I would ever choose to portray one of my characters."

"Liar," she ignored the long silent voice of Kennett growling in her ear.

Thoroughly chastised, the man turned to Frankie, only to be silenced when she held up a finger and pressed the button on her headset. She listened a moment before squeaking out an okay and turned to Clemency.

"That was Mum. She said to 'get your hot ass down to the car or she's leaving without you,'" she said with a small smile. "And Mr. Bennett, it's okay. I know that your anger wasn't directed to me personally."

Grumbling, Clemency shrugged back into her coat, buttoning it up to hide the damage. She hoisted her backpack onto her shoulder and handed Frankie her now empty coffee cup to dispose of. Ignoring the man, she wished the girl a happy holiday and turned to leave.

She made it through the crowded hall to the glassed-in foyer of the studio entrance before the man caught up with her. She could see Georgie waiting impatiently in the car outside.

"Please wait," he panted, reaching to grasp her hand. "Look, I know we've gotten off on the wrong foot. I just need you to know that I'm typically not such an ass. For some reason... whenever you're around... I don't know what happens..."

Clemency raised an eyebrow, looking down at her hand clasped in his. "I bring out the worst in you?"

"For some reason, yes," he replied emphatically as he released his hold on her to run his fingers through his hair. "Please let me make it up to you. Pay for a new sweater, buy you a cup of coffee at the very least."

"It's a little late, Mr. Bennett. I'm going home now," Clemency replied with a shake of her head. She pushed through the door and strode to the waiting car. Settling into the seat beside Georgie, she looked down at her hand, still tingling from his touch. As the car pulled away, she looked up to see that he had followed her out of the building. He looked so dejected. She smiled and raised a hand to wave goodbye as they passed through the studio gates.

They had driven several miles before Clemency noticed that her friend was watching her, one eyebrow quizzically raised.

"Did I miss something?" Clemency asked.

"Only me having an entire conversation by myself," Georgie replied. "I asked if that was Peter back at the studio, and then commented on the weather, asked about the script, then informed you that Roger and I were planning on eloping because I was miraculously pregnant with his love child. Then I asked why in God's name does the car suddenly reek of coffee."

This earned a loud guffaw from Roger and a weak smile from Clemency.

"The coffee smell is me. I had another accidental run in with--" Clemency froze and felt the blood drain from her face. "Did you say Peter?"

"Yes, my friend and, for all intents and purposes business

partner, Peter," Georgie replied. "I would have introduced you two, but when you told him to fuck off, I figured it best not to."

"Peter *Bennett*?" Clemency asked. When Georgie nodded, she wracked her brain, trying to remember the man she had seen on the TV screen all those years ago. She tried to compare it to the man she had encountered over the past month. "But he isn't *The* Peter Bennett, right? The actor I'm thinking about is old..."

"Sweetie, Peter *is* old," Georgie began before hesitating. "Actually, he's about the same age as me, but let's be honest, men age faster than women, right?"

"And you gave him a copy of *Tempest* to read?" Clemency asked.

"Well, yes. I may have mentioned in passing that he may be interested in a role," Georgie admitted. "I thought that's what you wanted."

"I don't think he's interested," Clemency said, turning to stare out the window as they approached the airport.

Half an hour later, Clemency was adjusting the glittery 'I Heart London' shirt Georgie had forced her to purchase, her coffee sodden cardigan disposed of in a nearby waste bin. Exiting the bathroom, she ignored her friends grin. It had come as a delightful surprise to find out that they would be sharing a flight as Georgie was heading further west to visit her daughter in California for the holiday. It prevented her from spending the entire flight worrying, so that by the time they landed in New York, Clemency felt rested and prepared for what lay ahead.

"You've got this," Georgie said, grasping Clemency by the shoulders so that she turned to face her, ignoring the swarm of people pushing past them. "And if you need me, I'm only a phone call away."

Clemency embraced her friend, realizing, not for the first time how similar she was to Carraig. Always bolstering her with words of confidence. With a forced smile she waved goodbye and turned toward the train platforms.

Now, back home, she found herself missing her friend dearly. Closing her eyes, she tried to summon up Carraig, but was met by only silence. Instead she turned to watch the surrounding farm fields pass by in the early afternoon sunset.

As the car pulled into the familiar driveway, she was happy to see that someone had made an effort to decorate for the holiday. A strand of lights blinked merrily around the front door. Thanking her driver, she rose to exit the car as a silhouette of a man and woman appeared in the large picture window. As their two shadows became one, Clemency dropped her bag back into the car. She stared numbly as the pair shared a lingering kiss before joining her bag. When the driver cleared his throat, she managed to mumble something about taking her to the closest hotel, and fifteen minutes later she found herself standing at a reception desk, fingers crossed that they had a room available. They resided in a small college town and with school out for the semester, luck was on her side. She managed to make it to her room before the first tears fell.

It didn't take long for her to cry herself out. She reasoned that this was not the end of the world. Hadn't she expected it? She just needed to get through the next few days... Still, it would have been nice to have the reassuring voices of her boys to bolster her confidence. Moving to take a shower, she smiled as she imagined Carraig and Benjamin off on a Christmas vacation together. She couldn't recall the last time their voices had invaded her thoughts.

Exiting the steamy bathroom wrapped in the plush bathrobe the hotel offered, Clemency's rumbling stomach demanded dinner. However, once that room service order had been placed, there was nothing preventing her from the inevitable. Picking up her phone, she pulled up the contact info for home. Before her husband could utter a greeting, Clemency launched into her list of demands.

"Hello Elliott. I just wanted to let you know that I have arrived and will be staying at the hotel in town. You will drop Lucy off her tomorrow morning, and I will be spending the next two days with our daughter. I will make sure she is home Christmas Eve so she can spend Christmas with you and your family. I assume you will be at their house for the day, so on Christmas I will be letting myself into our home so I can pack in peace."

She paused, waiting for her husband to find fault with this arrangement.

"Um... okay...," came his tentative response after a moment. "Why didn't you just come home?"

Clemency blew out a frustrated breath she hadn't realized she had been holding. "I did, Elliott, but it was clear that you had company. And while I may enjoy writing about threesomes, I don't necessarily wish to partake in them... At least with you," she added. "Now may I please talk with Lucy?"

He turned over the phone with no argument and as with many of her recent conversations with her daughter, she found her usually boisterous and outgoing child to be much quieter and subdued. Moving to answer the knock at the door, she tried to sooth Lucy's pleas to join her at the hotel immediately. Eyeing the bottle of wine on the cart that was wheeled into the room, she explained that this wouldn't be a good idea. She pleaded excessive jet lag, crossing her fingers behind her back at the little white lie. If anything, she would be dealing with a major hangover... Promising to see her daughter the following afternoon, Clemency disconnected the call, but before she could put the phone down, it beeped with a message from Georgie.

How's it going?

Clemency sent a picture of her salad and wine bottle in reply, but before she could even open the bottle, her phone began buzzing.

"Clemency's house of inebriation," she answered, trying to sound chipper.

"What the hell do you think you're doing?" Georgie barked. Clemency was taken aback by the anger in her friend's voice. She quickly brought her friend up to speed on what had happened since she had arrived home. "And so, you plan to drown your sorrows tonight and greet your daughter tomorrow all hung over and pathetic?"

"What the hell, Georgie?" You're the one who introduced me to this method of dealing with heartbreak in the first place," Clemency accused. "Now you're going all parental on me?"

"Sweetie, your heart isn't broken," Georgie pointed out, her tone softening. "Yes, it hurt to see proof of that prick's infidelity, but it did not break you. You had the presence of mind to get yourself somewhere safe and made alternative plans to see your daughter. Focus on the big picture - this is all temporary. In a few days you'll be back home in London, right?"

"Right," Clemency whispered.

"Okay, so, listen to Mumsy. Put the wine in the fridge, eat that sad excuse for a salad and get some sleep so you're ready to greet your daughter bright eyed and bushy tailed tomorrow," Georgie advised. "I love you, and I'm just on the other side of the country if you need me."

Clemency laughed and let out a slight hiccup. "I love you too. You're smart and beautiful despite being annoyingly always right."

"Can you please tell my daughters that?" Georgie said a tinge of sadness in her voice.

Doing as she was told; Clemency stowed the wine away in the mini fridge and ate her dinner. She was turning down the bed for the night when a light tap at the door took her by surprise. Shrugging back into the robe, she crossed the room. Opening the door, she was taken aback when her daughter launched herself into her arms.

CHAPTER NINE

"Lucy, sweetie, what are you doing here?" Clemency asked, holding her daughter tight. Oh God, it hadn't hit her until this moment how much she had missed her little girl.

"I needed to see you... I couldn't stay... Mommy..." Lucy dissolved into tears. Closing the door, Clemency led her daughter to the bed. Climbing in, she held her as she sobbed. She should have expected this. Why hadn't she heeded the signs? Lucy's sudden quiet elusiveness during their phone calls should have been a huge indication that something was wrong. Hell, the fact that Lucy had frequently taken to asking Clemency if she was okay should have been sign enough. What the fuck had Elliott done? What had he said to their daughter about their situation?

While Clemency was mentally kicking herself for being so caught up in her own life, her daughter's sobs had quieted and looking down, she saw Lucy's eyes flutter shut. Taking a good look at the girl, she noted that her sneakers were wet with snow and her gloveless fingertips were an angry red color.

"Sweetness, how did you get here?" Clemency asked, gently prodding the child.

"Walked," Lucy murmured, turning to snuggle closer to her mother. Walked? Shit, that was nearly two miles.

"Does your father know that you're here?" Clemency asked, and barely discerned Lucy shake her head before sleep claimed her.

Slipping off the bed, careful not to wake her, Clemency eased her daughter's shoes and socks off and carefully examined her feet. Crossing the room, she adjusted the rooms temperature before returning to crawl in beside her daughter, pulling her into her arms. She knew that she should call Elliott and let him know that their child was safe, but a part of her was happy to let him worry a little longer.

She hadn't intended to sleep, but it had been such a long day. When the sound of her phone vibrating woke her, she eased out of bed and padded to the bathroom, closing the door behind her before answering the call.

"Hello Elliot, by any chance have you misplaced something?" she said in greeting.

"Oh, thank God. Lucy's there with you?" Elliott began, sounding quite relieved. His next question was asked more angrily. "Why the hell didn't you call me to let me know?"

"I'm sorry," Clemency replied calmly. "I was busy consoling our distraught daughter and making sure she hadn't suffered from frostbite after walking for two miles in the co--"

"For God's sake, Cee Cee--" Elliot interrupted, but Clemency wasn't finished. She was no longer Cee Cee Oliver, and she no longer had to put up with his shit.

"Shut up, Elliott. Lucy is here with me, safely sleeping. I will return her home on Christmas Eve just as we had discussed. Just tell me what you have told her, so I understand what I'm dealing with here." She was met by silence on the other end of the line. "Elliott?"

She heard him clear his throat. "Um... about a week ago, Lucy walked in on me and Whitney..." he trailed off.

"You and Whitney what, Elliott?" Clemency asked and was greeted by more silence. "Fucking, Elliott?"

"No!" he quickly exclaimed. "No, we were just kissing, Cee."

"Okay, and how did you handle that?" Clemency asked and waited through more silence.

"I told her we would discuss the situation later," he finally replied.

"Okay... and when you discussed it? How did it go?" Clemency asked, struggling to keep the frustration out of her voice. She felt like she was pulling teeth here. On several of the brief phone calls she had shared with her husband during the past weeks, she had stressed that it was up to him to talk to their daughter. He had been vague whenever she asked how things stood.

"Well... I... I mean, we haven't really talked..." he stammered.

"Oh, for fucks sake, Elliott. You really are a prick!" Clemency shouted before disconnecting and tossing the phone into the sink.

"What the hell do I do now," she asked the empty room and waited in vain for an answer. She was sitting on the toilet, her head in her hands when Lucy's sleep tousled head appeared around the door.

"Mommy?" she asked looking around the small room in confusion as Clemency plastered a smile on her face. "I thought I heard voices..."

"I was on the phone, sweetie. Letting your father know that you were safe and sound," Clemency explained.

"Oh," the child said in response, her gaze drifting down to her bare feet.

"I can see that you have a lot of questions, love," Clemency said. "Why don't you get cleaned up and join me back in bed for a chat."

As she moved to let Lucy have the room to herself, her daughter finally gave a wobbly smile. "You sounded very British there, Mom. Calling me 'love'"

Reaching to the sink to retrieve her phone, she pulled Lucy into a quick hug and kissed her cheek before departing. Listening to the water running on the other side of the door, she paced the floor, tempted to message Georgie for advice. However, something stopped her. Her friend had seemed tense during the plane ride, and then there was the sadness in her voice when they ended their call earlier. She realized that this was more than a simple holiday visit with her middle daughter for Georgie and felt horrible for not being there for her friend. She was determined to make it up to her, but first things first, she had to focus on Lucy.

Her daughter exited the bathroom, freshly scrubbed and wearing only her shirt which she nervously tugged the hem down. Clemency smiled and held up the comforter invitingly and the girl launched herself into the bed. Joining her, she sat with her back against the headboard, pulling her daughter into her arms.

"So where would you like to start, Sweetness?" she asked, resting her chin on top of her daughter's head. She felt Lucy tense momentarily, before she shifted to rub her face against the soft fabric of Clemency's robe.

"Are you and Daddy getting a divorce?" she whispered.

Clemency didn't make it a habit to lie to her child, and she wasn't going to start now. "I don't know," she replied, before going on to explain that they were currently experimenting with being separated while she was working in London.

"But you're home now," Lucy was quick to argue. "Does that mean the separation is over?"

Clemency held back the tears that threatened to fall. This was going to be the hard part. She explained to her daughter how the past few weeks had just been the beginning. Now that she had completed the script, the real work was about to begin. "My contract is for a year, sweetness. I'll be returning to London after Christmas and we will get to work on casting." She briefly shut her eyes at the sound of her daughter's cry of dismay and was immediately greeted by the image of Peter Bennett. Only now, he bore the dark gaze of Kennett Shariq.

"Take me with you," her daughter's whisper shook the image from her mind.

"Oh, sweetie, if only that were possible," Clemency soothed, mindless to the tears that were now streaming down her face. "You still have the last few months of elementary school to get through. I know how much you have been looking forward to graduating with your friends. Never mind the fact that I'm going to be so very busy for the next few months. Besides the film, I still have a deadline looming with my publisher." Seeing the look of utter devastation on her daughter's face, she was quick to continue. "But come summer everything will have slowed down. My boss says that once we begin filming my responsibilities will have diminished and I'll have more free time. I'm hoping you will come stay with me then."

"Will that be all right with your boyfriend?" Lucy asked, taking Clemency by surprise by the abrupt change of subject.

"My boyfriend?" she asked.

"Well, Daddy clearly has a girlfriend. I've seen them together... Mommy she's practically my age," the young girl wailed, and Clemency bit back a smile. "Doesn't this mean you have a boyfriend, too?"

"No, sweetie, it doesn't. For one thing, I don't have time," Clemency declared.

"Liar," Kennett's voice echoed through her head. Closing her eyes, she was confronted by Peter Bennett's piercing blue eyes this time. "I may be an ass, but that doesn't stop you from wanting to know me better..." She opened her eyes to find Lucy watching her. Even from over three thousand miles away, the man still managed to be a menace.

"So, you've met Whitney?" she asked, trying to keep her voice chipper as she changed the subject.

They talked long into the night. Addressing everything from Elliott and his new girlfriend, to the boy who, much to Clemency's dismay, her little girl had developed her first crush over. She made it clear to her daughter that, while it was perfectly fine for her to be angry about the situation, Elliott was still her father and she was still required to show him respect. As gently as possible she chastised her daughter for running away.

When Lucy finally drifted off to sleep, Clemency settled back onto her pillows and began to ponder the subject she had been avoiding from the start. Divorce was inevitable. Even Lucy seemed to understand that. However, London was her home now. Could it also become Lucy's? Would Elliott fight her on that, or would she also have to face losing her daughter, too?

Her dream that night was a nightmarish combination of erotica and suspense. She was walking a deserted highway calling out for her lost child when she was brought to a halt by a man tackling her, knocking her to the ground. Instead of helping her up, he joined her on the hard pavement, his fingers creating chills of anticipation as they deftly unbuttoned her sweater. They were surrounded by the aroma of coffee, and she felt a stirring in her loins as he pressed his lips to hers.

Shooting up in bed, Clemency took a moment to determine where she was and what had happened. Falling back to her pillows, she stifled a giggle as the fleeting images of the dream faded along with the throb between her thighs. Holy fuck! Had she just climaxed from a dream? It had been so long, she hadn't recognized the feeling at first.

Their time together sped by in a blur of shopping, shopping and more shopping. Christmas Eve dawned with scattered snow showers and the hope for a white Christmas. After spending the morning at the hotel spa indulging in manicures, they returned to their room to find a bright pink head of hair resting on their pillows.

"Georgie!" Clemency exclaimed, instantly waking the intruder.

"Oh, good, I did get the right room," Georgie replied sleepily.

"What on earth? How did you get here?" Clemency asked.

Yawning and wiggling her fingers in a small hello to the child who was gaping at her, Georgie turned to her friend. "I realized that you needed me more than my ungrateful daughter, so I hopped a plane here this morning... last night... I'm not sure when, my time is all screwed up. What day is it? As for getting in here... well, I have my ways," she said with a grin.

Clemency laughed and threw herself into her friend's arms. "You're crazy, but I'm so glad you're here. Luce, this is my boss and new bestie, Georgianna Sutton. Georgie, *this* is Lucy. The best kid a mother could ask for... oh and quite possibly your biggest fan." The two women laughed as Lucy was barely able to squeak out a hello.

They spent the afternoon showing Georgie the sites of their

small hometown, but Clemency found herself sadly watching the time pass, and before she was quite ready for it, six o' clock and the time to return Lucy home had come. Promising to see her again soon, Georgie gave Lucy a hug goodbye.

"You've got this," her friend assured her, giving her hand a squeeze. "I'll be here when you return."

The first mile of the drive home passed in silence. However, as they pulled into the drive, Lucy turned to face her mother.

"I just wanted to let you know that if Georgie is your girlfriend, I'm totally okay with that," she said.

Clemency laughed and pulled her daughter into her arms. "She's not, sweetie, but I'm happy to see that you are open to such choices."

Chuckling over the fact that her daughter seemed almost disappointed by this, Clemency got out of the car and began retrieving their packages. Telling the driver that she would return shortly, she braced herself to face her husband who had stepped out onto the porch.

"Elliott," she greeted, handing up the bags.

"Cee," he replied, almost timidly. "You cut your hair... I don't like it."

Clemency laughed as she recalled her passionate response to Peter Bennett's identical declaration. "Your opinion no longer matters, Elliott," she said, tucking a curl behind her ear. "I'll be by tomorrow afternoon to pack. You'll be at your parents?"

He nodded, and Clemency reached to hug her daughter goodbye, reminding her that they would see one another again the day after Christmas.

"Boxing Day," Lucy said with a grin.

Returning to the hotel, she found Georgie contemplating the still unopened bottle of wine. She quietly returned it to the fridge before sitting to face her friend.

"Let's try a new way of handling heartbreak," she suggested, taking Georgie's hands in her own. "Talk to me."

Clemency listened as her friend unleashed her whole life story, starting with Donovan, the love of her life. She learned about the pain and heartbreak she suffered when he cheated on her when Frankie was still a newborn, and how her haste to retaliate had quickly led to husband number two and a second daughter, Alex. This was the 'ungrateful, wild child' who had opted to go skiing with friends despite the fact that her mother had flown thousands of miles to spend the holiday with her. Then there was Sammy, they youngest daughter, conceived with husband number three shortly before his sudden death. Georgie lamented that as an unexpected afterthought, Sammy felt neglected and unloved.

Feeling out of her depth, Clemency relented and retrieved the bottle of wine.

"Despite it all," Georgie said as she drained her glass. "I still can't help loving Donovan. It nearly kills me to stay friends with him and endure his constant flirting, but the alternative is not having him in my life which is just impossible to imagine."

"Was he the handsome devil I met on your steps with my menace the other day?" Clemency asked.

"Yes, and devil is quite an apt description," Georgie replied with a wry smile. "You never did explain what was up with you and Peter. If I had known that you had met and disliked him so, I never would have given him *Tempest* to read. I take it he's not interested?"

Clemency's description of her encounters with Peter Bennett, from the plane trip through to the coffee assault had Georgie rolling with laughter.

"Oh, sweetie, if that isn't kismet, I don't know what is," she said, wiping the tears from her eyes. "Don't you see... you two must be destined to be together."

It was long after midnight, and Clemency was too tired to argue with her friend. Although, secretly she realized that part of her hoped that her friend spoke the truth. Snuggling into her pillow, she drifted off to sleep with visions of Peter Bennett dancing in her head.

She was roused way to early Christmas morning by a knock on the door. Opening it a crack, she was surprised to find her husband on the other side.

"I was hoping that we could talk, Cee" Elliott said, rubbing a hand over the stubble of his unshaven face. Clemency glanced back at Georgie snoring away before turning to her husband.

"Give me a minute to get dressed. I'll meet you downstairs," she said, grinning at the shocked expression on his face when she closed the door. She quickly dressed and jotted a note to Georgie. On the elevator down, she belatedly realized that she had accidentally donned one of Georgie's lowcut blouses. Elliott also noticed, his eyes widening at her appearance as he rose to greet her.

"You look beautiful, Cee. You've changed," he said, leaning in to kiss her. Clemency stepped out of his reach, motioning to the waitress for coffee as she slid into the booth. "Is this because of her? Lucy mentioned that you had a friend with you."

"You can quit fantasizing, E. Georgie is merely a friend. Any changes that have occurred are thanks to you and our separation," she replied, smiling her thanks to the tired looking waitress who had appeared to fill her mug with coffee. "I assume you're here to discuss where things stand."

"Yes," Elliott said, rubbing his face again. "I'm not ready to make it permanent."

"You're not?" Clemency glanced up in surprise.

"No. I don't know where things are going, but we've had a good run, Cee. I don't think we should just throw it all away. Can't things remain the way they are for now while we see where things lead?"

Clemency hid her smile by taking a long sip of coffee. This wasn't Elliott talking, it was his mother. He always had been a mama's boy, and now it sounded like Mother Oliver was telling her son to get his act together and do whatever it took to keep his wife. Elliott, however, didn't seem ready to abandon his new, young prize just yet either. Still, Clemency recognized that she had the upper hand here.

"Okay, E. This is how things will go. I will remain married to you for now. But should I say the word, you will immediately agree to a divorce. No arguments. Agreed?" She began, a small smile touching her lips when he quickly nodded, looking quite relieved. "Now, going forward, I will be in the city for a week at the end of March, meeting with my publisher. This corresponds with Lucy's spring break so you will send her up on a train. I will return in May for her graduation and to bring her back to London to spend the summer with me, understood?"

Elliott nodded, and Clemency glanced away, ignoring the spark of interest in his eye. He wasn't accustomed to her take charge attitude, and the last thing she wanted was for her husband to find her attractive. She realized in that moment, that despite his plea for their marriage to remain intact, she was through. Digging into her plate of eggs, she pondered the thought as Elliott switched subjects and began talking about work.

They parted on friendly terms with Elliott promising to leave the front door unlocked for her that afternoon. Before he turned to leave, she stopped him.

"E, we both know that divorce is inevitable," she began. "Even Lucy has accepted it. I just ask that when the time comes for us to discuss our daughter, we can act as grownups. She is old enough to decide for herself where she wants to live."

"I know, but my mother--"

"Your mother has no say in this matter. You're a grown man, Elliott. Please remember that," Clemency said, gently laying her hand on his arm before turning to the waiting elevator.

Packing went quickly with Georgie's help, and Boxing Day was spent hauling boxes all over town. Several went into storage, while the rest went either to donation or the post office to be sent off to England. That done, Clemency and Lucy treated

Georgie to lunch at their favorite greasy spoon. Midway through the meal, Georgie answered a call from Frankie.

"Amelia Norris said what?" she asked. "Okay, there's a key to the flat on my spare keyring. Go see what's got the sisters in a tizzy."

"Is everything okay?" Clemency asked when Georgie ended the call.

"Apparently the Norris sisters are concerned about some packages that have been piling up at your door," Georgie explained.

"Packages? But we just dropped them off," Clemency replied. "I'm not expecting anything else."

"Maybe a crazed fan found out where you live," Lucy piped up. Clemency met Georgie's eye. That wasn't too farfetched an idea. While her book had achieved popularity stateside, it was still topping the charts in England.

They all put their forks down and listened in when Georgie's phone buzzed again. She listened to her daughter before giving a bark of laughter and instructed Frankie to move everything inside the flat. When she hung up, all she would say was that everything had been handled.

All too soon it was time to say goodbye. Giving her daughter one final hug, Clemency was surprised when Lucy pulled away looking serious.

"Mom, you should know that it's okay with me if you had a boyfriend. You shouldn't spend all your time working. You deserve to have some fun."

Overhearing, Georgie laughed. "I agree with you, Luce and I will see that your mum gets ample opportunity to enjoy herself," she said, pulling the child into an embrace, she leaned down to whisper. "And I have the perfect man lined up for her."

CHAPTER TEN

This was the longest bloody holiday ever, Peter thought as he impatiently watched his daughter perusing the nearby bookshelves. This was their annual Boxing Day tradition. In lieu of gifts, they spent the day following Christmas hitting as many bookstores as possible. Normally it was something Peter looked forward to and enjoyed. This year, however, he was struggling to appear festive and jolly for his daughter's sake. It didn't help his mood that every store they entered featured a massive display of *Tempest,* which meant that his thoughts were constantly dragged back to *her*.

She had said that she was going home, but that had been a lie. He may have scared poor Frankie into divulging the woman's address before racing over, stopping only to purchase a replacement coffee, only to find no one at home. He waited. Sitting on the stoop in the cold until Abigail Norris threatened to call the cops on him. Returning home, he bit the bullet and decided to ask Georgie about the woman, only to discover that she had flown off to the States to spend the holiday with Alex. He apologized to Frankie again for his earlier conduct and invited her and Sammy to spend Christmas with he and Gracie before returning home with the thought that perhaps Clemency James was purposely avoiding him.

He woke the next morning and realized that even if she was avoiding him, it shouldn't stop him from being the bigger man. He was determined to apologize. Pulling his laptop onto his lap, he began shopping for a replacement sweater. It was more involved than he anticipated, and an hour later he found his virtual cart full of items in a rainbow of colors. He couldn't help but imagine her in each and every one of them. If he were perfectly honest, he was imagining unbuttoning each sweater and the creamy skin he now knew he would uncover... In the end he narrowed his choices down to four in the hope that one of them was her favorite color.

That evening while walking with Gracie to their favorite restaurant, he stopped before the corner florist. He should send her flowers, he thought before asking Grace to give him a minute. He caught the florist as she was preparing to close for the evening and made her day, selecting three different arrangements to be sent to Clemency's flat the following morning. The remainder of the evening was spent ignoring his daughter's quiet contemplation of him.

When he tumbled off his office sofa Christmas Eve morning, his first thought was that he should have sent something Christmassy to her. On his morning jog, he accosted the florist as she was opening and added a poinsettia arrangement to his order, before impulsively adding a dozen red roses to the mix as well.

Two days had passed and nothing. The more he thought about it, the crankier he became. He had included his phone number with the apologetic message he had penned. Hell, if she didn't want to talk to him, she knew where he lived. A curt thank you card dropped into his mailbox at the very least would have been appreciated. Just forget about her, he told himself. She's not worth your anger.

Watching Gracie add another armload of books to her basket, Peter found himself aimlessly flipping through a copy of *Tempest* that he hadn't even realized that he had picked up. To be honest, he hadn't read the copy Georgie had pressed into his hands. He had ended up skimming through it enough to realize that it wasn't something that he'd ever consider doing. Adding the book to his basket, he decided to give it a second chance. After all, Georgie was the one to suggest it. He should at least try to determine which character she had in mind for him.

"You're reading that?" Grace squeaked when he added his selection of books to hers at the checkout.

"It's research for work," he explained, catching the cashier as she stifled a giggle. "Why? Is there something I should know about it?"

"No, I just know that a lot of the older girls at school have copies that they keep hidden under their mattresses," his daughter explained with a shrug.

Under their mattresses? Now Peter was truly intrigued. Later that night, halfway through the novel he was more than intrigued, he was fucking aroused. He had quickly decided that the character Georgie had in mind for him was The Magician. As he read yet another steamy scene between Kennett and Tempest, Peter found that he was stroking himself as he imagined the scene playing out in his head. Only in his vision, the raven-haired Tempest was replaced by the redheaded Clemency.

The next morning Peter was standing on his stoop stretching before his morning jog. Letting out another long yawn, he tried to drag his thoughts away from what had kept him up until the early hours of the morning. He frowned when Roger pulled to the curb and Georgie stepped out. She had a shit eating grin on her face as he bound down the steps to greet her, but he was focused on the lone long-stemmed red rosebud she was twirling with her fingers.

"Where'd you get that?" he blurted out.

"Good morning to you, too, Peter," his friend said, bringing the flower up to her nose. "This little thing? I just dropped my friend Clemmie off at home only to discover that some madman has spent the past several days having bouquet after bouquet sent to her while she was out of town."

"Out of town?" Peter repeated. She hadn't been ignoring him?

"Um hm, she went home to visit her daughter for the holiday," Georgie replied. "Speaking of... did you and Grace have a good Christmas?"

Suddenly everything seemed much brighter. He surprised Georgie by giving her a quick hug. "It was wonderful," he declared, pasting a kiss on his friends' cheek, the dour demeanor of the past several days forgotten. She had gone *home*. And what was more, she had returned. He still had a chance... His smile faltered. A chance at what? She could still choose to avoid him. Especially if she thought of him as a crazed madman, as Georgie had described. "Did she like the flowers?"

Georgie's laugh didn't boost his confidence level. "Let's just say she's feeling a little overwhelmed at the moment. Is there something you wish to tell me, Peter?"

His friend was looking at him expectantly, but he wasn't quite ready to voice his thoughts just yet. What if she didn't take to kindly to the idea that he was ready to get back in the game and had had set his sights on her young friend? Shaking his head, he turned to begin his run, but faltered after a few steps. "Actually, Georgie, there is one thing I'd like to know. Why did you think of me for the role of Kennett?"

"To be honest, you are probably the *last* man I would have thought of for that role. Clemency was the one who was adamant about wanting Peter Bennett," Georgie explained causing Peter's heart to give a hopeful leap. "Of course, that was before she realized you were Peter Bennett," she added with a laugh before entering her home.

"What the hell did that mean?" Peter asked the now empty street before turning to begin his run. As he turned the corner onto her street, he was quite tempted to go straight to the main source and question her. However, the mere thought of seeing her had his balls tightening. There was no way he could appear before her in this condition. There had to be some other way. His mind raced as his feet hit the pavement and by the time he had completed is usual circuit he had a plan. Skipping his own door, he ran up the steps to Georgie's and leaned on the doorbell.

"Yes, Peter?" Georgie smiled in greeting after wiping the initial look of annoyance off her face.

"I'll do it," he declared. "Get me a script. I want to audition for *Tempest*."

After giving him a bemused look, Georgie disappeared, returning momentarily with two scripts in her hand. Flipping through both, she finally handed him one. "That one is yours, is tomorrow too soon?" she asked.

Agreeing on a time, Peter felt the adrenalin kick in as he headed home to shower. It wasn't just the thought of seeing Clemency that had him excited. He realized that the prospect of working again also gave him a thrill.

CHAPTER ELEVEN

"Hey sweetie, I know I told you to take the day off tomorrow, but somethings come up and I'll need you at the studio in the afternoon." Georgie's voice came through the speaker on her phone and Clemency sneezed in reply. The perfume from the flowers permeated her entire apartment and she moved to open yet another window.

"Why?" Clemency asked, sneezing again. She had yet to determine which bouquet was responsible for setting off her hay fever. Fingering a velvety petal of one of the roses she hoped to God it wasn't them. They weren't really her favorite flower, but this arrangement was so beautiful that the thought of having to get rid of it saddened her.

"I just scheduled an audition," Georgie replied, causing Clemency to smile at the excitement she heard in her friend's voice.

"That was fast. We haven't even been home a full hour," Clemency froze. "Wait, we haven't even polished the script yet. Aren't we jumping the gun a little?"

"You'll soon learn that in this business it's sometimes beneficial to put the cart before the horse if it gets you what you want in the end," Georgie explained. "I'll send Roger for you."

Clemency sneezed as Georgie rang off. Perched on the edge of the couch, she reached for the packages. Opening the first one, she smiled when a soft, rusty orange cardigan fell onto her lap. Opening the three remaining bundles she laughed to find three more identical sweaters in blue, green, and red. The man really did not know how to quit while he was ahead. Sneezing again, she reached for the envelope bearing her name in neat block letters. She found a gift card to the nearby coffee shop along with a note card.

I truly am not the ass all our encounters have made me out to be. Please let us begin anew ~Peter

She smiled down at the card, tracing the letters with her fingertips. *Begin anew?* Who says that? And what exactly did he mean? Turning the card over, she saw it included a phone number. Was she supposed to call him? The card fluttered to the floor as she sneezed three more times in quick succession. Groaning in frustration she leapt to her feet and grabbed the two mixed bouquets. Exiting the flat, she knocked on the doors on either side of the hall. When they opened to unveil the Norris sister's suspicious faces, Clemency thrust vases into their hands wishing them both a belated happy Christmas. Returning to her apartment, she leaned against the closed door and took a deep breath. She paused and waited, then breathed a sigh of relief. Donning the green cardigan against the chill from the open windows, she moved to unpack and begin a much-needed load of laundry.

She was a bundle of nervous energy the next afternoon as she greeted Roger. This was her *first* audition. She had no clue what to expect, but she was excited, nonetheless. She entered Georgie's office to find her friend tearing a hole in the carpet as she yelled into her phone.

"I don't care what you have to say about this, Jason. Alexandra or Sasha or whatever the hell she has decided to call herself this week will stay in school and graduate or I will be cutting off her allowance, understand?" Georgie flung her headset onto her desk before flopping down on the couch beside Frankie and resting her bright head on her daughter's shoulder. "You are by far my favorite child at the moment, dear."

"High praise indeed, given my competition," Frankie replied with an eye roll. Clemency laughed at the girl's wry sense of humor. From day one, Frankie Sutton-McDougal reminded

Clemency of someone, but she was still struggling to determine exactly who.

"What's the plan? Who's auditioning?" Clemency asked. She missed the look that passed between mother and daughter, and the next moment Frankie had leapt to her feet to greet the delivery boy who had just popped his head in the door.

"You've eaten already?" Georgie asked, moving behind her desk and taking the salad her daughter passed her way. "Good, that will give you time to prepare while we have lunch. The audition is scheduled for three o'clock. We didn't want you to get nervous and begin over thinking everything, so we waited until now to fill you in. Here are the scenes that will be read. We'll be working in the small auditorium, go there now and read them over so you're ready."

Clemency just stared open mouthed. "What exactly are you saying? You surely don't expect me to read opposite..."

"Well, yes... Of course, normally we'd have someone lined up, or even use Frankie, but seeing as this was a spur of the moment thing and Frankie is feeling under the weather..." Georgie explained, her attention focused on her food. Clemency glanced to the dark-haired girl who was watching her wide eyed before she had the presence of mind to give a halfhearted cough. "Besides, this will give you the chance to hear your words out loud, feel them tripping over your own tongue. What's more, I'll get a sense for how you think your characters sound."

Clemency tried to argue, but quickly found herself shooed out the door. She made her way to the auditorium, her knees wobbling slightly as she made her way down the aisle toward the stage. The room was roughly the size of a classroom with several rows of seats facing a small platform.

Half an hour later the pages Georgie had given her sat, untouched, on a nearby table as Clemency continued to pace the stage. She couldn't do this. What the hell was her friend thinking?

The door at the back of the room opened and Georgie strode in followed by Frankie. When the familiar grey curls of Peter

Bennett appeared, it all became clear. She was going to kill her friend for this.

She was angry. He could immediately see a spark in her eyes. Well, good, he thought. I'm fucking pissed too. The script Georgie had given him was absolute rubbish, nothing like the novel he had read. Stalking down the steps to the stage he had made up his mind to read for the part but give a resounding 'no thanks' should he actually be offered the role. He softened slightly when he reached the platform and noted that she was wearing one of the cardigans. As her gaze darted around nervously before settling on his, he smiled when he saw that it brought out the green in her eyes, just as he had hoped it would.

Clemency turned away to pick up the script, noting the scene which was chosen first. She gave a tiny snort of derision. The trust scene. She had trusted her friend not to put her in an uncomfortable situation, not to push her before she was ready. She felt Peter move up behind her. His blue eyes when she had briefly met them were smiling, but there was something else behind them. Turning, she attempted to plaster a welcoming smile on her face, only to realize that he was every bit as angry as she was.

The light in the room faded until only the two of them were illuminated by a spotlight. She cleared her throat nervously. "Do we just begin?"

"Wait," Frankie called from the pool of darkness, and they heard her footsteps tripping down the stairs. "Here, Mr. Bennett," she said handing Peter a long dowel rod. "I'll be here, reading Benjamin's lines."

Clemency eyed the girl who gave another weak cough before turning to face Peter. Her eyes widened as she took in his appearance holding the cane. She didn't know if he had done it intentionally but dressed all in black, he was the embodiment of Kennett Shariq. It was all she could do not to swoon.

"You may begin with the first scene," the disembodied voice of Georgie commanded from the darkness.

Peter watched as Clemency visibly swallowed and closed her eyes. He hadn't expected to be reading opposite her, but he planned to make the most of the opportunity to be near her. He quietly moved up behind her. "We're going to teach you a lesson, Tempest," he said quietly into her ear, startling her with his sudden proximity. He pulled a chair out from the table and gestured for her to sit. "There have always been rules between you and me, Tempest. And when the three of us stood before our family and friends, we spoke vows. However, none of those rules nor vows touched upon what we are going to discuss today, and that is trust." He tapped the stick against the wall to emphasize his point and Clemency jumped at the sound. She barely recognized Frankie muttering Benjamin's lines off stage. "Pay attention and answer Benjamin," Kennett demanded.

"I asked if you trusted us," Frankie as Benjamin repeated.

"Yes," Clemency squeaked, jumping once again at the sound of the cane thwacking against the wall. The scene continued, Peter portraying Kennett perfectly, right down to his dark growl. Clemency, however, was getting more caught up in the whole theme of the scene - trust. She had trusted her husband of eighteen years. She had trusted Georgie. Now, like Tempest, Clemency felt betrayed by those around her.

As the cane came crashing down onto the table next to her, she snatched it from Peter's grasp and snapped it in two.

"I do trust, Kennett. I trust you more than any person in this whole damn universe given some of the punishments I have willingly submitted to during our long relationship together," she recited from memory before turning to face the darkened auditorium. "If anything, you do not trust me. Trust that I know what I am doing. Trust that I'm seeking a solution to this mess. Trust that I know my heart and what it is and is not ready for. You betrayed me, so take your fucking lesson and shove it up your ass and let me do the job I came here to do."

"And let's call that a scene," Georgie's tentative voice came from the back of the room.

"You went a little off script there," Peter observed, coming up behind her.

"Yeah, sorry about that. Let's call it author's prerogative," Clemency explained, moving to pick up the pages of the next scene.

There were no issues with the second scene because it had translated word for word from the book with no issue. Still, Clemency breathed a sigh of relief when it was over. She absolutely hated this. Unlike Frankie, sitting at attention in the front row. The girl looked like she would give her eye teeth to switch places.

The final scene took place much earlier in the story than the previous two. Tempest, a time traveler, had accidentally leapt to her Magician on the night of her wedding to Benjamin.

"Shit, fuck, and God damn it," Clemency exclaimed, whirling to face Peter. "No, no, no, no, no. I cannot be here. Not now!"

"Hello to you too, my Mighty Mistral," Peter recited, circling her. "Why can't you be here, Tempest? Did you neglect your powers again?" he murmured, his breath tickling the back of her neck. Electricity shot through her at his touch, his fingers softly tracing down her arms.

"I can't," she whispered.

"What can't you do, Tempest" he asked.

"Be with you," she replied. Peter pulled back. His lips had been a hairbreadth away from hers. Was she speaking as Tempest or herself? He was quite certain that the little speech she had made at the end of the first scene was directed toward Georgie. Was she trying to send him a message as well? He stepped back, pulling the script from his pocket, effectively breaking the moment. He purposely skipped ahead a page, ready for this to be over.

"So, you waited until now and you're stuck sharing your wedding night with me," he said, ignoring Georgie's objection coming from the darkness. Instead he focused on Clemency and the look of relief in her eyes when she realized what he had done.

"I won't fuck you, Kennett," she said giddily.

"No, I respect you, Tempest. No sex this visit, but you will be punished. For breaking rule number four just now, and for neglecting your powers. You know where to go. What to do."

"What do you have in store for me this time?" she asked as he moved alongside her, raising her arms above her head to mimic the frame Tempest was placed into. Clemency let out a little squeak and the spot on her back tingled where his touch gently indicated that she, like Tempest should bend over, placing her hands onto the ground.

"Magician?" he barely heard her whisper.

"Yes, my Mighty Storm?" he recited as he picked up a piece of the dowel rod and slapped it down on the table to mimic the paddling Kennett gives Tempest. Clemency jumped at the sound and Peter took a moment to pause and admire the sight of her ass in the air before moving to stand before her. He indicated that she could rise and one look at her told him that she was every bit as affected by the scene as he was. "Come for me my Wild Windstorm," he commanded, gazing down into her dilated eyes. The next instant, despite it not being scripted, his lips met hers. Unable to help himself, he moaned and gathered her in his arms, deepening the kiss as he felt her tremble.

"Oh, fuck," she gasped, pulling away. He let her go but reached for her again when he saw how unsteady she was. "You went a little off script there," she whispered, her wide eyes looking up at him.

"Actor's prerogative," he replied with a smile, catching himself leaning in on the verge of kissing her again. He watched her eyes get even bigger and let her go as she stepped out of his arms.

"Excuse me," she muttered before fleeing off the stage and out the door.

Peter ran a hand over his face and through his hair, moving to sit on the edge of the platform. "Frankie, dear, could you please leave us alone. I have a few choice words for your mother that your young ears shouldn't hear," he said to the girl gaping up at him. As the door closed behind her, he called out into the darkness. "What kind of fucking game are you playing here, Georgie?"

"No game," Georgie protested, her voice much closer than he had expected and he turned to watch her make her way onto the stage. "I was just introducing my two closest friends in the hope that they could help mend one another's broken hearts."

"My heart's not broken," Peter growled.

"Okay... maybe not broken. Perhaps frozen is a better description given that you were married to the ice queen for so long. I was hoping Clemency could help thaw it a little," Georgie said, ignoring Peter's glare. "I know you're angry at me for saying that, but you're also not exactly denying it."

Peter rubbed at his face again before deciding to ignore Georgie's analysis of his marriage to Vanessa. "Are you saying that... okay, I refuse to utter that ridiculous name... your friend, she has a broken heart?"

Georgie nodded and lowered herself to sit beside him before she proceeded to tell him about Clemency and her cheating husband. "I won't apologize for meddling," she said with a defiant tilt to her chin. "Clemmie told me all about your accidental encounters. I was just assisting the hands of fate. You two are perfect together, you can't deny it, I saw that kiss."

Peter groaned and fell back to lie upon the stage. "Please don't remind me about it," he said, pressing the heels of his palms to his eyes. What would his friend say if he admitted that he hadn't kissed a woman in nearly thirty years?

"Come on, Peter. I'm sure Clemmie would agree, you really brought the character of Kennett to life there," Georgie said, prodding him in the ribs. "I mean, that kiss... whew! It definitely had me squirming in my seat."

He sat back up in order to swat at her, but she merely laughed as she good naturedly bumped her shoulder against his. "Seriously though, I never saw you and Vanessa kiss that way. You can't deny that there is chemistry between you and Clemency."

He was quiet, staring out into the dark auditorium. "I never kissed Vanessa because I once overheard her telling one of her friends how lousy I was at it," he admitted to his friend.

He smiled at the look of shock on Georgie's face. "Is that why you have avoided romantic roles all these years? Do you realize how many thousands of women you have let down?" He shrugged in reply, refusing to look at her, but she hopped off the stage to stand before him, forcing him to meet her eye. "Peter Bennett, if what I saw here today was any indication... Damn it, this feels awkward because you're my best friend, but I swear, when you told Clemency to come and then locked lips with her, that woman *came*. You kissed her the way Donovan used to kiss me." Seeing the sadness in his friend's eyes, Peter opened his mouth to speak, but Georgie silenced him with a squeeze of the hand. "Just think about what I've said. I need to go make sure Clemency is all right."

CHAPTER TWELVE

Clemency had exited the auditorium and headed straight out the glass doors of the studio entrance. She had the presence of mind to stop and ask the guard at the studio gates for directions to the closest underground station, however, she was halfway down the block before she realized she had walked off without her purse and wallet. Hell, she didn't even have her coat, and while London had been enjoying another rise in temperature, her cardigan would be hard pressed to keep her warm. Checking her pockets, she was relieved to discover she did possess her phone.

After several more blocks, she spied a park across the street and dodged traffic before entering it. Shivering as she sat down on the edge of a, now empty fountain, she closed her eyes and thought of Peter and the feel of his lips on hers. Immediately she felt a surge of warmth and she knew that her cheeks were blazing. Clutching her phone to her chest, she knew what she had to do.

"Cee? What's wrong?" Elliott answered on the second ring and she realized the note of panic in his voice was due to her calling him at work. Of course, he would think something was wrong. Well he was right...

"I-I'm saying the word, Elliott," she blurted out before she could lose her confidence. "I want a divorce."

"Cee Cee, what happened? Is everything okay?" Elliott demanded.

"No, everything is *not* okay, Elliott. I just said I wanted a divorce," Clemency felt her voice raise an octave and a little old lady gave her a startled look before bustling on by.

"I heard you the first time," Elliott snapped. "I just wanted to know what happened to precipitate this."

"I kissed another man," Clemency whispered.

"Is that all?" Elliott breathed, sounding relieved. "It's okay, Cee. I forgive you. We can work through this."

Clemency gave a short manic laugh. He forgave her? "You don't understand, Elliott. I kissed a man, and... I mean, it wasn't even romantically... fuck, what I'm trying to say is that I felt more in this one kiss with a man who was practically a stranger, than I have felt in years with..." her voice trailed off and she was met by only silence at the other end of the line. "I'm sorry Elliot, but I can't go back."

She disconnected the call before he could argue, and immediately opened the ride share app and ordered a car to take her home.

Rush hour was not the most pleasant time of day to be stranded in the midst of London. By the time she made it home, Clemency was cold, hungry, and desperate for a shower to wash away the day's events. Finding Georgie perched on the steps leading up to her flat, her coat and backpack beside her did not improve Clemency's mood.

"I'm sorry," her friend said in greeting, handing Clemency the key to her apartment. "I should have trusted you more and not pushed."

Clemency acknowledge her silently before entering her flat. She headed straight through to the bedroom and the adjoining bath where she flipped the shower on to the hottest setting. Out of the corner of her eye, she saw her friend hovering in the doorway to the bedroom. Closing the door on her, she stripped and leapt into the warm stream of the shower, yelping as her frozen extremities began to tingle.

When she finally emerged from the steam ridden bathroom, it was to find Georgie sitting on the edge of her bed holding out a cup of coffee to her. She gratefully downed half the mug in one swallow before turning to her wardrobe. The towel she had tied around her fell away as she dug around for something warm to wear.

"Damn, I remember when my ass looked that good," Georgie said appreciatively.

"Your ass never looked this good," Clemency replied and saw the look of relief cross her friend's face.

"Are you okay?" Georgie asked as Clemency pulled a long-sleeved top over her head.

"I called Elliott," Clemency said, sitting down beside Georgie in order to add a warm pair of leggings to her outfit. "I asked him for a divorce."

"Does that mean--" Georgie began excitedly.

"It means nothing," Clemency interrupted. "Only that I realized that I can no longer go back."

"Do you feel up to going out for dinner? Maybe talk about it?" Georgie asked.

Clemency shook her head. "I need some time alone, Georgie. I'm going to go grab some takeout from that Indian place we had lunch at last week and come home to crash."

It had been a long day and Peter was looking forward to supper and a quiet evening at home. He was halfway down the block, trying to decide what exactly he was hungry for when he was accosted by a breathless Georgie.

"Oh good, I caught you," she panted. "I swear this is me meddling for the last time," she paused to catch her breath, before straightening and grasping the stitch in her side. "Clemency asked her husband for a divorce today. That must be a sign, right? You didn't hear it from me, but, if you're quick, you should be able to find her at Curry in a Hurry."

Peter watched as his friend practically skipped down the sidewalk to her own house before continuing on his way. He had a sudden craving for Indian food.

He was relieved to see her at the counter when he entered the small, hole-in-the-wall takeout joint. However, he suddenly felt awkward as he came up behind her. It had been so long... how exactly did one go about asking a woman out these days?

"Fancy meeting you here..." he began, immediately kicking himself for sounding cheesy before rushing on. "I was hoping perhaps you would be willing to join me for dinner? Give me a chance to apologize for being an ass... Perhaps we could get to know one another better..."

He was greeted with silence and he felt his heart begin to race as panic set in. Was this how men got shot down nowadays? He recalled getting slapped in the face a time or two in his younger days, but he had never had his advances blatantly ignored.

He was running his hands through his hair pondering his next move when the smiling waiter bustled up to hand over her order. Would she even acknowledge his presence, he wondered as the waiter looked up at him expectantly. The next instant she was in his arms, having turned around to run smack dab into his chest.

"Oh shit," she exclaimed as she fumbled, trying not to drop her food, while simultaneously yanking out earbuds. He removed the bag from her hands as she looked up to see who she had accosted, and he was happy to see a tentative smile pull at the corner of her lips.

"We really have to stop meeting like this," he said, his gaze lingering on her mouth.

Clemency licked her lips, struggling to keep calm. She knew meeting him again was inevitable and she had told herself that she would remain cool. She could do this. After all, she was a writer. She had words at her disposal. She could dazzle him with her wit.

"Um, oh, uh, hi..." she found herself stammering. Shit, fuck, crazy, she thought, immediately feeling her cheeks begin to burn. Where is your wit, you witless twit? She closed her eyes, silently pleading for help from Benjamin... Carraig... anyone.

"Don't look at me, I'm still swooning over that kiss," Carraig warned. Clemency's eyes flew open at the memory and found Peter gazing down at her, a grin on his face.

"Are you okay? I feel like I lost you there for a minute," he asked. Clemency nodded mutely and he would have continued, but the waiter was edging closer. "I'll have my usual, thank you, Raj," Peter said, pulling a few notes out of his wallet and handing them over. "Would you be so kind as to join me for dinner? Perhaps we can get to know one another a little better... you can tell me your real name..."

"My name is Clem--" she began, only to halt as he began shaking his head, his grin growing wider.

"That's your pseudonym. I want to know the real you," he insisted.

"No," Clemency declared, quickly sobering. "That person is dead, or at the very least on life support waiting for the plug to be pulled," she paled as she watched the smile slide off his face and realized what she had just said. "Oh, God, Peter, I'm so sorry," she said, laying a hand on his arm. Good going Clem... add insensitive ass to witless twit... "Georgie told me about your wife. I didn't mean to come across as inconsiderate there, it's just that I'm trying to make a new start, which includes embracing my new identity."

His eyes met hers and he found himself momentarily lost in their green depths. Her thumb, rubbing lazy circles on the top of his wrist was sending electric shocks throughout his body. Surely, she had to be feeling this too, right? As if reading his thoughts, her pupils dilated as her eyes widened and he smiled.

Unable to help himself, he bent to gently caress her cheek with his lips. "Make it up to me," he murmured in her ear. "Join me for dinner."

"I... but I already have my order to go..." Clemency stammered her eyes darting around in search of the bag of food she could have sworn was there a moment ago. She saw Peter holding it up as the waiter returned with a second bag. He waved away the change with a smile.

"Your place or mine?" Peter asked, sending a prayer heavenward that the indecision in her eyes wasn't about to lead to rejection. He watched as her demeanor changed, her uncertainty replaced by a wicked little grin.

"Your place would probably be best," she said, turning to the door. "My place currently smells like a funeral parlor. Some daft old man keeps sending me flowers."

Daft old man? He paused in the doorway, his brow furrowing at this description. Well, he certainly did feel daft lately, but old? He took a good look at her standing in the light of the streetlamp. Well fuck, he thought. Of course, you're old compared to her. He must have at least twenty years on her. You foolish man, where had the time gone, he wondered, before remembering Vanessa. Twenty-eight years of marriage made up the majority of his adult life. He was jolted from his thoughts by her touch, her hand reaching for his.

"Penny for your thoughts?" she asked, tilting her chin to look up at him.

He shook away the melancholy thoughts that had invaded his head and brought her hand to his lips. He watched her mouth turn up in a smile and acknowledge the reaction this had on certain parts of his anatomy. Fuck it, he thought. He may be a grey-haired old man who had no clue how to go about playing the field in this new century, but she made him feel like a giddy teenager. Without letting go of her hand, he led the way down the block toward his street.

Reaching his door, he handed her the bags to hold while he fumbled for his keys. The door open, he turned to find her eyes closed, her lips moving as though she were in silent conversation. He watched her until finally her eyelids fluttered open and she met his gaze.

"Anything you wish to share?" he asked, quirking an eyebrow at the horrified expression on her face. When she replied with a vehement shake of her head, he merely gestured for her to enter his home, noting as he did so the curtains on the neighboring house twitch. Georgie may have claimed to have given up on meddling in their lives, but it wasn't going to stop her from snooping.

He found Clemency standing in the foyer and immediately

saw his homes decor through her eyes.

"It's very... uh, bright," she said, relinquishing the bags of food. That of course was an understatement. The white marble tiles of the entryway bled into white walls and stairway leading up to a white ceiling. The family room he directed her too was every bit as sterile looking, with a wall of white bookcases and furnishings to match.

Peter had deposited the bags in the kitchen and had returned. Standing in the doorway, he watched her shiver as she took in her surroundings. "This was my wife's domain," he said quietly, drawing her attention to him. "I haven't gotten around to changing much since she..."

"I'm sorry, Peter," Clemency said, crossing the room to stand before him. He watched as she began to reach out to him, before dropping her hand back to her side. He felt vaguely disappointed. He had spent the past eight months shunning any attempts at consoling, but somehow would have welcomed hers. "I was afraid that white was your favorite color, and while it's fine in moderation, I just find it so... cold."

"Yes, well, you just very aptly described my late wife," Peter said with a bark of laughter. Seeing that the joke fell flat, he sought to change the subject as he turned to lead the way to the kitchen. "Speaking of favorite colors, did I manage to pick yours with one of the sweaters I sent you?"

"Nope," Clemency said with a grin. "Not even close. Thank you though."

"How about the flowers? Were any of them your favorite?" he asked. Clemency shook her head as she climbed up onto the barstool he gestured to. He stopped, on his way around the counter to turn to her. "Any chance you can help me out here? Enlighten me a little--"

But Clemency was shaking her head. "No way. It would only encourage you to send more and I already had to deal with my neighbors, the Norris sisters, all up in arms over all the arrangements sitting on my doorstep."

"Ah, Abigail and Amelia," he laughed. "I swear they were already a hundred years old when I signed on to my first film with the studio and roomed above them. Do they still fight like cats and dogs?"

She grinned and nodded, accepting the plate of food he had served up.

"I love this stuff," she said, forking bits of rice, chicken and sauce onto a piece of flat bread. "I tried curry once back home, and I swore it burnt a hole through my stomach, but Raj was a dear and let me sample everything until I found something I liked," Clemency realized she was rambling and tried to heed Carraig's voice telling her to keep calm, but she felt like a fish out of water here. It had been so long since she had been on a date... *was* this a date? she wondered, eyeing the food on his plate as he joined her at the counter. "What's that?"

"Jalfrezi," he replied, biting into a chili.

"Is it hot?" she leaned in to examine his plate more closely.

"Very," he said, arching one eyebrow in challenge.

The meal was a leisurely one. Clemency felt her nerves begin to settle as they fell into an easy conversation about various interests. They found that they shared similar tastes in books and movies but argued over the fact that he favored the Rolling Stones to her Beatles. All the while, he watched her surreptitiously eyeing his plate. When he got down to the last bite of his spicy, chili infused stir-fry, he shoveled it onto a bit of naan and held it out to her.

"You realize that curiosity killed the cat, right?" he asked as he dared her to try it. His breath caught as she accepted the challenge as well as the food straight from his fingers. A moment later, she was gasping and coughing, and he leapt to refill her water glass. She downed it in one gulp looking up at him with tears streaming down her cheeks.

They had turned to tears of laughter, but Clemency quickly sobered when Peter stepped forward and gently wiped one away with the pad of his thumb.

"I think I can provide much better relief," he murmured before lowering his head to hers. His lips were soft and gentle as they settled on hers, but when the first lightening bolt shot through to her very core, causing Clemency to gasp, he took it as acceptance and deepened the kiss. His tongue soothed her, just as he promised. She clutched at his shirt, pulling him closer. Her brain registering a distant pounding, but she wasn't sure where it was coming from. Perhaps it was her heart racing, or his beneath her hand...

Peter drew back unexpectedly, and dazed, she looked up at him, confused as the frowning, fiercely knit eyebrowed face looming over her momentarily transformed into Kennett. She let out a small whimper at the thought and he moved forward, placing his hands on her thighs as they braced his legs. His lips met hers again, one hand moving to grasp the curls at the nape of her neck, angling her head for better access. She moaned as the pounding resumed and he broke away again. But not for long. She met his dark gaze and he leaned in to capture her lower lip with his teeth. As he did so, the hand at her waist shifted and she felt the warmth of his touch caress the bare skin just under the hem of her shirt. In that instant she was lost.

"Oh fuck," she whispered into his neck as she fell forward. What the hell was this man doing to her? She felt a throb between her thighs and realized that twice now she had come just from his kiss alone.

"God, I can't wait to find out what he's like in bed," Carraig's voice said, causing her to shoot up. What the hell was she doing?

"Hey," Peter said, his hand moving to rest on her cheek, forcing her to look up at him. "It's okay."

Was it? Clemency wondered. What was she thinking? She was still married. She closed her eyes and shook her head against the chorus of voices that were vehemently declaring that she had done nothing wrong.

Seeing the look of panic in her eyes, Peter rested his forehead against hers. "It was just a kiss, love," he soothed.

"Oh, I don't know if I would say that. It looked like more than a mere kiss from where I'm standing," Georgie's voice said, causing them to leap apart.

CHAPTER THIRTEEN

"I'm sorry for interrupting," Georgie said, straightening from where she had been leaning against the archway. "I did knock... several times, actually--"

"Perhaps you should have taken the hint," Peter ground out angrily as he moved around the counter, but not before Clemency noted that he was doing so to hide his obvious arousal. She focused on her lap, trying to hide her grin.

"I thought you promised to stop meddling," Georgie," she asked.

"Yeah, like that was going to actually happen," her friend said, moving to inspect their plates. "How was dinner? Were you moving on to dessert?"

Clemency suddenly felt tired. "Actually, I think I'm going to head home," she said, hopping down off her stool. Rounding the corner, she gave Peter a shy smile before reaching up to peck his cheek. "Thank you for dinner."

He caught her before she could move away. "Give me a minute and I'd be happy to walk you home."

"You mean get away from here and all these prying eyes?" she asked with a quirk of her eyebrow.

"Um, perhaps your neighbors are less nosy?" he countered.

Georgie grumbled as they pushed past her out of the kitchen. "Just make sure you bundle up this time," she hollered after Clemency. "It's gotten even colder out there."

"Yeah, yeah, Mom," Clemency replied as Peter held up her coat. She turned to see that he was no longer smiling, if anything he appeared sad. He removed the knit hat from her hands and pulled it down over her head.

"This is crazy," he muttered. "I'm old enough to be your father. If Gracie were in your shoes I'd be after me with a pitchfork."

Clemency began to laugh, but quickly stopped when she saw how serious he had become. "Unless you became sexually active at a very young age, I highly doubt that, Peter. Georgie, tell him how old I am," she yelled over her shoulder only to find that their friend had joined them in the foyer.

"Stop looking like your dog died, Peter. This hot piece of ass just hit the big four-oh," Georgie declared, smacking Clemency on the rear. Laughing at the shocked expression on Peter's face, she rushed to reassure him. "Trust me, I've seen her driver's license and can also tell you her height and weight, but not her real name. She issued a vividly detailed threat regarding me divulging that so don't even ask. I have, however, also seen her ass, and I'm not exaggerating when I describe it as hot."

Holding the door open for them to precede him down the stairs, he couldn't help but agree with Georgie's assessment of Clemency's backside. He looked up to find her watching him and grinned when he saw her blush. Twelve years age difference... he could live with that.

Halfway down the first block he reached for her gloved hand. By the time they reached her street, he realized that he wasn't quite ready to let it go.

"Would you be up for some dessert?" he asked. Grinning as he watched her eyes widen as they both recalled Georgie referring to their earlier post-dinner lip lock as dessert. "I was thinking of something every bit as sweet as your kisses, but a little more calorie ridden," he added, nodding toward the coffee house across the street.

"That sounds lovely," Clemency replied, she, too, was not ready for the evening to end.

"Would you like coffee as well or is it too late for that?" he asked, as they entered the cafe.

"After what Georgie put me through today, I plan on playing hooky tomorrow, so coffee is good," Clemency said.

They parted, Clemency to find a table, Peter to place their order. Setting the tray down on the table a few minutes later, Peter found Clemency deep in conversation on her phone.

"Actually sweetie, I'm out right now... yes, I guess you could call it a date," she glanced up at Peter and blushed at his grin. "Luce, I'm not going to go into details right now. I love you and will talk to you tomorrow."

"Your daughter?" Peter asked, handing her a fork and nudging the plate of cheesecake in her direction.

"I usually call her at this time each night," Clemency hesitated, her fork poised above the pastry. "I asked her father for a divorce today. I wanted to see how she took the news, but, as usual, my husband has avoided telling her anything. I'll need to have that discussion with her tomorrow."

Peter listened as she opened up, telling him about her husband and his infidelity. It was nothing he hadn't already heard from Georgie earlier in the day, still he was drawn to Clemency's strength. He was drawn to her and soon found his hand had made its way across the table, his fingers entangled with hers. "What made you decide to make the separation permanent?"

Clemency stared at their joined hands, wondering what he would do if she said that he and that blasted kiss on the stage were to blame. "We're just fooling ourselves," she replied.

Peter waited for her to say more and was disappointed when she didn't. A small part of him had hoped that he had somehow played a role in her decision. Taking a bite of cheesecake, he changed the subject to something that had been bothering him all day.

"I have a question about the movie," he began. "Please don't take this personally, but is there a reason why the script you wrote is complete rubbish compared to the book?"

Clemency sputtered on the sip of coffee she had been taking and avoided his gaze, making him even more intrigued.

"I may have written that particular script especially for you," she finally admitted.

"You wrote a crap script for me?" he asked, not quite following. "I thought you *wanted* me in the role. Why would you write something I would hate?"

Clemency felt herself getting flustered. His voice had gotten lower and she could sense anger behind his words. He was so much like Kennett. "I... It's just that Georgie--"

"Georgie what?" he interrupted.

"Wow, he even growls like Kennett," Benjamin piped up.

"You've been a bad girl, Clemmie. Maybe he'll punish you like Kennett," Carraig added hopefully.

Clemency squirmed in her seat. "Georgie said you didn't do romantic scenes. I thought that if I could write a less intimate, more distant Kennett, you would be more inclined to, at least, consider the role," she blurted out.

Peter sat back and laughed. Leave it to Georgie. "I take it there's another script? One more true to the book?"

"Are you really considering taking the role?" she asked as she nodded.

"Let me see the other script first and I'll let you know," he replied. Although, he knew damn well that he would take the part if it meant getting to see more of her.

They lingered over their coffee, their conversation becoming more personal as they discussed their daughters. Despite being close in age, they realized that their children were night and day. While Lucy was a lively drama queen, always vying to be the center of attention, Gracie was a quiet bookworm. They learned that they both had yearned for a house full of children, but circumstances made them settle for devoting all their love and attention to one child.

Slowly the tables around them emptied, until finally a barista had to interrupt them to say that they were closing. Both were surprised to discover that they had spent hours talking and it was nearly midnight. The bell tinkled as the door closed and was quickly locked behind them and Peter saw that Clemency was peering at her phone. Something amused her and she let out a laugh as she quickly thumbed in a reply to a message and hit send.

"Something funny?" he asked as she pocketed her phone and accepted his hand.

"Georgie was just a little concerned that you hadn't returned home yet," Clemency explained. "I told her that I couldn't let you have your way with me if we were dealing with her constant interruptions."

Peter joined in her laughter, but at the back of his mind he was unable to shake the image of her writhing beneath him as he pleasured her. They reached her flat far too quickly, and their laughter faded. Clemency climbed the first step and turned to face him.

"I had a really good time tonight. Thank you for turning a really crappy day into something memorable," she said, looking down at him.

"I'm glad to have a chance to prove that I'm not some crazed madman who goes around threatening and assaulting innocent women," he replied. Her lips were at eye level and he couldn't resist the urge to lean in and lightly graze his own across them.

Clemency pulled back, already feeling slightly dazed. Surely, he couldn't make her come a third time, she thought before leaning forward to brush her lips against his a second time. He joined her on the step, pulling her into his arms as he deepened the kiss. She needed more... her gloves fell to the pavement as she yanked them off before her fingers wove their way through the soft curls at the nape of his neck, pulling him closer.

"Oh, fuck," she gasped as she broke the kiss and rested her forehead against his chest, struggling to compose herself.

"Yeah, I *really* want to," he admitted, his lips caressing the top of her head. "But I'm too much of a gentleman to do that on a first date."

Raising her head, she saw the mixture of mirth and desire in his eyes. "Goodnight, Peter," she said before brushing a final kiss across his cheek.

He bent to retrieve her gloves. "Goodnight..." he began, and she waited for him to finally say her name, but he shook his head as he placed the gloves in her hands. "Goodnight, my love," he said as he raised her hand to his lips.

CHAPTER FOURTEEN

"Goodnight, my love," Peter's voice bidding her farewell still rang in Clemency's ears the following morning. "My love..." She didn't care if he ever uttered her name, as long as she could live the remainder of her life hearing him tenderly call her his love.

"Don't forget the kisses..." Carraig added. Clemency grinned, pulling the blankets up as her hand snaked under the waistband of her soft flannel pajama pants. However, the mere thought of his lips on hers made the happy spot between her thighs twang in response before her fingers could even begin to work their magic. That didn't stop her from spending the rest of the morning lazing about in bed thinking about the previous night.

When she finally rose, it was to find several missed calls and messages waiting for her. Most were from Georgie's personal number with messages prodding her for details about her date. Then around nine o'clock, the messages became more professional, wanting to know what time she would be in. The earlier ones were kindly inquisitive, and Clemency imagined they had come from Frankie. However, it was clear that Georgie had reclaimed her phone, as the more recent messages were laced with a selection of colorful word choices. Amidst them all was a simple message from Elliott.

Are you sure?

The conversation with her husband felt like it had occurred a lifetime ago, so much had happened. But if anything, the evenings events had only solidified her decision. She thumbed in a one-word reply, before settling down behind the desk in the front room. As she waited for her laptop to boot up, she called the studio. Frankie's eager voice answered on the first ring.

"Frankie dear, please inform your mother that I will not be in today, I--" she halted as she heard Frankie relay the message and then cringed at the string of profanity laced threats that Georgie issued in reply. She managed to stop Georgie's daughter before she had to repeat the message. "Frankie, kindly remind Ms. Sutton that my holiday time included yesterday. I came in on my day off only to discover that I was summoned solely to be a pawn in her matchmaking machinations. I have priorities other than *Tempest* and I plan on seeing to them today."

She disconnected the call, and then as a precaution turned her phone completely off. The last thing she needed was any distractions, she thought, turning to her laptop and her current project. She was working against a deadline for the first time, and while the draft of her new novel was complete, it needed a lot of polishing. It was going to take more than one day of playing hooky to get it done in time.

By the time her laptop flashed a low battery warning, Clemency was surprised to discover that it was early evening. Her stomach growled and she realized that she needed to eat something more substantial than the coffee and candy that had gotten her through the day. A sugar crash was imminent. Shrugging into her coat, she opened the door to find Georgie on her stoop, white flag in one hand, a pizza box balanced on the other.

"I surrender," she said, waving the flag. "Please forgive me. I'll try to stop sticking my nose in your business if you say we can be friends again."

"That depends?" Clemency replied, trying to stifle a grin at her friend's antics. "Is that pizza for me and what's on it?"

"Well half of it is. I was hoping we could share... Your half is pineapple, bacon," she replied, giving an exaggerated look of disgust as she listed the toppings.

Clemency's stomach greedily rumbled at the thought and she held the door open. "I guess I'll forgive you this time. But only because you brought food."

She grabbed a slice straight from the box and ate it over the sink while Georgie busied herself gathering plats and napkins.

"What did you and Peter do last night after you left his place?"

"Seriously?" Clemency asked, gesturing toward the clock on the microwave. "You couldn't even make it two minutes before prying?"

"Okay, I said that I'd *try* to stop, not that I'd succeed," Georgie began. "Besides, I'm new at this whole girlfriend thing. Isn't this what we're supposed to do? It's like the equivalent of locker room talk. Oh my gosh, are we going to delve into specifics? Length? Girth?"

Clemency choked as she inhaled a bit of pineapple and it took several glasses of water and Georgie pounding on her back before she was breathing normally again.

"Look, Georgie," Clemency began before pausing. Having a close friend was new to her and she didn't want to hurt Georgie's feelings. "You and Peter have been friends for a long time, right? I'm just not sure that I feel comfortable kissing and telling. It feels... awkward. I mean... have you ever..."

Georgie's head shot up, and Clemency couldn't help but laugh at the look of utter horror on her friend's face. "Good God, no. He's way too old for me," she exclaimed. "Never fear, Clemmie. Whatever you say here will be kept in the strictest confidence. Now tell me more about this kissing..."

Clemency groaned. Her friend was hopeless. She went on to describe the rest of the evening while Georgie listened attentively.

"What was it like?" she finally asked. "I mean, you are seriously the first person I have seen him kiss, and that includes his wife. I know women who have swooned at the mere thought of it."

Clemency frowned. She realized that in all their discussions the previous night, Peter had never really touched upon his wife and marriage. He had made the offhanded comment about her being cold. Now Georgie was telling her that she had never witnessed any intimacy. She found herself feeling sorry for him but couldn't dwell on it because Georgie was beginning to physically prod her now, poking her in the ribs, and demanding details. She swatted her away, intending to ignore her, but then realized that Georgie had far more experience with men than she had. Perhaps she could tell her if what she had experienced was normal...

"Georgie, has kissing a man ever made you come?" she asked, turning away before the older woman could see the flush work its way onto her cheeks.

"Okay, now you're just making things up to get back at me," Georgie's tone was indignant.

"I'm serious," Clemency argued. "I haven't been with many men, and they were all before Elliott so I can't even recall their faces, let alone the sex. I just wondered if what I experienced yesterday with Peter was normal. Have I, somehow, been missing out on this all along?"

"You're saying that you climaxed when Peter kissed you? Which time, and what exactly do you mean?" Georgie asked.

"Every time," Clemency admitted, lifting her gaze to meet her friends' eye. "You saw the first one. It was like... WHAM! Instant pleasure. The others took longer to build up, but the result was the same."

"It's not normal," Georgie replied, her voice tinged with sadness. "It's special. I have only ever been with one man whose kisses affected me that way."

"Donovan?" Clemency asked.

Georgie nodded, picking up the, now empty plates and moving to the sink to wash them. When she had finished, she turned to face Clemency. "I realize that with everything happening so quickly with Elliott and now with Peter in the picture you're an emotional wreck. You're understandably afraid of getting hurt so you're talking yourself out of taking a chance with Peter, but I need you to know that he's a good guy... the best, actually. And he deserves to find happiness every bit as much as you do, and I truly believe that you two can find it together if you just give it a chance."

"I want to," Clemency whispered. "I really do. But, please, just let us go at our own pace, huh? I think Peter's every bit as gun shy as I am."

"Good. Now, subject change... I am giving you another day off tomorrow. But only because we need to go shopping. I insist that you accompany me to a New Year's Eve shindig-- No, don't interrupt me, this is not me meddling, I'm speaking as your boss. This party will have a lot of who's who in attendance, many of which may be good fits for roles in *Tempest*. It will be a good opportunity for you to meet them before we post the casting calls. Besides, as your friend... well, I need *someone* to kiss at midnight..." she added with a grin.

The following evening, Clemency was singing along to "I Am the Walrus" as she spun around in front of the floor length mirror that resided in the corner of her living room. Georgie was one dangerous lady to go shopping with. Clemency managed to limit her purchases to three of the dozen or so gowns that her friend had insisted she try on. Now she just had to narrow the three down to one for the following night's New Year's party. While she loved the flirty feel of the current choice as the fabric swished around her knees, her eyes drifted back to the midnight blue velvet that now lay discarded over the back of the couch. That one had clung to all her curves making her feel quite sexy.

"If my opinion means anything, I like the green one there best," Peter's voice came from the open doorway to her apartment. "It will bring out the green in your eyes."

"How'd you get in here? And if you're already trying to memorize lines for the film, you just quoted Hanish, not Kennett," she said crossing the room.

"Your door was unlocked, an unwise practice I might point out," he replied, his hand instinctively moving to readjust the spaghetti strap of her gown. "I did knock. You probably couldn't hear me over the screeching of The Beatles there."

Clemency suddenly felt under dressed in the slip of a dress.

She nervously crossed her arms in front of her to shield herself, but only managed to draw Peter's attention squarely to the swell of her breasts peaking over the low neckline. Seeing his quick intake of breath, she mumbled an apology before darting toward her bedroom.

"Did you just dis The Beatles again?" she yelled through the door as she lunged into her wardrobe for a change of clothes.

"I am the walrus, goo goo g'joob?" Peter hollered back. "Not exactly on par with Shakespeare there, love."

"Yes, I will grant you that it has a certain amount of absurdity... but it's endearing. I used to sing that song to Lucy when she was a baby," Clemency argued, pulling the hastily grabbed shirt over her head as she returned to the front room.

"*You're* endearing, but it's also absurd to think that The Beatles are better than the Stones," Peter said moving to stand before her.

"Lennon and McCartney are the best collaborative song writers in the history of music," Clemency declared.

"Jagger and Richards are better musicians *and* entertainers," Peter countered.

"The Beatles have more memorable songs," Clemency stated. Peter's response was merely to cock one eyebrow, so she continued. "Please Please Me."

"Ain't too Proud to Beg," Peter replied.

"All you Need is Love," Clemency placed her hands on her hips.

"I Go Wild," Peter stepped forward until he was toe to toe with her.

"Do You Want to Know a Secret?" Clemency grinned up at him.

"I Can't Get No Satisfaction," he said, reaching to toy with one of her curls.

"Come Together," Clemency said, refusing to be distracted.

"Is that a promise?" Peter asked. It took her a beat to catch the meaning behind his question. He saw a fleeting look of fear in her eyes before bending forward to brush his lips across hers.

When he pulled back and still saw uncertainty lingering, he stepped away, crossing to the other side of the room while he struggled to get his heart rate back to normal.

"So, am I interrupting your preparations for a hot date?" he asked. He grabbed the old guitar from the corner stand and moved to sit on the couch, praying that her answer would be no and breathing a sigh of relief when she shook her head.

"Can I get you anything? Coffee? A glass of water?" Clemency bustled into the kitchenette trying to find something to occupy her hands. "Why are you here?" she cringed as she realized that came out sounding harsher than she had intended. She grabbed a bottle of water from the fridge and proceeded to drain it.

Peter, meanwhile, smiled at the realization that he wasn't the only nervous nelly in the room. He plucked out the opening notes of "Paint It Black" as he began tuning the guitar.

"I missed you," he admitted. It had been nearly forty-eight hours since he had last seen her, and he couldn't seem to get her out of his mind. "I don't have your number, so I thought I'd drop in to say hello." He glanced up at her, giving her a lazy smile. "Hi."

"Hi," she repeated back with a sigh, suddenly feeling much calmer. She moved to perch on the end of the couch and asked for his phone. "Your daughter?" she asked, peering at the dark-haired girl making a face on the screen of the cell phone he handed to her.

He nodded and plucked a few more notes as he watched her out of the corner of his eye. It didn't take long for her to add her contact info, and she smiled at him as she instructed his phone to 'Call Clemency' and her own phone began buzzing across the kitchen counter where she had left it.

"There. Now I have your number as well," she said, handing his phone back to him.

"Just don't expect me to ask it to call that ridiculous name," he muttered as he slipped it back into his pocket.

"It's a perfectly legitimate name," she stated. "I'm the third generation to bear it."

"But it's not your given name? You use it as a pen name," he asked.

"Well, no. It's technically my middle name," she admitted. "It won't actually kill you to use it, you know."

"Best not to risk it. Georgie does like to point out how old I am after all..." he said, adjusting another nob. The guitar was now perfectly tuned. He was just afraid that if he set it aside, he wouldn't be able to resist pulling her into his arms instead. "What do people back home call you?"

"Cee Cee," she replied with a scowl, watching his long fingers deftly move over the strings.

"Ugh, that won't do at all," he admitted. Although... that does indicate that your first name begins with a 'C...' Is it Clementine?" Clemency shook her head with a smile. "Pity. Especially since you always smell of citrus."

"So, tomorrow's New Year's Eve. Out with the old, in with the new..." Clemency said, her nerves returning at the thought of him being aware of her scent. "Any good resolutions on the horizon?"

To get you into my bed, screaming my name as I make you come? Peter thought. Focusing his grin to the ground so she wouldn't see it, he shook his head. "I'm just sorry I can't offer to spend the evening with you, but I have a prior engagement."

Another woman? Clemency thought, shocked at the instant pang of jealousy. "That's okay, I, too, have a hot date tomorrow," she said, before sheepishly admitting that it was with Georgie when she saw the fleeting look of sorrow in his eyes. "I would be much happier ringing in the New Year curled up here on the couch."

"Me too," Peter said and the underlying innuendo was not lost on Clemency who flushed as the image of them stretched out on the sofa, their limbs entangled popped into her head. Once again, he moved to put distance between them. He placed the guitar back in its stand before circling the room, examining the books and knickknacks left by previous inhabitants. Clemency rose to her feet as he came to stand before her. "I want you," he stated simply. "You have been haunting my dreams from day one. I was married for twenty-eight years, and I will admit that it wasn't always happy. But I was faithful to my wife," he paused to run a hand over his face. "What I'm trying to say is that it has been a very long time since I have been with a woman. There are times... When I'm with you there are moments when I feel like... I'm not looking for a quick fuck. When I say that I want you, I mean I want a relationship. Something lasting. I know that it may be too soon for you to contemplate such a thing, but I'll wait. I--"

He stopped as Clemency reached up to gently trace her finger over the lines of his face. She met his eyes and found them searching. Sliding her hand around the nape of his neck, she pulled his head down to her, her lips seeking his. As the kiss intensified and he grasped her hips to pull her up against him, she felt his arousal. His lips trailed soft kisses across her jawline down to her neck and she found herself thinking about his words. This *was* happening awfully fast. He distracted her with a tiny nip, and she felt the coil deep inside her become impossibly tighter.

"Oh fuck," she gasped when his hand moved to graze the underside of her breast. The coil snapped and she was instantly flooded with pleasure.

"Is that an invitation?" he groaned into her ear.

Clemency froze. She tried to take a step back but found that her legs were unwilling to cooperate. "I'm sorry," she said with a small shake of her head. "It's just too soon."

"It's okay, my love," he said. He kept hold of her until he could mask his disappointment. "Like I said, we can take it slow. I should probably head home though, while I am still able to walk," he said with a grin.

"Happy New Year?" she said, looking up at him.

"Happy New Year," he agreed, brushing his lips across hers one last time. If she was in his life, he knew that it would, indeed, be happy.

CHAPTER FIFTEEN

"Can you please explain to me what we're doing here?" Donovan complained, gesturing to the sea of people around them. "This is the thanks I get for chaperoning your daughter back from Edinburgh for you? What was wrong with our traditional New Year's Eve poker game?"

"Thank you for bringing *your* god-daughter home from her grandparents," Peter said, grabbing a flute of champagne from a passing waiter before turning to his friend. "You and Georgie both have been harping at me to get out more. When I finally do, you complain about it."

"That's because I didn't expect to get dragged along," Donovan grumbled. "Oh and prepare yourself. Gracie spent a good portion of the flight trying to convince me to set you up with someone nice. She's awfully concerned about you being alone while she's at school."

Peter sighed as he scanned the room. "You need not bother."

"Do tell," Donovan said, watching a grin slowly spread across Peter's face.

She had worn the green dress just like he had hoped she would. She was smiling and chatting with the group of people surrounding her and Georgie, but he could see that it was forced.

Donovan followed his friends gaze and caught sight of Georgie. "Damn it man, you had better not be thinking about my wife," he growled.

"God no, she's way too old for me," Peter said with a laugh. "And you had better not let her hear you refer to her as your wife. She'll skin you alive," he added as he began to make his way across the crowded room."

"Ah, the enigmatic redhead," Donovan said when he realized who had caught his friend's eye.

Peter moved up behind her, ignoring the daggers Georgie was sending in his direction. Instead he glared at the young man who had been blatantly flirting with Clemency, causing him to falter before slinking away.

Watching the man break off mid-sentence before disappearing into the surrounding crowd confused Clemency. Then she felt a whisper on the back of her neck.

"Happy New Year, my love," Peter said grinning when she spun around in surprise. "Are you enjoying the party?"

"I am now," she replied, happier to see him than she realized. She had spent the day reliving the previous evening and was surprised to realize that she had regretted letting him leave.

"Happy New Year, my love," Donovan parroted, leaning down to peck Georgie's cheek.

Georgie, however, didn't take too kindly to her ex-husband's appearance and swatted him away. "What are you two doing here?"

"What do you mean?" Peter asked. "We went to university with Rupert Preston. He always invites us to his New Year's soiree."

"Yes, but you have never made an appearance before. Why start now?" Georgie asked.

"Well, to be honest, I never liked Rupert much, but this year I just couldn't resist," Peter said, turning his attention back to Clemency with a grin. "Care to dance?"

"Wait! You're supposed to be here with me... working," Georgie protested as Clemency took the hand Peter offered. "You can't just go off and leave me with him," she argued, looking at Donovan who just grinned back at her.

Clemency threw a belated apology over her shoulder as Peter led her to the dance floor. "I'm not very good at this," she admitted when he pulled her into his arms.

"Neither am I, but all I really want to do is hold you," Peter said, wrapping his arms around her as the lively beat of 'Brown

Eyed Girl' segued into 'Crazy Love.' "I know that musically, we have different opinions, but can we at least agree on the fact that Van Morrison is pretty spectacular?"

"Hmmm," Clemency agreed, trying to focus on not stepping on his toes rather than her bodies reaction to being close to him again. "*Moondance* is one of my top ten favorite albums."

He pulled back. "Surely you mean *Astral Weeks*?"

"Seriously?" she scoffed. "You have 'Caravan,' 'Into the Mystic,' 'Crazy Love,' not to mention the title track. It's the perfect album."

"Yes, I will not argue that it's great, but *Astral Weeks* in its entirety is a work of genius," Peter argued.

"Are we ever going to find something that we can both agree on?" Clemency asked with a sigh.

"We can agree on the fact that you're going to drive me crazy... love," he replied and they both laughed. "That and the fact that this has to be our song."

Clemency nodded in agreement as she gazed into his eyes. They swayed together, oblivious to those around them until the closing notes of the song were interrupted by the lead singer declaring that the band would be taking a fifteen-minute break. She felt a sense of physical loss when Peter stepped away. The last thing she wanted was to return to Georgie and schmoozing the other guests. She knew more than anything that she wanted to ring in the New Year in Peter's arms, preferably at home, in bed. She was on the verge of suggesting the plan when they were joined by Donovan.

"I don't believe that we have been properly introduced," he said, addressing Clemency. "Donovan McDougal. Peter's friend, and Georgie's former husband."

"Clemency James," she replied, offering her hand which he graciously took, raising it to his lips before freezing.

"Not *the* Clemency James? Author of *Tempest*?" Donovan asked.

"You've read it?" Peter asked, surprised.

"Georgie sent me a copy a few months ago, asking my opinion," Donovan admitted. "She was not amused when I told her I was all for participating in a threesome as long as I had a say in the third participants identity. Speaking of my former bride, she's looking for you. She insists that you're her midnight kiss."

Clemency glanced up at Peter before turning back to Donovan. "I'll pay you a hundred pounds to take my place."

"You're offering me money to kiss my wife?" Donovan asked, confused.

"Kiss her if you dare," Peter said. "We just need a distraction so we can slip away."

"Keep your money, dear. Seeing Peter happy is payment enough," Donovan said, giving her a quick peck on the cheek.

"Shall we?" Peter said, offering her his hand. In no time flat Clemency was happily ensconced in the passenger seat of his tiny Alfa Romeo 4c as they sped across town.

Her nerves had returned by the time they reached her place. She fumbled with her keys and tripped over the length of her gown when she moved to turn the light on.

Peter caught her before she could fall, his hands warm on her. "I'll get the lights, love. You go change into something more comfortable."

She took two steps toward the bedroom before she stopped and turned to face him. She watched as he shrugged out of his jacket and hung it on the back of a barstool. "I-- I need help," she said. "Georgie had to zip me up earlier..." she turned her back to him. His breath tickled the back of her neck as he smoothly lowered the zipper. The next moment she felt his fingers gently trace the same path down her spine. As they came to rest at the base, she turned to him, face upturned.

He groaned into the kiss as his hands explored the creamy expanse of skin he had uncovered. He wanted to touch her... feel *all* of her... Sensing his need, she broke the kiss and stepped back. Dropping her arms to her side to allow the dress to slide off her shoulders, she let it pool on the floor at her feet. She was so fucking beautiful, he thought. Standing in the dim light waiting for him. He gathered her into his arms, silencing her protest with his lips before carrying her to the couch.

"If you want me to stop, just say the word," he instructed. He hovered above her where she lay on the sofa. In reply, she reached up and tugged on his tie, unraveling it from its neat bow. She managed to slip two buttons of his shirt open before the need to touch her grew too great for him to resist. She arched her back as he ran his lips over her ribcage.

While she relished the feel of his lips traveling over her skin, she wanted... no, she needed more. They appeared to be on the same page, as Peter settled over her, one hand gently tweaking a hardened nipple as his lips sought out hers. She gasped at the feel of him pressing against her. He was... throbbing. God, she hated that word, but it was apt in describing what she was feeling. He was hard and throbbing, or was vibrating a better word?

"Peter?" she gasped.

"Yes, love?" he groaned into her ear, his teeth running along the ridge causing her to writhe.

"Peter," she said more forcefully as she pushed against his shoulder. He pulled away, trying to mask the look of annoyance that flitted across his face. Now she was having second thoughts?

She pulled him back, kissing away his worry. "I think you have an incoming call," she explained. "Either that or a sex toy in your pocket.

He rose and straightened his trousers over what Clemency thought was an impressive bulge. He growled something about the torture he would inflict upon Georgie if she was responsible for the interruption, but one look at his face as he examined his phone let her know that it wasn't their friend.

"Sweetie, what's wrong?" Peter said. Realizing that it was his daughter, Clemency rose to give him privacy. Suddenly feeling quite exposed, she moved to the bedroom in search of clothes. Peter found her there a moment later and was unable to hide the disappointment on his face as he watched her pull a top over her head.

"Your daughter?" she asked.

He nodded, welcoming her back into his arms for a tender embrace. "She's at a sleepover and someone said something hurtful so now she's insisting on returning home," he buried his nose in her curls, inhaling deeply. "I'm sorry."

"Never apologize for being a father," she said. Pulling back, her gaze was focused on his chest as she refastened the buttons of his shirt. "Gracie is your number one priority."

"I just... I'm finding it all so difficult suddenly. I don't know what to do with Gracie. She's fighting with friends, skipping classes and leaving school without permission. I don't know how to handle it all, especially when all I want right now is to be here in your arms," he ran his fingers through his hair. "God, I must sound like a selfish bastard."

"You sound like a frustrated father, nothing more," Clemency consoled. "Twelve is a rough age full of hormones, body changes, and petty jealousies among friends. I imagine it's even more difficult for Gracie without her mother. I'll let you in on a little secret from the Mom Playbook to make things a little easier for you."

Clemency moved to the front room, crossing to the kitchenette with Peter trailing behind her. Did she say hormones? There was no way that his little girl was dealing with that yet, was there? Turning from the fridge, Clemency handed him a small container. "Ice cream?" he asked.

"Ice cream," she repeated. "Go get Gracie, take her home and sit her down with this. Tell her to eat and start talking. Your job is to listen. Don't talk, there's no way you'll even be able to begin to comprehend, let alone solve her problems. Just be a sounding board. Let her get what she needs to off her chest."

"Ice cream and listen," he said. "I think I can manage that."

"I'll be here if you need any other advice," Clemency said, moving into his arms for a farewell kiss. "I plan on staying up to ring in the New Year with Lucy. Message me if you need anything."

"Thank you," he said, his lips lingering on hers. "For understanding... for everything... and Happy New Year."

"Happy New Year," she repeated, and as the door closed behind him, she truly believed that it was going to be just that.

CHAPTER SIXTEEN

The first week of the new year, however, proved to be more confusing than happy for Clemency. For one thing, except for a vague *Thanks for the advice* text message from Peter, she heard nothing more from the man. Advice was scarce as she discovered that Georgie had also seemingly disappeared off the face of the earth. This she learned when Roger failed to pick her up as usual. Giving up, she was halfway to the closest underground station when she received a call from Frankie.

"Mum, um, I mean Ms. Sutton won't be in for the next few days," the girls excited voice informed her. "You're to have the next week off."

"Week?" Clemency asked in surprise. Georgie had been gung-ho about plowing ahead with the project come the new year. "Is everything okay?"

"Everything is great," Frankie replied cheerfully before ringing off.

After shooting off a message to Georgie, wanting to verify that things were truly okay, Clemency settled down to put the finishing touches on her project.

Three days into the new year and Clemency had completed work on the novel. She should have been elated but looking around her empty flat she realized that she had no one to celebrate with. Picking up her phone, she dialed home. Lucy would at least feign interest and congratulate her, only she got Elliott's voice on the other end of the line, informing her that their daughter was still at school, rehearsing for the sixth-grade play. Her husband was unusually chatty, and lacking companionship, Clemency fell into an easy conversation with him.

"Are you still sure it's not too late for us..." Elliott finally asked toward the end of the call. She only hesitated slightly before assuring him that she still desired a divorce. Hanging up, she realized that she may have not secured Peter's affection, but she couldn't see returning to Elliott as a possibility.

But damn it, I want Peter, she thought with a sob as she cried into her pillow that night. As if hearing her cries, she woke the next morning to a call from the man, himself.

"I'm so sorry," he began before she could even ask where he had been. "I got called away to Wales, then ended up on location in the middle of nowhere with no cell reception. Please forgive me and say you're free for dinner when I return Sunday."

Clemency felt lightheaded with relief and fell back onto her pillows as they discussed his hectic week.

"All week long, all I have been thinking about is hearing the sound of your voice, and here I am doing all the talking," Peter finally said. "Although, once I get you alone again, I plan on using my mouth in a far more creative manner."

Clemency shivered in anticipation at the thought. Sunday morning, however, found her shivering for an entirely different reason. The scene outside her bedroom window was a winter wonderland. Snow covered the street below as great big flakes continued to fall from the sky. The call came a little after noon, and while it was expected, she was hard pressed to disguise the disappointment in her voice when she explained to Peter that, yes, the weather was every bit as bad as the forecasters were saying. She would not be seeing him that day.

It wasn't until she was preparing for bed that night that she realized she had never managed to contact Georgie during the week. She would be sure to badger her friend about her elusiveness during the morning drive. Yet, once again, Monday morning rolled around to find Clemency waiting in vain for a ride that never came. The sidewalks had been cleared of the previous day's snowfall, but that didn't prevent Clemency from mentally adding new boots to her shopping list as she slid more than once on the icy pavement. She arrived at the studio cold and cranky. Seeing Georgie cozily ensconced behind her desk didn't improve her mood.

"You're late," Georgie declared without looking up from the sheath of papers in her hand. "I need you down in design. Their concepts need both of our approval before they can move forward. You're scheduled to meet with the head of costuming at noon, and Val Jamison here at three."

Frankie offered up a sad smile as Clemency stumbled back out of the office. It took getting lost twice in the maze of hallways before she finally determined that the design department was located in an entirely different building located across a small garden courtyard. She spent the morning working with the artists there, signing off on most of their ideas while making note of the things she wanted to discuss with Georgie before okaying.

The costume department was in the same building, but as it was nowhere near the commissary, Clemency tried to ignore her growling stomach as she sat through her meeting there. The head of the department was dour, in her opinion, and she had to encourage the woman to be as flamboyant as possible in dressing Ziggy and Merry, the dwarves who were essentially interstellar fairy godparents to the main character.

She was quite famished by the time she made her way back to the main building and Georgie's office. There she was introduced to Val Jamison, a seasoned script editor who had worked with Georgie in the past. She had been brought in to work with Clemency to polish her script. Apparently, this entailed tossing her a highly marked up copy and telling her to clean it up.

As Val exited the office, Peter poked his head around the door. "Got time for a break, love?" he asked, returning her happy grin.

"No, she doesn't," Georgie interjected before Clemency could reply. "I need that script asap."

"*Actually* Peter, I would love a break," Clemency replied, continuing before Georgie could interrupt again. "I have been working straight through since nine this morning. I skipped lunch because you had me scheduled in meetings all afternoon. I'm hungry and tired, but I will return after a half an hour break to do your bidding."

Clemency stomped out of Georgie's office, but when she made to exit the outer office, Peter grabbed her by the arm and redirected her toward his door. Shutting it behind them, he instantly had her pressed against it, his lips crashing down upon hers. God, he had missed her. He coaxed her lips open, needing to taste her... and there it was, the gasped expletive that made him hard every time. Backing up to the couch, he pulled her along with him. As he fell back onto it, she straddled his lap. It was her turn to take command, her mouth exploring, trailing kisses along his jawbone, nibbling his ear. His hands rested on her hips, his thumbs teasing the bare skin above the waistband of her leggings. He wanted more but knew this was not the time and definitely not the place. It took all his self-control not to run his hands up under her shirt to explore the expanse of smooth skin he knew was waiting for him there.

Finally relinquishing his earlobe, Clemency sat up. "Hi," she said, feeling more than a little dazed.

"Hi," he repeated with a smile. "Miss me?"

"Maybe a little," she replied coyly before rocking against him.

His hands grasped her a little harder. "Not a good idea, love," he warned, watching her eyes widen in response. She leaned in to glide her lips across his and muttered another exclamation as her eyes glazed over. She was sexy as hell when she was aroused, he thought, then chuckled as the moment was interrupted by her growling stomach.

"You're breaks nearly up, love," he muttered against her lips. "What are your plans for the evening?"

"I'll be holed up in one of the fish tanks editing," Clemency said, not really looking forward to the task. "You?"

"Dinner meeting. If I get out early enough how about I stop by for dessert?"

"I like the sound of that," she said, unconsciously moving against him again as she lowered her head to nuzzle his neck. A rumbling from her belly indicated that it too approved of the plan, making them both laugh.

"Tell you what, you go get set up downstairs and I'll fetch you something from the commissary before I leave," Peter suggested.

Leaving his embrace was hard, and Georgie's scowl as she glanced at her watch didn't improve Clemency's mood. She grabbed her bag and beat a hasty retreat. Entering a fish tank, one of several glass enclosed workspaces where those without offices could work in solitude, Clemency flipped through the script. Noting the number of alterations, she pulled out the power cord along with her laptop. It was going to be a long night.

Thankfully, Peter did not underestimate her appetite. Piling a stack of takeout containers on the desk, he pulled her into his arms for a quick kiss before darting off to his meeting.

Hours later, surrounded by empty containers and with her desk lamp as the only light illuminating the area, Clemency realized that she was alone. Pulling off her headphones, she raised the volume on her music, letting the angry lyrics of The Clash wash over her as she worked. The loud music resulted in her missing the first text from Peter. It wasn't until the second one came through that her phone lighting up caught the corner of her eye.

Your lights are off. Am I too late?

Crap. She glanced at the time. It was already after ten and she was only about halfway through the script. Surely Georgie didn't expect her to get it all fixed in one sitting, she thought, not for the first time that evening. But recalling the woman's stern face gave her second thoughts. Picking up her phone, with a heavy heart she thumbed in a reply.

Still at work. No end in sight... Sorry.

She worked through the night, adding the final touches just after five in the morning. Too tired to return home, she lay her head down on the table, thinking that she just needed a minute or two to replenish her energy. Peter found her there an hour later. She was barely conscious of his presence as he gathered up her belongings and half carried her up to his office. Sitting behind his desk listening to her gentle snore, he wondered what had possessed her to work so hard.

She shot off the couch when Frankie entered the office with his morning coffee. The wide-eyed girl sat down the mug before backing out of the room, closing the door behind her. Clemency, however, was in a panic.

"Where am I? My computer... The script...Georgie..." her voice raised an octave with each statement, and Peter quickly rounded the desk to take her by the shoulders.

"The script is here," he said, pressing a jump drive into her hand. "You're in my office, Georgie is right across the way. Keep calm, love. Would you like my coffee?"

Clemency shook her head, her eyes enormous and hollow as she clutched the drive to her chest. He followed her as she tripped across the outer office toward Georgie's open door.

"You're late again," Georgie said, glancing up from her computer.

Peter frowned. What the hell was wrong with his friend? "She can't technically be late when she's never even fucking left in the first place," he growled.

Clemency missed the look of surprise on Georgie's face. "What's todays agenda?" she asked, placing the jump drive on the desk. She felt Peter's hands on her shoulders and gratefully leaned back into him.

"Auditions scheduled for one and four," Georgie replied. "You should go home and change. You look like hell."

As Clemency stumbled out of the office, Peter fished keys out of his pocket and handed them to her. "My car is just outside the west exit. I'll meet you there and run you home," he instructed. He watched her stagger down the hall, making sure she turned the right direction before turning to a curious Frankie. "Do me a favor love, cancel all my morning appointments. I know Jack will be hounding you any minute now, tell him I'll be in after one." He turned to Georgie's office, closing the door behind him as he entered it.

"I'm rather busy, can this wait?" Georgie said rather coolly.

"No, it can't... What the hell, Georgie," he began heatedly before stopping. He turned; his hand was on the doorknob before he swiveled back to face his friend. "Georgie Sutton, you are one of the most brilliant, innovative and talented women I have ever met. Someday, I imagine we will be celebrating your lifetime of achievement, and... I may be wrong here, but I'm betting that when my turn comes to get up and talk about how you influenced me, I'll be saying that I'm thankful that you introduced me to that woman. She's remarkable, Georgie. I'm already half in love with her. I don't know what has happened to put you in this piss ass mood, but please don't throw away her friendship."

He could see that she was shocked by his admission. Hell, he was a little stunned himself, he thought as he stormed down the hall toward the exit. He found Clemency in the passenger seat of his car, her head resting on the window, sound asleep. He prodded her awake once he pulled up in front of her place and, with a yawn, she told him to make himself at home while she took a quick shower.

Fifteen minutes later, he peered into her bedroom to find that she had showered and was now sound asleep on her bed, wrapped only in a plush robe. Unable to help himself, he set the alarm on his phone before kicking off his shoes and climbing onto the bed to join her. Laying there watching her eyes flutter behind closed lids, he pondered his earlier declaration. Was it possible to fall in love so quickly? He tried to recall what it had been like with Vanessa. It had taken them ages to declare their feelings, and if he were honest, he would admit that he had only done so because she had expected him to.

A wet curl fell across her cheek and when he reached to gently tuck it back into place, she mumbled his name and rolled closer to him. He shifted so that she lay with her back against his chest and breathed deeply. Closing his eyes, Peter found himself surrounded by her citrus scent and he slept.

Clemency woke to find her robe open and Peter's hand resting on her ribcage just below the swell of her breast. Attempting to turn to face him, his eyes fluttered open and his lips settled on hers. He deepened the kiss as his palm cupped her breast causing her to shudder at the pleasure that had immediately flooded her. He drew back to gaze down at her, seeing that she was now fully awake, her body flush with arousal. He dipped his head for another brief kiss before moving lower and capturing the hardened peak of a nipple between his lips. She cried out and arched her back, but his hand continued to travel over her body, trailing further south until it reached the junction of her thighs. He let out a long low groan. She was so wet... so ready for him, and yet he knew that they had mere minutes before his alarm alerted them that it was time to return to the studio. He had meant it when he said he wasn't looking for a quick fuck. When he finally took her, he meant to take his time and savor it. For now, he would settle for bringing her pleasure.

Rising on one elbow, he was determined to watch her face as he slowly dipped a finger into her. She threw back her head and moaned as he withdrew the digit to circle the engorged bundle of nerves before sliding back into her. She gazed up at him, her eyes dazed as he repeated the motions. When he added a second digit and pressed the palm of his hand to her, she cried out his name and he could feel her muscles clenching as she climaxed.

"You're beautiful when you come," he whispered against her lips and she cried out once again, her voice competing with the alarm sounding off from the bedside table. "Time to return to the real world, love."

"But what about you?" she asked shyly, reaching out for him

"There will be time enough for that, my love," he replied, moving to slip his shoes on. "For now, we have appointments to keep."

"Tonight?" she asked hopefully.

"We'll see," he answered, not sure how long his day would run. "For now, get dressed, I'll see what I can scrounge up for us to eat."

CHAPTER SEVENTEEN

That night was a bust, as was the remainder of the week. One of them always seemed to be caught up in meetings or auditions, and Clemency found herself burning the midnight oil on more than one occasion. However, they did manage to spend a few quick breaks together and almost managed an entire lunch on Thursday before Frankie popped her head into Peter's office to warn Clemency that Georgie was on the warpath and looking for her.

For the life of her, Clemency could not figure out what had gotten into her friend. Georgie's mood had not improved, if anything it had gotten worse. When Clemency and Peter were caught attempting to make plans for the weekend, Georgie pounced, glowering at them both as she issued demands that would keep Clemency hard at work straight through till Monday.

The second week of the new year proved no better. Clemency could have sworn that she was told that this project would be highly collaborative. But Monday morning Georgie swept into the office announcing that she had cast the role of Tempest, to a woman Clemency had found to be completely wrong for the part. The week went downhill from there. It didn't help that Peter was, once again, stuck in Cardiff. By Friday she realized that she had spent the entire week either on the verge of tears or in a murderous rage. She couldn't continue this way.

The final straw came that morning. Entering the office, the first thing she saw was the whiteboard they had erected listing the characters and the potential cast they had in mind. Someone had crossed off Peter's name and circled the name, Colin

Fletcher, an actor that Clemency had detested from the moment he had opened his mouth.

Hoisting her bag onto her shoulder, Clemency turned and walked out of the office. Unsure of what to do next, she recalled that Peter had pressed his office key into her hand before he had left, telling her to use it as a refuge should she need to. Thankful, that the outer office was empty, she slipped through the door as Georgie's loud voice was heard coming down the hall. Her bag hit the floor as she fell back onto the leather sofa. She had effectively trapped herself, she realized. But it was only temporary. She knew what she needed to do, she just needed to find the nerve to do it. Closing her eyes, she waited. Only Carraig and Benjamin's voices with their sage advice never came. Instead, she fell into a deep sleep.

She woke feeling refreshed. Noting the time, she saw that it was early enough to call her daughter before Lucy headed off to school. The sound of her child's voice bolstered her nerve and as she hit disconnect, she powered up her laptop. The letter didn't take long to type and as Peter's printer whirled to life, she picked up her phone again. Ignoring the stream of increasingly angry messages from Georgie, she shot off a text to Peter, letting him know what she had planned.

His *I'll support you no matter what* gave her a much-needed boost to her courage. She was packing everything up when her phone rang.

"I'm on my way home," Peter said by way of greeting. "I should be there in time for dinner. Are you game?"

"That sounds perfect," Clemency replied.

"I'm not making excuses for Georgie, but she's not typically like this," Peter said with a sigh. "I'm sorry--"

"It's okay, I've made peace with my decision," Clemency replied when he faltered. They chatted for a few more minutes, but before he rang off, Peter hesitantly offered a suggestion. After pondering his advice, Clemency found herself sneaking out of the office and down the hall toward the commissary before returning to finally confront Georgie.

"Where the hell have you been?" Georgie ground out when Clemency entered her office. The speech she had prepared vanished from her head, so she simply stepped forward to hand over the letter of resignation she had prepared. She watched her friend's eyes widen in surprise, but when Georgie opened her mouth to argue, Clemency set a pint of ice cream along with a spoon on the desk in front of her.

"I quit, Georgie. As my letter states, working with you has become increasingly impossible. However, I'm willing to give our friendship one last chance. Either eat and start talking or tell me to fuck off," Clemency declared as she took a seat across from Georgie.

She watched as the woman opened and then closed her mouth before reaching to lift the lid off the ice cream container. She glared across the desk at Clemency.

"You offered Donovan money to kiss me New Year's Eve," she accused.

Clemency was taken aback. <u>This</u> is why her friend had been so angry? "Oh my God, Georgie, did he do something to hurt you? I swear it was done in jest. Peter and I just wanted to spend some time together."

Georgie swiveled her chair around to face the large picture window. "I slept with him," Clemency barely heard her whispered confession. "Over two decades of fighting off his advances..."

Clemency rushed to her friend's side. Kneeling in front of her, she took Georgie's hands in hers. "Sweetie, tell me. What did that bastard do?"

"You're beginning to sound like me. He didn't do anything," she sighed. "We spent four glorious days together, barely making any effort to leave the bed. He told me that he loved me... had always loved me... and then, he left."

"He left?" Clemency asked.

Georgie nodded. "Fled back to his Scottish Highlands with nary a word. Left me stuck here watching you and Peter basking in constant post-coital bliss."

Clemency let out a bark of laughter as she rose to her feet. "Bliss, yes. Coital, no," she admitted, continuing when she saw the look of surprise on her friend's face. "How do you expect us to do anything when you have me here working day and night?"

"I never expected--" Georgie began.

"Where's that script, Cinderella? Go down to design, Cinderella. You're late again, Cinderella..." Clemency interrupted.

"I guess I have been a little bitchy lately," Georgie admitted.

"A little?" Clemency asked, nodding to the letter sitting on the desk. "I can't do this anymore, Georgie. It's not what I signed on for."

"You signed a contract," Georgie pointed out.

"Two of them, actually," Clemency agreed. "I spent the day pouring over them. The first was for the rights to *Tempest*. That's fine. It's yours. Do what you want with it. The second was for my collaboration. It stipulated the use of the flat and a stipend, otherwise payment for my services would be conducive with the completion of the project. I can be packed and out of the flat by the end of the weekend and you can pay me for my services up till now... or not... I really don't give a damn right now, I'm over this shit, Georgie."

"Where will you go?" Georgie asked.

"I-I don't know yet," Clemency replied. She hadn't thought that far ahead. Hearing Lucy's voice today made her realize just how much she missed her child, but the thought of leaving Peter left her feeling empty inside.

"I'm sure you could move in with Peter," Georgie said, shuffling the papers on her desk. "Are you in love with him?"

Clemency turned her back on her friend, pivoting to stare blindly out the window. "That's a personal question. We're speaking professionally at the moment."

"Okay, fairly put. As your employer, I refuse to accept your resignation," Clemency turned at the sound of her letter being torn in two and opened her mouth to argue, only to be interrupted by Georgie who commanded her to sit. "Time to renegotiate. What are your demands?"

Clemency took her time as a myriad of ideas struggled to take shape. "Set hours," she said as she lowered herself back into the seat facing the desk, but Georgie was vehemently shaking her head before Clemency could even get comfortable.

"Impossible. Especially once filming begins. I can assure you that you role in the production will get easier, at least until we've gotten to the editing stage. But this is not a nine to five job. How about if we compromise and I guarantee no more over-nighters?"

Clemency nodded, but her attention was already focused on her next demand. She glanced to the whiteboard. "Tempest and Kennett recast."

"I assume you still desire Peter in the role?" Georgie said, leaning her elbows on the desk as Clemency nodded. "Will he take it?"

"I think I can sway him to accept the part," Clemency said with a grin. "He wants to see the real script first though."

"Done," Georgie declared, rising to make the changes on the board. "This works, I got word today from Colin Fletcher. He wants to read for the part of Carraig of all things... We are, however, stuck with Kaitlyn. She's signed a contract. But I think we can make it work."

Georgie readily agreed to the remainder of Clemency's demands. Most were things they had already decided upon, but Clemency wanted to make sure to get them down on paper. Namely Lucy joining her for the summer, and a two-week holiday break at the end of July.

When Peter poked his head in the door an hour later, he found both women laughing as they discussed casting ideas and upcoming auditions. When Clemency finally caught sight of him leaning against the door frame, she wasted no time bounding into his arms.

"Hello to you too, my love," he said when he finally relinquished her lips. He grinned to see that her eyes had glazed over. "Are you ready for dinner?"

Clemency glanced over her shoulder to see a shadow pass

over Georgie's face as her friend attempted to look busy. She pulled Peter out the door before looking up at him apologetically. "I'm sorry--" she began.

"But you're going to have to cancel," he finished for her. "Is everything okay?"

"We've worked out our professional differences. I'll be staying," she explained, happy to see his broad smile at the news. "Georgie just needs a friend right now. I hope you understand."

"Say no more, love," Peter said, brushing a quick kiss across her lips. "Gracie will be home this weekend and we have plans, but I'm just a phone call away. How does a late supper on Sunday sound?"

"Wonderful," Clemency replied. "And speaking of phone calls, do me a favor and call Donovan and find out what the hell he's up to." She refused to say more, not wanting to betray her friends trust. Instead, she watched him leave and pondered Georgie's earlier question. Could she possibly be falling in love with him? She thought about how his kisses made her toes curl as she turned back to the office.

Georgie looked up in surprise, but followed Clemency's orders to grab her purse, they were leaving.

"What about Peter?" she asked, following Clemency out the door to find Roger already waiting at the curb.

"He can wait. You're more important," Clemency replied. As they climbed into the back of the waiting car, Clemency found her friends eyes assessing her.

"You've really gone three weeks without making it to the bedroom yet? Are you sure that *you* can wait?"

"I never said that we haven't made it to the bedroom," Clemency replied coyly. "As for me, all my nerve endings still erupt into a happy dance whenever that man kisses me, so I'm good."

"Clemmie, Clemmie, Clemmie, are you going to kiss and tell?" Georgie asked.

"Only if you do, Georgie. Only if you do..."

CHAPTER EIGHTEEN

Clemency grimaced as Georgie sloshed tequila all over the place as she attempted to refill her shot glass. She had suspected that her friend had cheated and remained sober during their last foray into the bottom of the bottle, now she was certain.

"Donovan just said, see you soon and left," she asked, mopping up the spilled liquor.

"'S right," Georgie replied. "Nearly two weeks and not a peep." She threw her drink back and missed her mouth, causing Clemency to cringe at the sight of the droplets staining her friends white silk blouse.

"Let's get you out of these clothes," she said as she pried the glass out of Georgie's grasp and prodded her toward the bedroom.

"Are you trying to seduce me Cal... Call... shit, how do you even say that name of yours?" Georgie threw over her shoulder.

"I'm just thinking that your outfit there cost more than my first car, and you're going to be fairly cranky come tomorrow when you sober and see the damage," Clemency replied as she rummaged through her wardrobe for a change of clothes. Moving to the bathroom to wash up, she returned to find that her friend had managed to complete half the task of changing clothes before passing out face down on the bed. She climbed in and pulled the comforter over them with a sigh, trying not to think that it was supposed to be Peter sharing her bed tonight.

The following morning found Clemency sitting on the edge of the sink as Georgie heaved her guts into the toilet beside her. Her phone buzzed as she handed a wet washcloth down to her miserable friend.

"Good morning, love," Peter's greeting was far more chipper than she felt. "How are you ladies doing this morning?"

"I'm fine and dandy," Clemency replied as Georgie's efforts echoed off the tiled walls of the small room. "The thing you're hearing that sounds like a velociraptor in the midst of its death throes, however, is Georgie." She hopped off the sink and moved to the bedroom, ignoring the hand her friend had raised in a rude gesture.

"I just got off the phone with Donovan," Peter said. "His mood is the exact opposite of Georgie's. Says he's looking for someone to take over his practice and is planning on moving down here. Seems determined to make things work with Georgie."

"She'll most likely have something to say about that," Clemency replied.

"About what?" Georgie asked from the doorway.

"What was that Gracie?" Clemency heard Peter say as she turned to her friend.

"I'll have something to say about what?" Georgie demanded.

"I'm on the phone Gracie... No, it's not Georgie... It's a friend," Peter continued in Clemency's other ear.

"Clemency, tell me," Georgie said, taking a step toward her.

"Peter, I gotta go,"

"I have to go, love," they both said at the same time before ending the call.

"Daddy, who was that?" Grace asked.

"I just told you, it was a friend," Peter explained.

"A girlfriend?" his daughter prodded. "You called her 'love.'"

"Yes... it was a friend who happens to be female," Peter replied, swallowing nervously. "Are you ready to hit the museum?"

He felt like a relic on display as his daughter assessed him, and he couldn't help but examine her just as closely. Clemency had said that twelve was a year full of hormones and body changes, but he still saw his little girl standing before him. Okay... she may be may have embraced a bulkier wardrobe as of late and she was hunching over more than usual. Did he need to take her to a doctor for that? Had he missed some sort of spinal deformity?

Peter let out a breath he hadn't realized he had been holding when his daughter shrugged her shoulders before skipping off to grab her coat. Once a month father and daughter enjoyed traipsing through one of the many museums the city had to offer. They would seek out the less exciting objects in a collection, the ones often found crammed into the dark corners of displays. They enjoyed making up stories about them, and today was no exception. As they examined a pre-classic Mayan vessel housed in the British Museum, Peter told the story of a young girl who would always bring her poor old dad his morning coffee in said cup. Grace, on the other hand, insisted that it had been used by a Mayan prince who would drink the blood of his enemies from it. Moving on to the next room, Peter couldn't help but wonder how Clemency would fare at this game. Knowing her, she would blow them both out of the water with her imaginative tales.

Grace didn't bring up the subject of the mornings phone call again until later that evening when she came upon Peter fiddling with his phone.

"Are you texting?" she asked incredulously.

"Yes, Gracie," he replied. "I'm not so ancient that I can't comprehend modern technology and communication."

"It just looks so... odd. Who are you messaging?" she asked, trying to peer over his shoulder.

"A friend," Peter muttered as he finally completed keying in the simple four words *How was your day?*

"The same friend from this morning?" Grace inquired and seeing that his daughter would not be satisfied until he answered all her questions, Peter set his phone down and gave her his undivided attention.

"Yes, Grace, the same friend," he replied.

"Is she your girlfriend?" she asked tentatively, and Peter saw a glimmer of hope in her eyes.

He sighed. He wasn't ready to get his daughter's hopes up. "She's someone that I'd like to get to know better, Gracie. But right now we're both very busy with work so it's hard for us to find time to get together."

"You can go now. See, she says that she misses you," Grace said excitedly as she read the message that appeared.

"I'm not going to go and leave you here all alone," Peter explained patiently. "We have dinner plans tomorrow. In the meantime, I have plans to kick a certain young tushy at Scrabble."

"In your dreams, old man," Gracie exclaimed before running off to set up the game board.

Sunday seemed endless as Peter's thoughts continued to drift to his evening plans. He was able to sneak in a quick call to Clemency mid-morning and she agreed with his plan to bring takeout over to her place rather than going out. He nearly skipped down the steps when the time came for him to return Grace to school. He then had to bite back the string of expletives when six blocks into the drive he had to turn back because she had forgotten her clarinet. He swore he aged another decade waiting for their order at the restaurant, but he finally pulled up to Clemency's flat and was smiling nervously at the Norris sisters peering at him through their cracked doors.

His knock was instantly answered, and he was unceremoniously yanked into her flat and the bag of food ripped from his grasp before Clemency launched herself into his arms. As far as greetings went, he could get used to this, he thought as her mouth moved against his.

"We're having sex tonight," she whispered into his ear and he chuckled in reply. "I'm serious. Me... you... tonight. No more interruptions, Peter."

"I'm not arguing with you, love," Peter moaned as she ran her teeth along the edge of his ear. He pulled her up and she wrapped her legs around his waist. "Supper can wait. Bedroom?"

She moaned in what he assumed was agreement, as she was focused on weaving her fingers through his hair as her lips traveled over his jaw to his neck. He miraculously made it across the room to the doorway of the bedroom without tripping and set her down on her feet. As he did so, she ran her hands down his chest and teasingly brushed against the bulge that was making it so very difficult for him to walk, before moving her hands up under his shirt, pushing it off over his head. She immediately pounced on his bare chest.

"I need to feel you," he rasped as she lightly grazed his nipples with her nails. His hands clutched at the hem of the cami she wore, yanking it up before dropping to his knees. He slid his hands inside the waistband of her lounge pants and pushed them down as he nuzzled her belly. Damn, every part of her smelled of citrus. He would never be able to eat an orange again without thinking of her. He lightly trailed his fingers up her body as he rose to his feet, suddenly feeling the need to take it slow.

He saw the same desire in her eyes as they met his and she tentatively reached out to unfasten his trousers. He lightly traced his fingers over her arms as his pants pooled at his feet and he felt her knuckles brush against him. He stilled her hand. Stepping out of his shoes and remaining clothing, he picked her up before walking the remaining steps to the bed with her in his arms.

Clemency suddenly felt timid as she lay beside him. Her hand rested on his hip, but curiosity got the better of her and she slid it lower, her fingers tracing his hard length. God, the man was perfect she thought as he nipped at the sensitive juncture of her neck and shoulder. She lifted her head and held his gaze as she wrapped her fingers around him, giving him a firm stroke. A smile tugged at the corner of her mouth at his response, his head falling back as he uttered one breathless word. The next minute, however, he was gazing back down at her, a frown creasing his brow.

"Do you hear music?" he asked. She froze, listening for a moment before leaping from the bed.

"That's Lucy's ringtone," she exclaimed. "Something must be wrong for her to be calling me now," she explained, reaching for her phone. "Lucy, honey, is everything all right?"

"They're having sex!" her daughter cried, and Clemency realized that she had inadvertently hit the speaker button.

"W-what? Who's having sex?" she asked, looking around in panic. Her eyes fell to Peter, but he looked every bit as perplexed as she.

"Daddy and Whitney," Lucy exclaimed. "They're totally doing it!"

"Right now?" Clemency asked, looking at the bedside clock. Was her husband really banging his girlfriend at three in the afternoon while his daughter was at home?

"No, but she was here this morning when I returned home from my sleepover. She must have spent the night and I bet they did it," Lucy explained. "Mommy, I need to see you, can we switch to video chat?"

"Okay, sweetie, but give me a minute. You kind of caught me in the middle of a date. I'll call you right back," she said looking to Peter apologetically. He smiled and handed over her shirt and pants while he moved to don his boxers and t-shirt.

A few minutes later she was climbing up onto a barstool at the kitchen counter, smiling at Peter as he dished up their dinner. Pressing the connect button on her phone, her smile faltered when the strained face of her daughter appeared on the screen.

"You're wearing that on a date?" Lucy blurted out causing Clemency to grimace. She realized that the camisole top she usually wore around the flat was not exactly the most fashionable attire. "Are you having sex, too?" Lucy asked incredulously.

"No, Luce, I'm *definitely* not having sex," Clemency replied, trying to keep a straight face as Peter choked on his bite of chili pepper. "That is quite a personal question, sweetness, and not something I plan on discussing with you, understand?" She watched her daughter sheepishly nod. "Now, we have discussed the fact that your father and I are divorcing. You knew that he was seeing Whitney. None of this should have come as any great surprise. So there's no real need for you to be so upset, is there?"

"No," Lucy muttered. "It's just that Daddy never talks to me.

He just does stupid stuff like this and expects me to just accept it."

"That's just how your father is, sweetie," Clemency explained. "Confrontation makes him uncomfortable so he will avoid talking to you about things he thinks will make you angry or sad. If you truly feel uncomfortable with Whitney sleeping over, or anything else your father does for that matter, you are going to have to be the one to say something. Otherwise, he will be completely oblivious to your feelings." Clemency glanced up to see that a cloud had descended over Peter's face, but when she questioningly quirked an eyebrow, he just shook his head and turned away.

"... it will be so much easier when I come to stay with you," Clemency turned her attention back to the phone to hear her daughter say.

"You really think so?" she asked. "I just admitted to you that I'm dating someone. How is that different from your father and Whitney?"

"Well, to begin with, you, like, warned me ahead of time. You didn't throw Whitney in my face and say, 'by the way, I'm hittin' that!'" Lucy explained.

"Luce, I'm certain that never in his life has your father said those words," Clemency said in exasperation.

"Okay, he didn't say that exactly, but come on, Mom, she's like half his age. It's like he's having a mid-life crisis," Lucy complained.

"Age is merely a number, sweetie. If your father is happy with Whitney, all we can do is be happy for him," Clemency sighed.

"Is this your way of warning me that you're also having a mid-life crisis, Mom? Are you dating some young stud?" Lucy asked jokingly and Clemency was happy to see that Peter was amused by the question.

"Young, no, stud, yes," Clemency replied as she grinned and winked at him.

"Oh, my God, Mom, is he there right now?" Lucy exclaimed in horror.

"Yes, Luce. What part of 'I'm currently on a date,' did you not understand?" Clemency asked.

"Can I meet him?" Lucy asked after a tentative pause.

Clemency glanced at Peter who shrugged and nodded before rounding the counter to join her. "Lucy, this is Peter. Peter... Lucy."

Her normally outgoing daughter was quite shy to begin with, but within minutes she and Peter were happily chatting away. This gave Clemency a chance to dig into her food. She was shoveling the last bite into her mouth when she heard Peter wrapping up the conversation as he paced the living room.

"One last thing, Luce, can you tell me what your mother's name is?" she heard him ask.

"Cee Cee," Lucy replied, confused by the question.

"No, those are her initials. She has been going by her middle name here, but I'm curious to hear what her first name is.

"I don't know," Lucy said, amazed that she never knew her mother's greatest secret. "I can ask my dad though."

Clemency laughed as she accepted the phone back from Peter. "Good luck, I threatened him with bodily harm should he ever utter the name outside of our wedding vows. I think my secret is safe."

"I like Peter," her daughter said when Clemency's face reappeared on the screen.

"I'm glad, sweetie. I do too," she said watching the man in question as he cleaned up their dishes. "It's getting late here, and I have an early morning so I'm going to say goodnight now."

"Okay, Mom. Love you," Lucy said.

"Love you too," Clemency said, and as she disconnected, she found that she was looking at Peter.

Moving to stand before her, he pulled the phone from her hand. His kiss was soft, but she noted that a cloud had, once again, descended upon his features.

"What's wrong?" she asked, reaching up to trace the lines of his face.

He silently shook his head before turning back to the bedroom. She followed, trying to hide her disappointment when she watched him step into his trousers. "Your daughter knows about sex," he said quietly as he sat down on the edge of the bed.

"Yes," Clemency agreed, wondering where this was leading. "I have always been open with Lucy about her body from a young age."

"But she's only eleven and she knows what sex is," he repeated.

"Well, yes... I mean, she understands that it's an intimate act shared between two people. The subject naturally came up when I discussed her changing body and menstruation. I'm sure she's talked about it with her friends and probably picked up a few misconceptions, so I'll need to touch base with her again soon... Peter? Are you okay?"

"Menstruation?" he squeaked in reply before clearing his throat. "How often do you er... have these talks with her?"

"Every few months or so. Usually it occurs when something crosses her radar -- something she saw on TV, or read about in a book, that requires further explanation." Clemency explained. "Peter, what's wrong?" she asked as she watched him run his hands over his face.

"Gracie," he whispered.

Grac---- oh..." she began before the reason for his terrified look dawned on her. "Maybe Vanessa..."

She stopped as he began to violently shake his head. He rose from the bed and began pacing in front of her. "What the fuck am I doing? God, I must be the world's most clueless parent here... no make that clueless man," he amended pausing to face Clemency. "We almost made love tonight and I never gave a single thought to protection... Aren't people supposed to have some long, in depth interview process before hopping into bed nowadays?"

"Peter, please calm down," Clemency implored. "First of all, I'm clean. And given your admitted celibacy, I assume you are too. As for Gracie, you're not clueless, just a little behind. I can hel--"

"It's not all about diseases, love. I thought you were the expert here," Peter ranted as he moved to the front room. He wasn't sure where this anger was coming from, but now that he had begun, he was powerless to reign it in. "Heaven forbid should I have gotten you pregnant. Wouldn't that have been a great example to set for our girls?"

Clemency froze in the doorway to her bedroom. A long-buried pain welled up inside of her as the image of her holding his child flashed before her eyes. She wasn't sure why he was lashing out at her, but now it was her turn.

"Getting me pregnant would have been a fucking miracle," she yelled as tears streamed down her face. "I'm broken, Peter. That's why I wasn't concerned about protection."

He took a step toward her but was met by the bedroom door slamming in his face. He stood listening to the sound of her sobs fade as he heard the shower in the adjoining bathroom start up. He had two choices, stay or go. He chose the latter.

CHAPTER NINETEEN

The fight had been silly. That was Clemency's first thought the following morning as she washed the tear stains from her face. Georgie was quick to second the thought assuring her that Peter had just been scared.

"His little girl is growing up and he's terrified that he's going to make a proper mess out of it all," Georgie told her over coffee that morning. "Just be patient, he'll come around."

What neither woman realized at the time was that Peter *had* come around. In fact, the moment Clemency's door clicked shut behind him, he had realized that he had made the wrong choice. He wanted nothing more than to pull Clemency into his arms, admit that he had been an ass, and beg her forgiveness. Unfortunately, the fates were plotting to make this feat quite impossible.

To begin with, he was called out of town Monday and Tuesday. Grumbling the entire drive to Cardiff, he swore that he would never again mentor another young director. He lost track of the number of times he picked up the phone to call her, before deciding that his apology should be done in person. He just didn't know when that would be... he was due to fly to the States Thursday morning.

He returned to the city late Wednesday afternoon, making a quick stop at the studio on his way home for some papers he wanted to take on his trip. He hoped to be in and out and on his way to see Clemency, so he was understandably frustrated when Georgie poked her head in the door and requested that he stop by her office.

"I don't have time--" he began as she disappeared.

"Make time," her voice commanded from the outer office. Throwing the papers into his bag, he traipsed after her. Entering her brightly decorated office, he was on the verge of launching into the list of reasons why he couldn't just 'make time,' when he spied reason number one sitting on the sofa, her gaze squarely focused on the laptop that was shielding her.

She was pale, and there were dark circles under her eyes. All his fault, he realized. He took a step toward her and her head shot up, her eyes wide with fear. A rustling behind him made him aware that they were not alone.

"...Peter, please take a seat," Georgie said, gesturing to the chair beside a woman with a severely cut head of silver hair. "You've worked with Leslie before... She's helping us nail down the cast for *Tempest*." Georgie continued.

"I absolutely agree with Clemency that you'd make an excellent Kennett," Leslie gushed causing Peter's head to swivel around, his gaze landing once again on the woman sitting quietly on the sofa. Meanwhile, Georgie had launched into her proposal, officially offering Peter the role and outlining the shooting schedule. He heard none of it, his focus solely on the woman on the couch, willing her to look up and meet his eye.

"...Peter," Georgie's loud voice called his attention back to the purpose of the meeting. "I was asking if you had any issues with the proposed schedule?"

"Uh, no... other than some meet and greets that are already set which will require a couple of long weekends, my schedule is clear. I'll get you the exact dates. And if the two weeks in July is concrete, I can plan a holiday with Gracie," he replied.

"Does that mean you're on board?" Leslie asked, practically bouncing in her seat.

"That depends," Peter replied. "Is it a unanimous decision to want me in the role?"

Leslie nodded enthusiastically as Georgie also gave a curt bob of her head. Peter's eyes, however, had settled back on Clemency.

"Clemmie," Georgie's voice was much gentler now, and Clemency's head shot up at the sound of her name. "Peter asked if you still want him." The corners of his mouth tugged up in a smile as her eyes met his and widened in surprise. "In the role of Kennett, that is," Georgie clarified.

Clemency nodded; her eyes still locked with his. "Yes, I still want him," she replied, and for the first time in days, Peter breathed a little easier. She still wanted him...

"Leslie, why don't I walk you out," Georgie said, rising from her desk. Peter also rose to his feet, but only to prevent Clemency from also making a quick getaway.

"God he's hot. I can't wait to see him as Kennett," Leslie could be heard saying as she and Georgie departed. It was just the thing to break the tension in the room as Clemency was unable to suppress a giggle.

"I'm sorry," they both said at the same time, and Peter felt instant relief as she smiled up at him.

They were locked in an embrace when Georgie returned.

"Glad to see the two of you have kissed and made up," she observed as she shuffled the stacks of papers on her desk. "Now get out of here before you start tearing off one another's clothes."

"Do you have plans for the evening?" Clemency shyly asked.

"I'm all yours, love," he replied, turning to Georgie while Clemency moved to pack up her belongings. "I haven't heard from Donovan in a few days. How are his plans to move down here coming along?"

"They're currently on hold," Georgie replied. "I explained that if he and I were going to attempt to have a relationship again, it would be done at my speed, not his. Speaking of relationships... are you two planning on going public with yours? Right now, Frankie and I are the only ones aware of it, but you know how the rumor mill works here. One little spark and the news will spread like wildfire."

"Why would we be news?" Clemency asked, hoisting her bag onto her shoulder, looking even more confused as Georgie laughed in reply and Peter directed her out of the office.

"Well, love, I'm not sure if you realize this, but I'm fairly famous..." Peter began, earning a well-deserved swat from Clemency. "I'm just saying... I'm well known, and while your face isn't necessarily recognizable, your name is. The fact that we're involved would be considered newsworthy. Georgie is just saying we need to decide if we want to out ourselves now or wait for it to happen on its own."

This wasn't something Clemency had anticipated. "What's your opinion?"

"I have always been a fairly private man. I have never been one to answer questions about my personal life, and I don't really plan on starting now," Peter replied, holding the car door open for her. "Are you hungry? Would you like dinner now, or go straight home?"

Clemency, still preoccupied with pondering the previous subject, answered. It wasn't until Peter pulled into the spot outside her flat that she realized that she was starving.

"Actually, would you mind if we got something to eat first?" she asked, joining him on the sidewalk. "We could wal--"

"That's it, Frankie. I'm done," a woman yelled as she stormed out of the adjacent walk-up. "Find someone else to be your knight in shining armor. We're through. I mean it this time."

Clemency watched open mouthed as Georgie's daughter appeared on the top step of the stoop, and silently watched the angry woman stalk down the block. She had known that her friend's daughter lived nearby with her partner, but this was the first she had seen of them. Spying them, Frankie gave her a wry smile.

"Sorry you had to see that. Jenna has a flair for the dramatic. I'm glad to see you two have made up though," she said. "Give Jenna a week or two to cool off and I'll be in your shoes."

Peter slipped his hand into hers as Clemency watched the young girl turn her back and reenter the house. "She didn't sound happy about the prospect of a reconciliation," Clemency said as she let him lead her down the street.

"I don't think Frankie has been happy since Alex left," Peter explained, continuing when he saw Clemency's confused look.

"Her sister, Georgie's second daughter. They were extremely close growing up, until one day about ten years ago now, Alex decided to go live with her father. I think on some level, Jenna became Alex's replacement. Only Frankie never found the same closeness with her that she shared with her sister. I know this isn't the first time they have quarreled."

"That's a shame. Frankie's such a nice young woman... she... she reminds me of someone... It has been bugging me for weeks, but I just can't place my finger on who.." Clemency said. Peter was looking down at her waiting for her to continue, but they had crossed the street into the retail district of their neighborhood, and she was suddenly distracted by the sight of the drug store on the corner. Telling Peter that she wouldn't be more than a minute or two, she darted into the shop.

Agreeing on Italian food, they made their way to the restaurant which happened to be located next to a small bookstore. Once again, Clemency promised to be quick as she darted through the door. She found Peter perusing a small display of *Tempest* when she returned to the front of the shop with her purchases.

"Would you like a signed copy?" she joked.

"I would kill for a signed Clemency James," the middle-aged woman at the register said as she rang up her purchase. "They're pretty rare. I hear she only did a handful of signings."

Peter was grinning at her as he handed over a copy along with a pen. Taking note of the cashier's name, Clemency inscribed it before handing it over with a smile.

"I guess I've decided to out myself," Clemency said to Peter as they left the stunned bookseller clutching the book to her chest.

The restaurant was quiet, and they were led directly to a secluded corner table. After giving their orders, Peter watched as Clemency began digging through her purchases. After much opening of packages and moving of items between bags, she handed him a flat rectangular sheet of cotton. He felt his cheeks blaze at the realization of what he was holding.

"That, my love, is a pad," Clemency explained and grinned as he quickly handed it back to her. "They come in many sizes, thick and thin, with wings and without. These should be adequate for a young girl. Put this bag under the sink in Gracie's bathroom. Give this to her to take back to school with her."

Clemency waited until the waitress put their drinks on the table, enjoying the sight of Peter as he squirmed in his seat. She then handed him a small, glittery cosmetic bag.

"This is an emergency kit that Grace should keep with her at all times. It has a few pads, a pocket calendar to mark the start and end of each period, and a bar of chocolate... because, really, we need all the chocolate in the world during that time of the month. Add a pair of spare undies and she's set," Clemency continued before handing him the final bag. "This has a book I got for Lucy when we began discussing the joys of puberty. It's good at answering basic questions without being overwhelming. There is also a book for you on what questions to anticipate and how best to answer them."

By the time their food arrived, Peter was no longer feeling quite as panicked, and instead was extremely grateful. "How do you suggest I go about broaching the subject with Gracie?" he asked as he dug into his pasta.

They discussed several scenarios and as the meal progressed, Peter even thumbed through the books, asking questions as he began to relax more. As the waitress cleared their plates and placed the to-go box of tiramisu in front of them, Peter placed the books back in their bag and reached for Clemency's hand.

"Thank you," he said sincerely. "I'm truly sorry for flying off the handle the other night. The realization that Grace was growing up and I was neglecting her took me by surprise and scared the shit out of me."

"Ignorant, Peter, not negligent," Clemency explained. "Big difference. Especially since you just sat her for the past hour and willingly allowed me to educate you. All you need to do now is let Grace see that you are approachable."

Night had fallen as they walked hand in hand back to her

place. Reaching the park, Peter slowed as his mind drifted back to the angry words they had thrown at one another.

"The other night... You said... you claimed that you were broken," he said, turning her to face him.

Clemency shuffled her feet; she had hoped that he had forgotten that part... "I had a miscarriage. Nine years ago now," she admitted, staring up at the moon. "I nearly died, but the doctor said it was a fluke and that once I healed, I would be able to try again... I was never able to conceive after that."

Unable to find the words to console her, Peter merely drew her into his arms. While he could never fully comprehend the physical loss of a child, he could commiserate with her. He had once dreamt of a house full of children, only to find himself pleading with his wife to carry 'the accident' that was Gracie to term.

They walked the remainder of the way back to his car in companionable silence. He stowed his packages while Clemency gathered her bag, but then he surprised her by saying that he should get going, he had an early morning.

"Oh, I thought you wanted dessert," Clemency said, holding up the takeaway bag from the restaurant.

"I want dessert very much," Peter admitted. "I just thought it might be too soon... after dinner and all..."

Clemency answered his sheepish smile with a grin of her own as she reached for his hand. They nodded hello to the Norris sisters as they made their way up the stairs.

"He has a nice ass," one old lady shouted across the hall to her sister.

"No, you cannot make a pass, you daft old lady," the other shouted back. "He belongs to Nancy. Besides, he's young enough to be your grandson!"

They were barely able to contain their laughter. "I like them," Peter declared as the door closed behind him. "They think I'm young."

"They also think you have a nice ass," Clemency said, moving into his arms and letting her hands settle onto his behind.

"Something I'm inclined to agree with."

He lowered his head to kiss her. Softly. Slowly. Relishing the feel of her lips... her scent... her taste... It had been nearly three days since he had last seen her... touched her... and it had been pure hell. The kiss became more urgent as he delved deeper, and there it was, the gasp of pleasure from her as she threw her head back to gaze up at him in wonder.

"Oh, fuck," she whispered as she grasped his arms.

Is that an invitation, love?" he asked, nuzzling her ear. He pulled back in time to see her slight nod before gathering her into his arms and crossing to the bedroom in a few large strides. "I apologize in advance... but that's exactly what it's going to be... We've been thwarted too many times and the need to be inside of you has become far too great."

He set her on her feet and made quick work of pulling her top off over her head. She, however, was not arguing. Instead, she was struggling to push his jacket off his shoulders and had begun popping buttons off his shirt in her haste to feel his bare skin against hers once again. He stilled her hands and took over the effort to disrobe while his clothes were still intact, watching her as she shucked the remainder of her clothing and moved to lie upon the bed.

He watched her eyes widen as she got a good look at him before he moved to join her. Beginning at her feet, he trailed soft kisses up her body, feeling her squirm until he finally met her lips, his body nestled against hers.

"You're so damn beautiful," he murmured against her lips. He was struggling to retain control, not wanting to rush to quickly. It wasn't easy though. Not with her writhing against him.

"Damn it, Peter, stop with the sappy platitudes," she moaned from beneath him. He raised himself up on his elbows to gaze down at her and she took the opportunity to wiggle, parting her thighs to allow him to settle between them, his cock sliding over her slick core. "Shut up and fuck me like you promised," she commanded.

His hip bucked and she cried out as he pushed into her. He

paused, looking down to make sure she was okay, only to have her wrap her legs around his waist. "Don't you dare stop now," she growled, raising her hips to grind against him.

He knew that it had been awhile, but he swore it had never been like this before. It was as though he had been listening to a certain piece of music his entire life, only to suddenly realize that he had only been hearing one, lone instrument play its part. Suddenly, with Clemency, he was hearing a full orchestra. She was a one-woman symphony full of little cries and gasps. He tried to determine exactly what he did to make her let out such a low, sultry moan, but there was no chance to experiment. Clemency was an active participant in this orchestration, meeting him thrust for thrust. When she grasped his shoulders and called out his name, he was lost. It was by far the most erotic sound he had ever heard in his life, and he couldn't help but also call out as he emptied himself into her.

They lay together, a tangle of limbs. "You wouldn't have happened to shout out my name there at the end?" she chuckled in his ear.

"Who me? Never?" Peter denied, his hips thrusting forward making her cry out and spasm around him. "Ridiculous name. It shall never cross my lips."

"Never? I bet you a hundred pounds I can eventually get you to say it," Clemency quipped.

"You're on," he replied, reluctantly moving to sit on the edge of the bed, reaching for his trousers. "This was the last thing I wanted to do, love, but I was serious when I said that I had an early morning."

"Oh," Clemency replied, sitting up and clutching the bed sheets to her chest. Being with her was the last thing he wanted to do? It certainly didn't feel that way a few minutes ago...

"I meant leaving you," Peter clarified. "I'm flying to Atlanta tomorrow. I had hoped that our first time would last all night. I long to wake up with you in my arms and make love to you as the sunlight streams across the room."

"Something to aspire to..." Clemency said, leaning into his

caress and placing a kiss on the palm of his hand. "When do you return?"

"Sunday, and I'll call as often as I can," Peter said as he leaned in to kiss her goodbye. One kiss led to another, and before he knew it, Peter was once again pulled down onto the bed as Clemency moved to straddle him. He was more than a little surprised to find that he was already hardening as his hands moved to cup her breasts. Fuck it, he thought, as she pitched forward, her lips seeking his. He could always sleep on the plane.

CHAPTER TWENTY

It turned out to be the longest bloody weekend of Peter's life. He had honestly enjoyed meet and greets in the past. He reasoned that it was a way of giving back to the fans. But in reality, it had been an escape. Now that he no longer had a reason to avoid being at home, he was beginning to see the events with the same eye as some of his more cynical celebrity guests - as meet and *gropes*.

He missed Clemency. Only their frequent conversations and messages to one another kept him from losing his mind. He listened, heart breaking, as she described the loss of her parents and brothers, and in turn he related tales of growing up as the eldest in a large family outside Edinburgh.

She bolstered his morale throughout the day Saturday, causing him to grin whenever his phone vibrated with yet another incoming message from her. Sometimes they were pithy messages, other times inspirational quotes.

There is nowhere you can be that isn't where you're meant to be...

He frowned down at the message. It sounded vaguely familiar.

A few minutes later he was struggling to keep a smile plastered on his face as a young woman gushed about being his biggest fan when he felt another telltale buzz in his pocket.

Life is too short, there's no time for fussing or fighting, my friend.

Fussing or fighting? His handler made a subtle cough to alert him to the approach of the next guest as he pocketed his phone. Was she referring to the fight they had? He thought that they had made up... The woman making her way toward him stumbled when she saw the grin that appeared on his face as he recalled exactly how they had made up.

He finally realized what she was doing several guests later when the third message appeared.

Close your eyes and I'll kiss you. Tomorrow I'll miss you. Remember I'll always be true.

He was tempted to continue the lyrics until he realized that they would culminate with 'and I'll be sending all my love to you.' His heart skipped a beat at the thought. He had already confided in Georgie that he was falling in love with Clemency... He pondered his reply while he greeted the next group.

When his handler indicated that there would be a five-minute break, he whipped out his phone and began typing a message as quickly as he could.

I am just living to be lying by your side, but I'm just a moonlight mile on down the road.

As the break ended and the first guest was being led in, he received her reply.

Elementary penguin singing Hare Krishna. Man you should have seen them kicking Edgar Allen Poe... Brilliant lyrics. So deep...

He let out a bark of laughter, startling the woman entering the room. He had to quickly explain that he was amused by a message from his girlfriend, not the woman's elaborate costume. It was the shortest meeting of the day as the woman seemed even more despondent to hear that he had a girlfriend.

It had been a long day and Peter had just returned to his hotel room when he eagerly answered his phone. Instead of Clemency, however, it was his publicist, on the other end of the line. Apparently social media was abuzz with the rumor that he was no longer on the market.

"Is it true?" Emma demanded.

"Yes, I'm seeing someone," Peter admitted. "But as usual, my private life is private. I will not be answering any questions about it."

"Does this mystery woman have a name?" Emma persisted.

"What did I just say?" Peter's voice went up a decibel as he made his exasperation known.

"I'm sorry, it's just that this is *huge* news," Emma replied. "You would have been on all of the most eligible bachelor lists last year if it hadn't been seen in poor taste given that your wife had just died. Now you're saying that you're definitely off the market?"

"Most definitely," Peter confirmed. "Look, Em, while I have you here, can we discuss the meet and greet schedule for the year? I'm going to be tied up all summer with a new project and I'm just not wanting to be away from home as much anymore. Is there anything we can do?"

"The contract for Boston in March has already been signed, so that one is set in stone. I've been negotiating the others so consider them nixed," Emma replied. "Is it true, then that you took a role in Sutton's adaptation of *Tempest*? Oh my God, you're not dating Georgianna, are you?"

Peter laughed. "Yes, to the first question, a resounding hell no to the second. I'll call you when I get home."

He had never been happier to stand in an interminably long TSA line as he was Sunday morning. Things began going downhill when the first alert came over the PA system - his flight was delayed. As he sat morosely watching the hands on the clock above his gate tick by, he resigned himself to the fact that he would not be spending the evening in Clemency's arms. When they finally announced that the flight would be boarding, he rang her, wanting to at least hear her voice and apologize.

"You daft man, you are not in control of the weather, there's nothing to apologize for," she replied.

"I know, I'm just disappointed. I wanted to spend time with you tonight. I know we both have a busy week ahead," he said.

"You are welcome to come by no matter what the hour," Clemency invited. "But I also understand if you want to go home and rest, too," she added, not wanting to sound desperate to see him. It had also been a horribly long weekend for her.

It was just after two in the morning when a light tap at her door roused Clemency from the couch where she had nodded off.

"Are you wearing anything under that robe?" the exhausted man leaning against her door frame muttered.

"Nope," Clemency replied succinctly. Taking his bag, she set it aside and led him through the flat to the bedroom. She got him out of his jacket, but when she reached to unbuckle his trousers, she feared that he was going to keel over. As the pants fell to the floor, she nudged him to sit on the edge of the bed and was barely able to catch him and direct his head to the waiting pillow. She removed his shoes before climbing in beside him and pulling the comforter up over them. In his last moment of consciousness, Peter turned and gathered her in his arms.

It felt like he had just shut his eyes, when a blaring alarm had him shooting up in bed. He only had a vague memory of the car ride that brought him home to Clemency. The woman in question, however, was nowhere to be seen. A moment later the sound of water running ceased and his heart began to race when she stepped into the room still clad in the robe from the night before.

"Are you wearing anything under that robe?" he asked again, this time much more alert.

"Nope," Clemency replied with a grin, tossing the towel she had been using to dry her hair aside before moving to kiss him. As she leaned forward, the robe parted, and he tugged on the tie before running his hands over her still damp skin. "Welcome home," she murmured, then let out a squeal of surprise when he flipped her onto her back and deepened the kiss.

"I won't be home until I'm buried deep inside you," he growled as he struggled to push his boxers down over his arousal.

Clemency gasped as he slid into her. Yes, this is definitely home, she thought as they began to move together.

It was another quick fuck as neither had the time, nor patience to draw it out. Thoroughly sated and relishing the feeling of Clemency's muscles sporadically clenching him, Peter frowned.

"Is there a reason why I keep hearing the Wicked Witch's theme from *The Wizard of Oz*?" he asked.

"Oh, crap," Clemency exclaimed, struggling to get out from under him. "That's my phone. Georgie's calling. I'm late."

"That's Georgie's ring tone?" he laughed.

Peeking out the window to see the SUV waiting at the curb with an impatient looking Georgie inside, Clemency let out another string of curses and grabbed for her clothes. "I changed it a few weeks ago when she was being so bitchy and haven't had a chance to change it back," she explained.

"Dare I ask what mine is?" Peter said with a grin. He was sitting up in bed enjoying the flurry of activity happening around him. He could get used to this, he thought.

"Crazy love," she replied as she paused to give him a quick kiss. "Lock up when you leave and message me when you have an idea of what your schedule is like. Love you."

Peter sat there grinning like an idiot as he heard the front door slam. She had said that she loved him...

CHAPTER TWENTY-ONE

Shit, fuck, crazy, Clemency thought as she climbed into the seat next to Georgie. She nodded a greeting to Roger and Frankie in the front seat before muttering an apology for keeping them waiting. The car fell silent and remained that way for the drive. Not that Clemency noticed, she was too busy panicking. Surely, she did *not* just tell Peter that she loved him...

Arriving at the studio, Georgie immediately sent her daughter away and closed the office door.

"Okay, sweetie, do you care to explain why you were late? Or perhaps why your shirt is on backwards? Or why you were as white as a sheet when you got in the car?" Georgie asked.

Clemency cursed as she glanced down at her top. Turning her back on her friend, she attempted to wriggle it around. "Peter got home last night," she muttered, straightening her clothes before falling back onto the couch.

"I figured as much," Georgie replied, taking a seat. "You have an air of morning sex about you. But that doesn't explain the look of shock on you-- Oh God. Don't tell me this was your first time... Does Peter have some sort of freakish anomaly? Does he have a tiny prick?"

Clemency began laughing and once she started, she couldn't stop. Tears streamed down her face before she was able to finally curb her hysterics as Georgie just watched with a bemused expression on her face.

"He's perfect," she assured her friend with a hiccup. "Completely and utterly perfect. And being with him is..."

"Perfect?" Georgie guessed, enjoying seeing her friend at a loss for words. "If that's the case, what's the problem."

Clemency hesitated. "I may have accidentally told him that I loved him before dashing out of the apartment."

It was now Georgie's turn to laugh. "Define accidentally."

"It just sorta slipped out... I didn't mean for it to..." Clemency replied, rising to pace the floor.

"You *don't* love him?" Georgie asked.

Clemency froze. "I do... or at least I think I do. But it's too soon..."

"Says who?" Georgie asked. "I told Donovan that I loved him on our first date. That was nearly thirty years ago, and I still love that man more than any man on the face of this earth."

"How are things with him?" Clemency asked, changing the subject.

"Back to square one," her friend admitted. "I may love him but trusting him is an entirely different matter."

Their heart to heart was interrupted by Frankie who had returned to inform them that everything was ready, and Leslie was in the auditorium waiting for them. It was the first day of casting calls. They had nailed down a handful of the main roles, now they were casting a wider net in an attempt to fill the rest.

It was the start of the busiest week yet for Clemency. If she wasn't sitting in on auditions, she was touching base with the art and costuming departments. She even had a preliminary meeting with the folks responsible for hair and makeup. Several hours each day were also spent working with Val Jamison on the script. Now that it had been polished, they were reading it aloud to get a feel for how Clemency, herself, imagined the characters speaking. Frankie would often join them, reading opposite Clemency as Val jotted down notes.

It was on Thursday afternoon that it finally dawned on Clemency why Frankie seemed so familiar to her. As Val packed up her notes for the day, Clemency touched the young girl's arm and asked her to remain behind in the fish tank they were working in.

"Frankie, when your mother first introduced us, she said that you wanted to work in the film industry, but hadn't quite figured out where you fit yet... Why haven't you told her that you want to be an actress?" Clemency asked. The young woman was shocked by the question and immediately began to sputter half-hearted denials, but Clemency stopped her with two simple words. "You're Tempest."

Frankie plopped down onto a chair. "The last thing mum wants is for any of us girls to go into acting."

"But it's what you love, isn't it? I can see it in your eyes when you read lines," Clemency asked.

"My friend Simon dragged me to a drama club meeting when we were still in school. I fell in love with it then and continued on, studying it at University," Frankie admitted. "But I have always kept it a secret from mum."

"Speaking as a mother, I would hate it if Lucy kept something she loved hidden from me," Clemency said, reaching to give Frankie's hand a squeeze. "I think you should audition for *Tempest*. We may have already cast that horrible woman in the lead, but you would make an excellent Haven or Mila."

Frankie looked horrified at the idea and protested vehemently as she fled the room. Clemency sighed as she gathered her own belongings. It was just after four and if she hurried, she could escape before Georgie caught her and set her on another task. She and Peter had only managed to see one another in passing all week, and he had been in Wales for the past two days, but he was due home tonight. Nothing had been said about the slip of her tongue on Monday, but she had caught him watching her closely during the fleeting moments they had gotten to spend together.

She had been looking forward to seeing him that evening, but as she stepped out of the shower, she was disappointed to find a message waiting for her.

Change of plans, Gracie wants to meet for dinner. Can I come over after?

Tossing the phone onto the bed, Clemency glanced around

the room. It had been a long day... Hell, it had been a long week and she was tired. Dropping the towel, she had wrapped around her, she climbed under the covers. Telling herself that she was *not* wallowing, she reached for the phone.

Maybe another time.

The last thing she wanted was for their relationship to become a series of booty calls, Clemency thought before falling into a fitful slumber.

The following day was Friday and it was chock full of auditions. By midmorning Clemency was feeling weary and felt the beginnings of a headache coming on. Georgie, however, was like a bulldog with a bone. She was determined to end the week by nailing down all three main leads. Clemency had begun losing enthusiasm for the project. Sure, Peter cast as Kennett was her dream come true, but she still cringed every time she thought of the woman cast to portray Tempest. She was still on the fence about the man cast as Carraig. She had detested Colin Fletcher when he had initially read for the role of Kennett. Almost as much as Frankie had, the poor girl had fled the auditorium before the man had uttered two lines. As Carraig... he was different, and on a good day Clemency admitted that he worked. Today they were auditioning Benjamins, and it was not a good day.

The first two readings were adequate... nothing to write home about. By far the highlight for Clemency was watching Frankie reading opposite. She really did make an excellent Tempest. Peeking at Georgie who sat alongside her, Clemency wondered how the brilliant woman was so blind to her daughter's talent. Midway through the third reading the side door opened and Colin popped his head in. He apologized for the disruption, but instead of leaving, he moved to take a seat in the front row. The poor actor auditioning never had a chance. Frankie stood on the stage like a deer caught in the headlights. The lines, when she read them were wooden at best when she wasn't flubbing them altogether. Finally calling a halt to the fiasco, Georgie took her daughter aside and after a moment of discussion, Frankie fled the auditorium, a look of relief on her face. When she returned, she had Peter and Kaitlyn in tow.

As Frankie slid into the seat beside Clemency, Georgie led the two actors to the stage.

"We're in for a treat," she said, explaining that the remaining contenders would read opposite set cast.

"Treat or nightmare?" Clemency muttered after the first actor completed his audition. She found herself slouching in her seat, wanting to hide from the disaster she had just witnessed. Frankie, beside her was in a similar position, but Clemency suspected that she was trying to hide from Colin who was still sitting in the front row, a grim expression on his face. Probably wondering what exactly he got himself into, Clemency thought as the next hopeful made his way down the aisle. He stopped to ruffle Frankie's head of dark curls and the girl sat up with a smile.

He was good, that much was clear, and that was saying a lot given how horrible Kaitlyn was. It wasn't just her acting that was off, although the girl seemed to think Tempest had a split personality and would change the tone of her performance midline. No, the woman herself was horrid, often stopping to berate the poor man auditioning, telling him exactly how she thought he could have added more inflection to the dialogue. When Georgie called an early end to the morning session, Clemency could see the anger in Peter's eyes as he leapt off the stage and made his way toward their friend.

"I know, I know," Georgie said, brushing past him. "I'm working on it," she added over her shoulder as she moved to take Kaitlyn aside.

Clemency thought Peter would argue, but instead he turned to drop into the seat next to her. "Fancy a little lunch, love?"

"Actually, I'd kill for some ibuprofen and a nap," Clemency replied as she rubbed her temples.

"Done," Peter proclaimed, digging his keys out of his pocket and handing them to her. "There's a bottle of paracetamol in the top drawer of my desk. I'll go fetch us something to eat while you rest."

He entered his office twenty minutes later to find Clemency curled up on the leather couch fast asleep. God, he wished he could sleep so peacefully, he thought. He hadn't gotten a decent night's rest since the night he had spent with her. He hadn't slept that well in years and the sex the following morning had been pretty spectacular as well. He stifled a yawn as his thoughts drifted back to the simple two words, *Love you*, she had tossed at him as she departed. His heart swelled every time he thought of them. Sitting there watching as she let out a subtle snore, it was all he could do to refrain from sweeping her into his arms and repeating the words to her. The door slamming open as Georgie flew into the office prevented him from acting on his desires, and he saw Clemency shoot up at the sound of their friend's loud voice.

"I agree with you that Kaitlyn is complete rubbish," Georgie declared, sitting down in the chair in front of the desk and claiming the sandwich he had gotten for Clemency. "We're stuck with her, so let's start brainstorming ideas for getting this to work."

Peter gave Clemency a smile of apology and handed over the remains of his salad to her. She smiled her thanks and popped a crouton in her mouth before grabbing a copy of the script. The three of them spent the remainder of the lunch break making notations that they hoped would help the actress embrace the character of Tempest better. By the end of the hour, they had a plan. Staying behind to clean up, Peter noted how little Clemency had eaten. Catching up with her at the door to the auditorium, he stilled her hand as it reached to open it and pulled her into his arms.

"I've barely seen you all week," he said. "Are you..."

"I'm fine," Clemency was quick to answer, before finally relaxing in his embrace. "I've missed you. Is everything okay with Gracie?"

"Hmmm... She just wanted to let me know that she had an

event at school this weekend and wouldn't be coming home," Peter said, nuzzling her neck. Inhaling her scent had such a calming effect on him. "Were you upset that I had to cancel last night?"

"No!" Clemency exclaimed, stepping out of his embrace as Leslie rounded the corner. The woman's gaze lingered curiously on them as she entered the auditorium. "I was a little disappointed, yes. But, Peter, you are first and foremost a father. I understand that and would never get angry over you needing to spend time with your daughter."

"I was just a little concerned," Peter explained. "You've been so quiet, and you hardly ate any lunch."

"I'm just tired," she replied with a sigh. "I haven't slept well since... well, since Sunday night."

"Me either," Peter said with a grin. "Why don't we have dinner at my place tonight. I'll cook."

Clemency agreed with a smile and Peter leaned down to brush a kiss across her lips as the door opened and Frankie's voice informed them that Ms. Sutton requested their presence so they could 'get this day from hell over with.'

CHAPTER TWENTY-TWO

Clemency glanced up and down the street as she bound up the three steps to knock on Peter's bright blue door. The rest of the afternoon had preceded much like the morning had and Georgie ended up calling it quits after the second gentleman left the stage practically in tears due to Kaitlyn's treatment.

"We need to talk," Georgie muttered to her before moving off to address the men waiting their turn in the foyer. "Gentlemen, due to unforeseen circumstances, we're going to need to reschedule. Please see my assistant, Fran--" The rest of the sentence was cut off by the closing door and Clemency wasted no time in gathering her belongings and heading out the side entrance. Glancing at the purple door of the adjoining home, she felt a spark of guilt for abandoning her friend, but the prospect of a lovely evening with Peter after the week she had endured was too great to resist.

The door in front of her opened and an arm reached out to pull her inside. As it slammed behind her, suddenly Clemency found herself pushed up against the door as Peter's mouth found hers. Okay... strike lovely evening and replace with exciting, she edited as she moaned into his enthusiastic greeting.

"How the bloody hell do you expect me to keep reading those bloody scenes knowing that you wrote them and are sitting right there watching me?" he panted into her ear as he kept her pinned to the door with his body. "You don't know what it does to me."

Actually, she had a fairly good idea as she had watched him

squirm a time or two during the risqué threesome scene that was part of the audition script. Plus, she was quite certain that the evidence of the effect her writing had on him was currently pressing into her thigh.

"If you can't handle a simple snippet during the audition, however, do you plan on surviving the actual filming?" she asked coyly, adopting an innocent expression as she glanced up at him from under her eyelashes.

"You little minx. I should punish you for this," he growled, dipping his head to nip at the sensitive spot at the base of her neck.

"You're really beginning to sound like Kenn-- Peter, what are you doing?" Clemency gasped as he unexpectedly lifted her into his arms.

He paused to look down at her. "I'm taking you upstairs to my bed where I plan on having my way with you. Is that okay?"

Clemency nodded dumbly as she suddenly couldn't find her voice. He was going to have his way with her... it was like a scene from one of her novels.

Entering the bedroom, Peter felt breathless as he set her on her feet. It wasn't because he was over fifty years old and had just carried her up a flight of stairs either. She just looked so beautiful standing there in the fading sunlight waiting to see what he planned on doing next. He shook his head; he had no plan... Without even thinking he had her pressed up against the wall again, his hands lost in the short curls of her hair as his mouth devoured hers.

"I need to know," he said when he finally pulled back to rest his forehead against hers. "I need to know if these scenes of yours were written from experience, or if they're pure fantasy?"

"You want to know..." she paused confused, but when his hands moved to cup her ass and pulled her up against him, it dawned on her what he was asking. "Now you sound more like Benjam--"

Peter pulled away abruptly and Clemency was shocked by the loss of his touch. "I'm not one of your characters, love. I'm not Kennett. I'm not Benjamin. I'm Peter."

"I know," she whispered, reaching out to trace her fingers down his jawbone. He was Peter and he was hers. She was still in awe over it all. Stepping closer, she rose on tiptoes to brush her lips lightly across his. "You are Peter, and this is real. Everything else is pure fantasy."

"Everything?" he asked, pulling her close once more, his hands grasping at the folds of her skirt until they found their way under and the only thing separating them from her bare ass was the thin, lacy fabric of her underwear.

"Well..." she hesitated, and he had her up against the wall again, her legs wrapped around his waist as he pulled her shirt over her head. She was finding it increasingly difficult to keep her thoughts straight. Was he asking her if she had ever been with more than one man at the same time? God no, that was pure fantasy. However, other acts she had described...

She whimpered as he freed her breasts, and the satin confines of her bra was replaced by the velvety touch of his lips. She arched her back wanting more and let out another whimper when he returned her to her feet. He dropped to his knees, pulling her skirt and panties down together until they pooled at her feet and she stood completely bared before him. Suddenly feeling self-conscious as his gaze fell to the scar that was evidence of the c-section that had brought Lucy into the world, her hands fluttered to try and shield herself.

"No," he commanded, grasping her arms and holding them firmly at her side. "I want to see you. All of you. You are so fucking beautiful." He moved a hand to lightly trace the faded scar and Clemency convulsed as his finger transitioned from the numb scar tissue to a more highly sensitive area. "... and you're ticklish," he added with a grin.

"You're evil," she began to chastise before he suddenly buried his nose in the juncture between her thighs. Her head fell back against the wall as she felt his tongue snake out to take a tentative taste. "Fuck, Peter," she moaned, weaving her fingers lightly through his silky hair.

"Soon love," he groaned. "That is the main course. I'm relishing the appetizer first."

While his tongue was working wonders, Clemency couldn't bring herself to find the release he was seeking from her. She was too tense. There were too many thoughts racing through her head, and she couldn't focus. She cried out when he relinquished the bundle of nerves that produced so much pleasure and sat back on his heels to look up at her.

"I want you to come, my love. Tell me how to please you," he pleaded.

"Kiss me," she said without even thinking.

He rose to his feet and placed his palms on the wall above her head. Leaning in so the only thing touching her was his lips, he grazed them gently across hers. She moaned, tasting herself and he drew back to look at her, one eyebrow raised. She gave a sheepish grin before reaching to pull his head back down to her. She didn't have to prod, he deepened the kiss, gliding his tongue into her mouth so she could taste herself on him more fully. This was her undoing. She broke the kiss and cried out as the coil unfurled deep inside her.

Peter moved quickly. One hand held her up while over the sound of her heart pounding in her ears, Clemency heard the rasp of a zipper as he tried to divest himself of his trousers.

"I need--" he gasped as her hands joined his in pushing his pants down over his hips. The next thing she knew, she was back up against the wall with her legs wrapped around his waist and he was there, deep inside her. His lips sought hers out again and she felt a pulse deep inside as the coil began to tighten once more. There wouldn't be enough time for another build up... His need was too great. Instead, Clemency pulled back and watched him, relishing the feel of him pushing into her and watching the pleasure play out across his face.

"Come for me, Peter," she whispered and was rewarded when he slammed into her one final time and threw his head back with a howl of triumph. She wrapped her arms around his neck and held him close until their heart rates settled, but instead of returning her to her feet, Peter turned and carried her across the room to his bed.

"You're staying here tonight," he replied in answer to her questioning look. "I want you in my arms come morning."

He pulled the comforter up over them and they succumbed to sleep as the setting sun illuminated the dust motes hovering above them.

It was dark when Peter woke, and it took him a moment to realize where he was. Since Vanessa's death, more often than not he had taken to sleeping downstairs on his office couch. He grimaced at the realization that he should have prepared better, changed the bedding at least. Then again, asking Clemency over had been a spur of the moment decision. Glancing down at her gently snoring beside him, he realized it was the right decision. Having her in his bed felt right.

He carefully extricated himself from the bed and grabbed his pants before padding downstairs to the kitchen. Recalling the meager lunch she had eaten, Peter realized that if he was hungry, she must be starving. Opening the refrigerator, he was happy to see that his housekeeper had stocked it well for the weekend. Pulling out a dish of lasagna he placed it into the oven to warm up along with a loaf of garlic bread.

As he waited, his eyes landed on the blazer he had absent-mindedly tossed across the back of a barstool and he remembered the impromptu purchases he had made on his way home. Was everything pure fantasy... he wondered as he pulled the small bottles out of the coat pocket. And if so, was there any chance that he could make them a reality?

He finished reading the label on the second bottle when the oven timer dinged. Placing both bottles into his pocket, he prepped a tray with plates of food and made his way back up-stairs. He found Clemency sitting up in bed looking a little lost, but she smiled broadly when he entered the room and his heart skipped a beat at the sight. Setting the tray down across her lap, he leaned in for a kiss and once again had to mentally calm him-self down as he felt every fiber of his being jump to attention at the contact.

He could tell that she was feeling self-conscious sitting there. After watching her cross and then uncross her arms in front of her bare chest, he finally took pity on her and handed her his shirt.

"I hope you're hungry," he said placing a hand on hers to still her from buttoning the shirt. "That's enough, you look quite lovely."

"I didn't know you could cook," she said changing the subject as her cheeks continued to blaze.

"I'm okay in the kitchen when I have time, but this is courtesy of my housekeeper, Mrs. Bea. She comes in a couple days a week to make sure Gracie and I aren't wallowing in filth and starving to death," he explained.

"Well, my compliments to the chef. This is excellent," Clemency declared as she dug in. As Peter had suspected she was hungry, she all but licked her plate clean. He felt himself becoming more and more aroused as her tongue darted out to claim the last bit of sauce from her finger.

He rose to remove the tray, and when he turned back, he saw that the uncertainty from earlier had returned to her eyes.

"Were you sure about what you said earlier?" she asked. "About me staying here tonight?" He nodded. Approaching the bed, he reached out to caress her cheek. "Even at the risk of Georgie seeing me sneak out of here come morning?" she added with a smile.

"Who said I was going to let you out of my bed come morning?" he asked, easing the shirt off her shoulders, watching her eyes widen imperceptibly. "It's Friday, love. We have all weekend together. Shall we return to our earlier discussion regarding fantasy versus reality?"

"What do you want to know?" she squeaked as his fingers moved to trace little circles around her nipples.

"Everything," he whispered. "Your writing is quite descriptive. What have you done? What haven't you done? What would you like for me to do to you?" He watched her squirm and shake her head and could only imagine the images flitting through her mind. "Talk to me love."

"The stories... they're just that... fantasies put to paper," she protested.

Placing his hand under her knees, he pulled her down the bed until she was lying flat on her back. Trailing a line of soft kisses up her body, he noted her cry of pleasure when his attention turned to her breasts. They were quite sensitive, and she arched her back to jettison the pebbly hard nipples toward his waiting lips.

He was more than happy to feast upon her, but he had other things on his mind and his cock twitched to remind him that it wasn't going to wait around all night. She was still half wearing his shirt. Grasping two ends and taking inspiration from the character she had written for him, he tied them together, effectively pinning her arms to her sides.

"How about this? Fantasy or reality?" he asked, the intensity in his voice causing her to shiver.

"Well, it's definitely reality now," she admitted with a giggle, trying to mask her nervousness.

He flipped her over as he moved to stand. Circling to the foot of the bed where she had to strain to see him, he eased his trousers off, pulling the bottles from the pocket before discarding them. The first vial contained massage oil, which he set aside. He figured if they followed his plan to spend the weekend in bed together, at some point their aching muscles would need some relief. The second, he placed where it would be easily accessible before returning to the bed and straddling her legs.

Running his hands over the smooth skin of her ass, he began with gentle caresses before transitioning to a firmer kneading motion. She squirmed under him and he shifted as he realized that she was trying to part her thighs for him. His cock leapt at the first fleeting sight of his goal.

After counting to ten, he moved so that he was perched over her, his prick naturally nestling in the crevice of her ass cheeks. "And this?" he whispered against the back of her neck, hoping she would comprehend his intention. "Fantasy or reality?"

He felt her tense momentarily, before a shiver ran down her body.

"Both," she finally breathed, and he felt her push back against him. "Ancient reality. Long cherished fantasy."

He was flooded with relief. In six simple words she had told him that, not only was she game, but this part of her was his, and his alone. He knew it was silly to be jealous of some faceless, soon to be ex-husband, but he was happy to know that he was getting some part of her that the jerk had somehow been neglecting. Sitting back up, Peter reached for the second bottle. Clemency let out an audible gasp as he drizzled several drops of oil between her cheeks.

"This is also an ancient reality for me," he explained as he eased her onto her knees and grabbed a pillow to place under her. "What I do recall is that you need to talk to me. Let me know immediately if I'm going too fast and hurting you. Understand?" Clemency nodded and he could see a look of dazed pleasure already clouding her eyes. "No, love. Use words. Tell me you understand," he chastised as he slipped between her slick folds, penetrating her with one solid stroke.

"I understand," Clemency cried into the mattress.

Trying to think of anything except the sensation of her muscles involuntarily clenching around him, Peter coated his fingers in the lubricant and gently began to tease the tight ring of her rosebud. He eventually had to grasp her hip with one hand to stop her from moving against him. When he finally managed to breech her tight entrance with a second finger, he had to withdraw his prick completely as she had completely come undone. The sound of her screaming his name as she climaxed quickly skyrocketed to the top of the list of his favorite things in life. He wanted to be patient, but his cock was demanding satisfaction.

"May I proceed," he asked.

"Please," Clemency whimpered and he paused. Was that an affirmative, or had she had enough?

He wasn't sure what exactly provoked him. Perhaps Kennett was beginning to influence him more than he had thought, but he smacked her ass in frustration. "I told you that I needed communication, damn it!"

He heard the ripping of seams as she strained her arms to rise on them. As she turned to look back at him, he could see the quiet reserved woman had vanished, in her place was a rebellious vixen. "Please, Peter. Slide your cock up my ass and fuck me!"

Far be it from him to disobey a direct command... He counted to ten in as many languages as he could muster to prevent the urge to bury himself to the hilt in one swift stroke. By the time he had finally sheathed himself, they were both panting and a thin sheen of sweat covered both their bodies.

She gasped when he began to withdraw but pleaded with him not to stop when he hesitated. She was so fucking tight, he thought as he worked to develop a steady rhythm. It was as though a vice was gripping him and he knew that he wouldn't last for very long. Hearing her cries and realizing that they were beginning to sound more frustrated, Peter looked down to see her tangled arms straining to reach between her legs.

"Fuck, Peter! I need to come again," she demanded. That was all it took. His hips bucked forward once again as he exploded into her. In the pure bliss of the moment, he somehow had the presence of mind to reach under her to assist her in her demands. He wasn't sure what he did... he must have brushed the right spot in the proper manner, because all of a sudden, she became impossibly tighter and she sang out his name once again.

CHAPTER TWENTY-THREE

The day was slipping by, Peter thought as he noted that the sun's rays no longer stretched across the bedroom floor. He was hesitant to get up. After their second round the night before, he and Clemency had shared a leisurely shower before tumbling back into bed in a tangle of limbs. Sometime just after daybreak, he had awoken to Clemency's lips wrapped firmly around him. He had relished the sensation for as long as he could before hauling her into his arms and making love with her.

He couldn't recall a more wonderful night, and now, watching her gently snoring on the pillow beside him, he realized that he didn't want it to end. He wasn't just thinking about the sex even... he wanted *her* in his life. Her smile, her laughter, and, yes... her touch. His thoughts drifted back to the two simple words she had uttered to him Monday morning. Love... yeah, if he were honest, he would admit that he had fallen, and fallen hard for Clemency. Something was just stopping him from vocalizing those feelings. It was too soon...

"Penny for your thoughts," she whispered, and he felt her hand on the side of his face.

I love you and want to spend the rest of my life waking up to you in my arms, he thought. Instead, he turned to press his lips to the palm of her hand.

"I didn't realize you were awake," he replied.

"Barely. What time is it?" she asked.

He rose on one elbow to peek at the clock on the nightstand. "Half past ten," he said. Not as late as he had initially thought. He pulled her into his arms as he settled back down. Over the sound of Clemency's low moan of pleasure, Peter's brain registered the sound of a slamming door.

"Daddy? Are you home?" His daughter's voice called from below.

"It's Gracie," he said unnecessarily as he leapt from the bed and tripped over his trousers. What was she doing home? He thought she had plans to stay at school for the weekend. Zipping up his pants he paused when he saw his panic mirrored in Clemency's eyes as she sat clutching the bed sheet to her chest. Willing his racing heart to settle, he sat on the edge of the bed. He could handle this... hadn't he just been thinking about spending the rest of his life with this woman? She would have to meet his daughter sometime, why not now? "Get dressed, love. I'd like for you to meet my daughter," he said, raising her hand to his lips. She looked uncertain for a moment, before giving a tentative smile and nod.

"There you are," Grace said, looking relieved as Peter appeared at the top of the stairs. "Did you sleep up there last night?"

"How did you get here? I thought we had discussed you not taking the underground by yourself," he countered.

"Sam was coming home for the weekend so I hitched a ride with her," Grace explained. "I needed to come get something to wear for tonight. Can you take me back?"

Sam was Georgie's youngest daughter. Peter's mind was racing as he hit the bottom step. That probably meant...

"Gracie?" Georgie's voice came from the stoop as she pushed open the front door. "Sweetie, I don't think your father's ho--Oh, good. Peter, you are here."

"Why wouldn't he be here?" Grace asked turning to Georgie.

"Yes, why wouldn't he be here?" Donovan added his own voice to the mix, coming in behind Georgie. "We have plans to go golfing this afternoon. Gads man why aren't you dressed ye--Oh. Hello," he said in surprise as Clemency appeared at the top of the stairs.

She suddenly understood the phrase 'a deer caught in the headlights' as four pairs of eyes turned in her direction.

"Daddy? What's going on?" Grace asked as Clemency met Peter's gaze. Bolstered by his smile, she gathered her courage to descend the steps to stand by his side.

"You, and you... Out," Peter declared, pointing to Georgie and Donovan.

"But, golf, mate," Donovan whined as Georgie pushed him toward the door.

Instead of following, Georgie turned to face Clemency, one eyebrow raised. "You skipped out on me yesterday," she accused. However, she was unable to keep her angry appearance as her face slid into a grin and she leaned in to give Clemency a peck on the cheek. "Good luck," she whispered in her ear.

As the door closed behind her friend, Clemency turned to find Peter's daughter accessing her.

"Gracie, honey... I'd like you to meet..." Peter began and Clemency looked up at him expectantly, waiting to hear her name finally cross his lips. He gulped and she took pity on him when she saw the flash of anger appear on his daughter's face.

"Clemency," she said, stepping forward, hand outstretched. The girl ignored it, continuing to glare at her father. "It's okay, Grace. Your father is quite aware of my name. He just thinks it's ridiculous and refuses to say it."

The young girl finally turned to her, relief replacing annoyance as she reached out to accept Clemency's hand. "You're his girlfriend?"

Clemency hesitated, but Peter was quick to come up beside her, placing on arm possessively around her waist. "Yes, Gracie. We've been seeing one another for several weeks now."

Grace's reaction took them both by surprise, as she threw herself into her father's arms. "Oh, Daddy, I'm so happy. You've been so sad and alone for so long."

Peter's eyebrows knit together in a frown as he looked down at his daughter's head. He thought that he had done a good job of masking his feelings, but apparently this young girl was far more observant than he had realized.

"I think I should go and let you two spend the day together," Clemency said, inching toward the door.

"Oh, please don't go," Grace said, turning to grasp Clemency's hand. "Sam and her mum were going to come over to help me, but you're here now and that's even better."

Clemency looked to Peter who shrugged back with a smile. "What exactly do you need help with, sweetie?" she asked.

"Clothes," the girl said with a roll of her eyes. "School is requiring me to attend a dance tonight and I need something to wear."

"Well, I definitely can't be of help there," Peter said with a clap of his hands. "How about I see to lunch while you ladies inspect Gracie's closet. How does Chinese sound?"

Clemency vehemently shook her head. She was still off fried rice after her last experience with Georgie.

"Pizza," Gracie declared.

Peter groaned. "Okay, but you're not contaminating my pie with your foul toppings so be prepared to take leftovers back to your dorm."

"There's nothing foul about pineapple on pizza," Grace argued and, to Peter's surprise was quickly joined by Clemency.

"Pineapple is great on pizza," she declared. "Especially with--"

"Bacon," they both said together.

"Have you tried it with ranch sauce?" Clemency asked Grace.

"No, but it sounds delish!" the girl exclaimed and they both turned to face Peter.

"So, one pizza with pineapple, bacon, and ranch?" he relented with a grimace. Grace nodded before turning to skip up the stairs, while Peter turned to Clemency. "And here I thought you were the perfect woman..."

"Perfect woman?" Clemency replied with a snort. "You hate my name... my hair... criticize my excellent taste in music... and now my choice of pizza toppings. I'm beginning to wonder why you keep me around in the first place."

He pulled her into his arms and lowered his lips to hers. As he deepened the kiss, he felt her shiver as his tongue glided against hers. "I keep you around because you're so easy to pleasure," he whispered in her ear as he nuzzled her neck. Sensing that they were being watched, he glanced up to spy his daughter gazing down at them from the landing. The smile on her face was absolutely radiant. God, he hoped he was doing the right thing. The last thing he wanted was to risk both their hearts.

Fifteen minutes later Peter poked his head into Grace's room to let them know that he would be back soon with lunch. Clemency nodded and waved absentmindedly as she held up yet another frilly lace dress. They had unloaded the contents of the girls closet onto the bed which sadly matched the dress in both its pinkness and childishness. Clemency was struggling to find a diplomatic way of questioning Grace about her fashion choices. The last thing she wanted to do was hurt the girl's feelings.

"They're horrible, aren't they?" Grace finally said as she fingered the velvet of another dress. "My mother picked them all out for me... but they're all wrong for tonight."

"I wouldn't say horrible exactly..." Clemency began. Atrocious, dreadful, and hideous maybe... "It's just that you're twelve, right? My guess is that your mum bought all of these when you were still a little girl. I mean, just look at the labels, you've outgrown most of them. You're becoming a young lady and need clothing to reflect that, not these childish frills."

"But I need something now... for tonight," Grace said, tears of frustration springing into her eyes.

"Are you really required to attend a dance?" Clemency asked, thinking that a school dance at age twelve would have been her worst nightmare.

"Please don't tell Daddy, but my class participation isn't so great. Headmistress and I struck a deal. If I attend a handful of events, I won't risk getting a bad mark," Grace explained.

"Hmmm, well I think the solution is obvious," Clemency said, rising from the bed. "We need to go shopping."

"Shopping? Like together?" Grace asked wide eyed.

"Well, my daughter likes to frequently point out to me that I'm horrid at the whole girl thing so I thought I would see if Georgie and Sam would like to join us if that's all right with you," Clemency said. "Why don't you work on sorting out this mess while I give them a call. Anything that no longer fits, toss into a bag and we can see about donating it."

Georgie readily agreed to the plan, saying that Roger would be out front in an hour. Hearing Donovan's voice in the background, Clemency asked to speak with him. She assured him that if he could arrange a later tee time, Peter would be all his for the afternoon.

Returning to Gracie, she found the girl adding the last piece of clothing to the donation bag. "Some of them still fit, but I don't ever plan on wearing them," she admitted. They had just turned to address the dresser when they heard Peter return. Agreeing to tackle it later, they headed downstairs to lunch.

"You mentioned your daughter," Grace began as she took a bite of pizza. Her eyes widened in appreciation of the new taste combination.

"Yes. Lucy. She's just a few months younger than you. She's smart and outgoing, always wanting to be a part of everything happening around her," Clemency explained.

"Does she live here with you?" Grace asked.

"No, she's with her dad now, but I'm hoping she'll come visit during the summer," Clemency replied. Peter watched a shadow of uncertainty flicker across her eyes as she spoke and reached to give her hand a squeeze.

As they ate, they listened as Grace chattered on about all the things they should show Lucy when she came. Peter had never seen his daughter so animated; it was like she was suddenly a different person. When he was finally able to get a word in edgewise, he asked if they had solved the clothing conundrum.

"Not exactly," was their vague response. They both leapt from the counter at the sound of the doorbell a moment later. "We've taken steps toward solving it though," Clemency explained as she shrugged into her coat and reached for her purse.

"We're spending the afternoon shopping."

He watched as Grace skipped out the door without so much as a farewell, before grabbing for Clemency. "You're just going to leave me here alone? What happened to spending the weekend in my bed?"

"You won't be alone," Clemency said, shifting so he could see Donovan standing beside the car, aimlessly tossing a golf ball in the air as he chatted with Georgie. "You don't judge my choice of pizza toppings, and I won't criticize your idea of sport, deal?"

He grumbled good naturedly as he followed her down the steps and held the car door open for her. Leaning down, he brushed a soft kiss across her lips before pulling out his wallet and handing her a credit card. "Buy Gracie whatever she wants," he instructed.

"I heard that," his daughter's voice came from the back seat. "Clemmie, I want a pony!"

"Within reason," he amended, before leaning down to whisper in her ear. "And buy yourself something sexy for tonight."

"Well that was a rarity," Donovan said as they watched the car depart.

"What?" Peter asked.

"Seeing you kiss a woman," Donovan replied. "I've known you for over thirty years and can probably count on one hand the number of times I've witnessed it. Hell, I stood up with you at your wedding and I think the kiss I just witnessed showed more passion than the peck you gave Vanessa. What changed?"

Peter tensed. His friend usually knew better than to touch upon such a personal subject. The last time he had, it was to ask why Peter was planning on marrying such a heartless bitch. Peter had decked him for that. Now, he wondered why he hadn't listened to Donovan more closely back then.

"What changed is that I have stopped heeding the criticism of a cold, heartless, bitch," Peter replied, purposely throwing his friends words back at him.

"Good," Donovan replied after a moment pause. "Golf?"

◆ ◆ ◆

They were able to quickly find the perfect dress for Gracie at the first boutique Georgie took them too. But as the girl turned toward the cashier, Clemency stopped her.

"I'm guessing most of the clothes in your dresser are going to also need replaced," she said. "Why don't you have a look around and see if there's anything else you like."

Georgie's daughter, Sam was only a few years older and quickly took charge, dragging the young girl off as Clemency moved to gaze outside the window at the street below.

"Where on earth do Peter and Donovan go to golf in February?" she asked Georgie as she watched the first few snowflakes begin to drift down from the sky.

"Golf is just code for, 'let's hit the pub, get pissed, and play darts,'" Georgie said with a laugh. "So... any more L-word?"

"Shhh..." Clemency urged, looking around to make sure Peter's daughter wasn't in earshot.

"Oh, stop worrying. Sammy's probably introducing the child to denim," Georgie said.

"Which would not be a bad thing considering the amount of satin and lace that girl has in her closet," Clemency stated.

"Yeah, Vanessa treated her more like a china doll than anything else," Georgie said, smiling as her daughter approached with an armload of clothes.

Looking around for Grace, Clemency finally spotted her hovering near the lingerie section, a look of pure trepidation upon her face.

"Is everything okay, sweetie," Clemency asked. She thought Grace was going to jump out of her skin when she placed an arm around her shoulder. She nodded mutely; her gaze focused on the floor. "Gracie--"

"I need a bra," the girl blurted out, taking Clemency by surprise. Facing Grace, Clemency grasped her by the shoulders and took a good look at her. She needed a bra? There was nothing there yet... Then it dawned on her, recalling the conversation she had overheard in the park last November.

"Sweetie, do you really want a bra, or perhaps some cami's to make it easier to change clothes during gym class?" Clemency asked gently.

Relief flooded Grace's eyes. "The second one," she muttered.

Taking her by the hand, Clemency led her into the section and assisted her as she chose a selection of camisoles and sports bras.

Peter leaned on the door frame of his daughter's bedroom watching as Clemency added the finishing touches to Grace's hair. His little girl looked so beautiful and grown up. Peter's heart caught in his throat when he realized that this was how it was supposed to be all along. Vanessa had treated Grace like a mannequin, dressing her up as she saw fit and, like a mannequin, Grace had always been stiff and quiet. He could tell by his daughter's posture alone that she was now wearing what she wanted. She looked comfortable and if her animated chatter was any indication, she was happy. Clemency had made that possible in one single afternoon. He shifted slightly, alerting them to his presence.

"Daddy! What do you think?" Grace asked, skipping over to twirl in front of him.

"I think you look positively radiant," he declared as he bent to kiss her cheek. "Are you ready to head back?"

"Just about," she said, turning back to the bed. "I just want to sort out some of these to take back with me."

Clemency saw his eyes widen at the sight of the pile of loot they had acquired that day. "We'll meet you downstairs when you're ready, sweetie," she told Grace, grabbing Peter by the hand and dragging him down the hall toward his room. Once inside, out of earshot, she pulled his credit card out of her skirt pocket and handed it back to him. "We went a little overboard, I know... If money is an issue, I'd be happy to--"

She was interrupted by his mouth on hers. As she wound her arms around his neck, pulling him closer, she felt him slide the card back into her pocket.

"Money is never an issue where my daughter is concerned," he said as he broke the kiss. "Keep the card. If there is anything you or she need, use it."

She watched wide eyed as he turned and left the room. Had she insulted him? Was he upset that she and his daughter had bonded so easily? She didn't think that was it, but she couldn't account for his sudden intensity. Leaving the room, she reached the bottom step of the stairs in time to bid Grace goodbye. She wished her luck at the dance and was rewarded with an eye roll.

"I'm just required to 'attend' the dance. This new purse is big enough for a book. My plan is to find a quiet corner and read for a few hours," the girl said with a smirk.

Clemency laughed as she pulled her into her arms. "You are definitely a girl after my own heart."

She felt Peter watching them closely, and as Grace bound down the stairs to his waiting car, he loomed in front of her. "You'll be here when I return?" he asked, gazing down into her eyes and smiling when Clemency gave a quick nod. "Wearing something special, I hope." Clemency felt her cheeks flush as she thought of the scrap of fabric she had managed to sneak into the pile of clothing purchased. "Interesting..." Peter breathed, noting her reaction.

The drive to Grace's school was the longest twelve blocks he had ever driven. Hitting every red light certainly didn't help, nor did his daughter's persistent chatter. His mind raced, trying to imagine what Clemency had purchased. Was she donning black leather and curling up on his office couch? White lace in his bed? A French maid's costume in the kitchen? As he pulled up before Crestwood Academy, he realized that his daughter was looking at him expectantly.

"I'm sorry, Gracie, did you say something?" he asked.

She looked down at her lap. "I asked if you were in love with

Clemmie?"

Peter thought back to his morning musings. He didn't make a habit of lying to his daughter and he wasn't going to start now. "Yes. I think I am," he admitted. "Are you okay with that?"

Grace nodded enthusiastically. "I think she's wonderful. And I can tell that she makes you happy."

He gave his daughter a hug and watched as she entered her dorm before turning the ignition and returning home to the woman who did, indeed, make him happy.

CHAPTER TWENTY-FOUR

The month of February flew by in a flurry of activity. Valentine's Day weekend, Peter took Clemency to a flower shop and gave her an ultimatum - either pick out a bouquet of her favorite flower, or he would purchase every arrangement in the store and have them delivered to her flat. Seeing the look of panic on her face, the florist asked Clemency what she liked.

"Daisies," Clemency said with a gulp. "Simple, white daisies."

They left the shop with Clemency holding a large bouquet and Peter looking quite pleased with himself. That evening they had a disastrous double date with Georgie and Donovan. Their friends bickered as Donovan pointed out to Georgie that he couldn't prove his fidelity and willingness to commit to her if she wouldn't allow him to move to London. Peter ended up spending the evening on Georgie's couch trying to convince her that Donovan had a valid point and maybe it was time for her to take a leap of faith. While next door in Peter's kitchen, Clemency tried to convince Donovan that a grown man didn't need permission to live where he wanted. By the end of the evening, Clemency and Peter fell into bed together, too exhausted to do anything other than hold one another.

The remaining two weeks of the month they considered themselves lucky to find five minutes to spend together. Georgie had made a big push on auditions, wanting to finalize the cast, while Peter worked with Jack to add the finishing touches to his project.

Peter had given Clemency a key to his place and in the span

of a few short weeks, most of her belongings had migrated over. He didn't mind. He was happy to find her citrus scent lingering in his bathroom. Happier still to find her head resting on his pillow when he stumbled in after the increasingly frequent late nights. However, as the dreary February days transitioned into a stormy March, Peter found that he was becoming more and more frustrated with Clemency's tendency to wake him in the middle of the night. He wouldn't mind if she wanted to have her way with him, but no... he would often waken instead to the bright light of her phone and the scratching of a pencil on paper as she jotted down notes.

"I can't help it," she cried when he called her on it after the third night in a row. "I'm at the beginning of a new project and just getting to know the characters. If one of them decides to whisper in my ear in the middle of the night that they have a craving for whipped cream in the bedroom, I need to write it down before I forget."

"Whipped cream?" he croaked, gaping at her.

"Think about it, love," Clemency whispered against his lips before rising to dress for the day.

Peter did think about it, and was intrigued, making a mental note to add whipped cream to the shopping list. However, he was also bloody exhausted, so staying home that morning he phoned a friend who also happened to be an interior designer.

That weekend Gracie was home and Peter discussed his plans for remodeling her mother's bedroom, asking her if there was anything she wanted before he donated all her belongings. In the midst of their conversation he got called back to the studio. Returning home, he discovered that Grace had invited Clemency over and the two of them had begun sorting through Vanessa's possessions. He had only returned briefly to explain to his daughter that he had to work all weekend, yet again and he would take her back to school.

Grace gave him a confused look. "Why can't I just stay here with Clemmie?" Clemency's head shot up at the sound of her name. She had taken to returning to her flat on the weekends that Grace came home. Yet, once again, the girl was more perceptive than either of them realized. "Daddy, I know she stays here most of the time anyways. You can stop hiding it," Grace said with a roll of her eyes. Peter looked at Clemency and shrugged, grinning when he saw the blush appear on her cheeks.

Rising to her feet, Clemency pressed a kiss to Peter's lips. "Go... Work... We'll stay here and clean, and then have a girl's night."

As Grace folded the last of her mother's clothes, adding them to the bag of donations, Clemency was digging through the back of the closet, her fingers brushing against a small wooden chest.

"Hey, sweetie, this box may be perfect for you to keep all of your mementos in," she said, pulling it down from the shelf. Opening it, she found a bundle of letters and notes. Glancing at the writing on one of them, Clemency's eyes widened in surprised before she quickly folded it and stuffed the bundle into the back pocket of her jeans. Turning to hand Grace the chest, she assessed the small pile the girl had set aside. "Honey, is this all you wish to keep?" Grace looked at the collection of items she had randomly selected and Clemency could see the hesitation in her eyes. "What is it, sweetie?"

"I don't really want to keep anything," the girl whispered. "I don't want to remember my mother. I'm glad she's gone," she declared more forcefully before fleeing the room.

Stopping long enough to stow the bundle of letters on Peter's dresser, Clemency followed the sound of sobbing and found Grace curled up on her bed. She didn't hesitate. Lying down beside the girl, she gathered her into her arms and held her until the tears subsided.

"Do you want to talk about it?" Clemency asked quietly.

"My mother didn't want me," Grace declared, turning to face Clemency. When Clemency tried to protest, Grace continued. She told me, quite frequently that the only reason I existed was because Daddy forced her to have me."

"Oh, sweetie," Clemency had no answer to this other than to hold Gracie tight. "I know it's hard to imagine, but someday you may regret not keeping some part of your mother. Let's go add a few items to the box, stow it away and call it a night. We'll make dinner and find something to binge watch, deal?"

A few minutes later, as she added the last piece of jewelry to the small chest, Grace turned to Clemency. "Were you speaking from experience just now?"

Swallowing a lump in her throat, Clemency nodded and explained about the unexpected deaths of her parents and brothers. "...I couldn't cope with going through their belongings at the time. In my haste, I got rid of it all. I now regret that I have nothing but memories to share with Lucy."

Closing the door on the room, Clemency sought a more lighthearted tone for the remainder of the evening. Pulling out her phone and selecting the video chat option, she rang up her daughter and introduced the two girls. They immediately discovered they had many things in common and Clemency listened to their chatter and giggles as she puttered around the kitchen.

Peter found them crashed on the sofa early the next morning when he finally stumbled through the door. Seeing his daughter asleep in Clemency's arms, he knew he couldn't keep quiet any longer. Gently shaking her awake, he motioned for Clemency to follow him. She yawned and frowned as she trailed him up the stairs. Closing the bedroom door behind them, he turned and drew her to him, his lips crashing upon hers.

"Well hello to--" Clemency began when they finally parted, only to be interrupted by Peter.

"I love you," he declared. "We've been skirting around it for weeks now, but you need to know that I'm in love with you and probably have been since that blasted plane ride last November."

"I love you, too, you daft old man," Clemency said as she pulled him down to kiss her again. She was relishing the little happy dance his kisses still caused her lady bits to break out in when she heard Grace call her name. "Did you just get in? Why don't you get some sleep. Grace and I have plans with Georgie and her girls this morning. I'll wake you when we get back."

Brunch was followed by shopping. First clothes, then at Grace's insistence, books.

"I already finished all the ones I got for Christmas and Lucy suggested a few I want to try," the girl explained. An hour later, while waiting for the cashier to ring up their purchases, Grace caught sight of the nearby *Tempest* display and put two and two together. "Oh my gosh, Clemmie, that's you!" she exclaimed.

Heads turned, and Clemency felt a moment of panic as voices began whispering and people stared at her. When copies of her book began to be pressed into her hands with pleas for an autograph, she pasted a smile on her face and complied until Georgie finally intervened. As her friend pushed her toward the exit, she overheard an observant fan who recognized Georgie speculate about a *Tempest* movie.

"I guess the cat's out of the bag," Clemency said with a forced laugh as she slid into the backseat of the car.

"In more ways than one," Georgie agreed. "I'm pretty sure I saw the cashier take note of Peter's name on the credit card you used. I think you have officially been outed."

Sobering at the thought, Clemency declared that it was time to return home.

"No worries, love," Peter declared when she described the events that had transpired on their outing. "I'll give my publicist a ring and warn her. This isn't a catastrophe. It was going to come out sooner or later."

Leaving Peter to make his call, she went to see if Grace needed help packing for school. Entering the girl's room, her eye caught the glittery cosmetic bag she had created for the girl sitting prominently on the bed. Following her gaze, Grace moved to pick it up.

"I realize now that you're to thank for Daddy having that mortifying conversation with me," she said. "Can I ask you a question or two?"

"Of course, sweetie," Clemency answered, moving aside a few stuffed animals to sit beside the girl.

"It's just that, many girls have already started... you know..." Grace began.

"Their period," Clemency provided. "There's nothing wrong with the word. The floor will not open up and swallow you if you say it."

"Right. Their period," Grace repeated more confidently. "I just wanted to know when mine would start."

"Oh, love, there's no real way of knowing that. It will happen when your body is ready," Clemency replied.

"And it will just happen? No warning?" Grace looked horrified at the thought.

"There may be cramps beforehand, but that's not guaranteed. That's why when you do begin menstruating it's important to keep track with the calendar. Even that won't necessarily be accurate for the first couple of years as your body adjusts. Becoming a woman's not easy, sweetie, but it's worth it in the end."

"I'll second that," Peter said from the doorway.

"Daaaaaddddy," Grace complained. "You already had your chance to explain this."

"And we can discuss it further on the way back to school if you want. Are you ready?" he asked with a grin.

Clemency was laughing at the banter between father and daughter when her phone began playing 'Lucy in the Sky with Diamonds.'

"Hey, Luce, is everything okay?" she asked.

"Can I talk to Grace?" her daughter said in greeting.

"Is that Lucy? I need to ask her something," Peter said at the same time.

Clemency threw her arms up in exasperation before handing her phone over. "If anyone wants to talk to me, I'll be downstairs."

Several minutes later, Clemency turned from the sink where she was rinsing dishes. She dried off her hands as Grace came bounding into the room, backpack slung over her shoulders.

"Lucy and I exchanged contact info so we can chat while I'm at school," she announced as she grabbed the box containing their leftover pizza. "Tell Dad I'll be waiting in the car. Love you, Clemmie."

"Love you too, Gracie," Clemency said to the girls retreating back, and realized how true that simple statement was. She loved Peter and Grace. They had become her family, but she still felt as though a large part of her heart was missing. She dearly longed for her daughter.

"Thanks for the advice, Luce," Peter said, entering the kitchen. "Here's your mum." Handing her the phone, he leaned in for a kiss before motioning that he would be back in a few minutes.

"Sweetie, what secrets of mine have you divulged now?" Clemency asked her daughter.

"Don't worry, Mom. Daddy refuses to tell me your name so it wasn't that," Lucy said. "Peter just wanted to know your favorite color."

Clemency laughed, wondering what the man was up to now. She chatted with her daughter, making plans for their New York City meeting in a few weeks. Before hanging up, Clemency asked to speak with Lucy's father.

"Hello Elliott. I just wanted to touch base and see where we stood on the divorce," she said in greeting.

"Oh... um... good?" came his hesitant reply and Clemency immediately knew something was wrong. Elliott was the world's worst liar.

Peter, followed by Georgie entered the kitchen a few moments later to find Clemency cursing up a blue streak. They perched themselves on the barstools behind the counter, settling in to watch the fireworks.

"For fucks sake, Elliott. We agreed on this. When I said the word, you were going to see to it that it happened. No questions asked," Clemency shouted into the phone.

"I didn't think... I mean, you said that you had kissed a guy... that wasn't such a big deal... I figured you'd come around," Elliott faltered.

"Come around?" Clemency repeated in astonishment. "Come

around and what, Elliott? Join you and Whitney in our bed?"

"No! I just--"

"First of all, Elliott, you never think. That's your problem. If something is too difficult to handle, you avoid it," Clemency interrupted. "Second, my kissing Peter was a big deal because I have since fallen in love with him and would very much like to be free of you so I can see where our relationship may lead."

"You're in love?" Elliott whispered as Clemency turned to meet Peter's gaze.

"Yes," she replied with a grin.

"Are you going to marry him?" Elliott asked.

"I don't know, but I'd like to have the option available," Clemency said, running a hand through her hair. "Look, Elliott... I'm giving you until the end of the week to provide me with proof that you have filed for divorce. If you haven't, I will get my own lawyer on it, and I promise you, I will play dirty. Does your family even know about Whitney yet?"

The threat worked as Elliott cleared his throat and promised he would get things done. Clemency set her phone down to a round of applause from Peter and Georgie as Peter circled the counter to take her into his arms.

"Clemmie, you do realize that you admitted that you're in love with Peter, right?" Georgie said. "He was sitting right here and I'm pretty sure his aged ears heard you loud and clear."

"Oh, I heard her all right," Peter said, lowering his head for a lingering kiss. "And I love her right back."

"Sorry, Georgie, I knew there was something I had forgotten to tell you this morning," Clemency admitted.

Georgie threw her hands up in mock disgust. "If you're not going to be a proper friend and dish out all the juicy details, I may as well leave," she exclaimed. "Oh, and why on God's green earth did Peter bring home a bag full of whipped cream?"

Clemency laughed as she peered into the bag Peter had set on the counter. "Research, love," she replied with a wink in Georgie's direction. "It's for a threesome scene if you wish to stick around..."

The look of horror on both Peter and Georgie's faces at the idea had Clemency doubling over with laughter. As Georgie made a beeline for the front door, she turned to impart the news she had come over to deliver in the first place.

"You two have definitely been outed. Social media is abuzz with the news of your relationship."

The following weekend, Peter and Clemency made their public debut by attending a local film festival. While it was a small affair, Clemency was still required to nervously paste on a smile as she stood beside Peter, camera flashes blinding them as paparazzi shouted questions. She instantly knew that this was something she would always hate, and on the ride home she asked Peter how often he had to endure such events.

"I used to do them fairly often, but only because it's what Vanessa lived for," he replied. "I take it you didn't enjoy yourself?" Clemency was hesitant to disappoint him, but eventually she shook her head before turning to gaze out the window at the passing scenery. "We will, of course, be required to attend the *Tempest* premier next year," Peter said reaching for her hand. "But if you'd like we can live like hermits until then."

"That sounds like absolute bliss," Clemency replied as they pulled up in front of the house. Making plans a year in the future also felt perfect.

Half an hour later, Peter exited the bathroom to find Clemency waiting for him to help her out of her gown. She was staring at the dresser where she had placed the bundle of letters she had found the previous week.

"Peter... there was--" she began.

"I know," he interrupted as he lowered the zipper on her gown. "Thank you for keeping them from Grace. I destroyed them."

Clutching the fabric of her dress to her chest, Clemency turned to face him. "She was unfaithful to you... The entire time... And you stayed... Why?"

"For Gracie, of course," he replied, turning away from her. "Why else?"

He returned from the closet a moment later wearing his robe to find Clemency standing where he had left her.

"I didn't," she whispered, fear in her eyes as she gazed across the room at him.

"You didn't what, love?" he asked taking a step toward her only to watch as she tripped back away from him.

She swiped at a tear as it fell, quickly turning to pull a nightshirt out of the dresser. "I didn't stay, Peter. I was faced with the same situation. I have a young daughter and a spouse that I discovered was unfaithful, and I left. What does that make me in your eyes?"

He crossed the room, placing his hands on her shoulders and turning her to face him. "Mine," he declared. "It makes you mine. That, and stronger and wiser than I could ever be. I was so wrapped up in work when I first discovered Vanessa's indiscretions. When I finally confronted her, she threatened to take Grace and run if I so much as hinted at wanting a divorce. She wanted to have her cake and eat it too, and I let her in order to keep Gracie in my life."

Clemency thought about Grace's confession and her heart hurt for these two lost souls. Despite knowing that it was wrong to think ill of the dead, she hoped that Vanessa was burning in some fiery pit. Stepping into Peter's embrace, she let him lead her to bed.

CHAPTER TWENTY-FIVE

Spring had sprung and the weather most days was quite lovely. This didn't prevent Peter from being in a foul mood though. He ignored the chirping birds as he sat in the garden with Clemency and Gracie. They were coordinating their schedules for the rest of the month and his pen had worried a hole into the page of his date book as he glared at the meet and greet trip scheduled for the following weekend.

"I have to leave early Thursday for a weekend trip to Boston," he finally said with a sigh. "I'll be back Sunday night. Can you two survive without me that long?"

"Actually, no," Clemency replied. "I'm also flying out Thursday. I'm meeting Lucy in New York. Can you join us after your convention for a few days?"

Grace let out a howl of protest. "No fair. I've always wanted to go to New York. Plus, it's spring holiday that week. You can't just leave me here all alone."

Well, fuck, Peter thought looking back down at his calendar. He had Gracie's holiday penciled in for the week after. Now what were they going to do?

"It's brilliant," he looked up to see Clemency grinning. "Peter, are you flying directly to Boston?"

"No, Georgie arranged the tickets and for some reason we're flying into New York and taking the train," Peter replied.

"She booked you on the same flight as me," Clemency explained. "All we need to do is add a ticket for Grace and we're all set."

Grace was bouncing in her seat. "I'm going to New York? Really?"

Peter already had his phone out, calling the airline and making the necessary arrangements.

When Peter left to take his over-excited daughter back to school, Clemency phoned her daughter to make sure Lucy was okay with a minor change in plans. Thankfully, she found her to be excited at the prospect of meeting Peter and Grace. Everything was working out perfectly...

...that was until she entered the office the next morning to find Georgie in the midst of a complete meltdown.

"Kaitlyn is out," she declared. "She's entered rehab, her contract has been nullified."

Clemency let out a celebratory whoop that was echoed by Frankie. Georgie, however, looked less than thrilled.

"Come on, Georgie. This is a good thing. That woman was horrible, both for the part and as a human being," Clemency soothed.

"Agreed, but she was our lead. Unless we can come up with a replacement in the next few days our schedule is screwed and I'll need you back here next week for auditions," Georgie explained.

There was no way Clemency was missing out on her week with Lucy. Especially now that Peter and Grace would be joining them. The wheels in her head were turning as she made her way across to the costume department for her first meeting of the day.

It wasn't until mid-afternoon that she got a break and was able to sneak into Peter's office, closing and locking the door behind her.

"Do you have a minute?" she whispered as he looked up from behind his desk.

"If you're here to make the fantasy of you, me, and that couch a reality, I'm all yours, love," he said with a grin.

Clemency faltered, glancing over at the couch. Damn, now she had visions running through her head and she didn't have time to get distracted. "Well... no... actually, I came to see you about something else. Did you hear about Kaitlyn?" she asked quietly as he rose and rounded the desk. He nodded and leaned back, crossing his arms and listening as Clemency launched into her plan.

"Frankie?" he asked in astonishment. "Frankie McDougal? The little girl whose bruised knees I used to kiss and bandage? You want *her* to play Tempest?"

"Trust me, Peter... she's perfect for the part. We just need to get Georgie to see it. Can I count on you to help?" Clemency begged.

He watched as she licked her lips nervously, knowing full well that he could never deny her. "Tomorrow afternoon in the auditorium," he agreed. "Just make sure to get Georgie and Leslie there first and keep them quiet. Now... how about that couch?" he asked with a wiggle of his eyebrows.

The following day found Clemency sitting in a dark theater between a still grumpy Georgie and a confused Leslie.

"Would you please explain what the hell we are doing here?" her friend whispered again.

"I asked you to trust me," Clemency whispered back. "And for fucks sake, keep quiet or this won't work at all."

Georgie let out a squeak of surprise when the side door opened, and Frankie walked onto the stage.

"Hello?" the girl called into the darkness before the side door reopened and Peter strolled in followed by three other gentlemen.

Lord love him, Clemency thought. He really came through. She may have to give in and fulfill his office couch fantasy after all.

"Mr. Bennett," Frankie said. "I got your memo, but I'm confused. What's this all about?"

"Well, you see, Frankie, me and the boys here," Peter began, gesturing to the men gathered behind him. "We need your help. Now that Kaitlyn is gone, we need someone to run lines with and Clemency says you're just the person to help with that."

"You want to run lines?" Frankie asked confused. "All of you? Right now?"

Peter knew that he had overdone it. He had approached Simon Foster and Liam McKenna about helping him, but when Colin Fletcher got wind of what was happening, he also insisted on joining the party.

"Not the whole script, mind you," Peter clarified. "Just a few scenes. I'm told you understand the proper inflections and emotions Clem-- I mean, the author is looking for."

Clemency snickered at Peter's near slip of the tongue. She turned to glance at Georgie to find the woman sitting on the edge of her seat intently watching the stage.

Peter handed Frankie a script and the men began running scenes with her. If anything, Clemency found her to be even better reading opposite professionals. The only time she faltered was in the scene with Colin.

When they had finished, Clemency sat back in her seat with a grin, watching the silent communication occur between Georgie and Leslie.

On stage, Frankie looked slightly shaken as she closed her script and handed it back to Peter. "I hope that helped, Mr. Bennett," she said with a weak smile.

"I think it helped immensely," Peter replied with a grin before turning to face the darkness. "What do you think, Georgie?"

"I think it was absolutely brilliant," Georgie said. She had already made her way to the stage and took her surprised daughter into her arms. "I think we have finally found your niche in the industry, love."

Later that night, Georgie leaned against Clemency as they sat together on her sofa. They had gathered for a celebratory dinner, that had gone south when Frankie's partner, Jenna, had stormed out in a fit of anger. Muttering a quiet thank you, Frankie meekly followed.

"She probably hates me for setting her up that way," Clemency said as the door slammed behind the two girls.

"Jenna definitely does," Georgie agreed. "It means she has less control over my daughter, and for that I thank you." Clemency looked at her questioningly, but Georgie just shook her head and added more wine to her glass. "I'm not entirely sure that I'm happy with Frankie entering the profession, it's a rough mountain to climb. But I do know that she has something that many other young women entering the fray don't have."

"What's that?" Clemency asked.

"Me," Georgie replied with a grin. "So, I guess this means your holiday is still on... tell me about your plans."

They were an hour into their flight and Peter glanced across the aisle to see his daughter still talking a mile a minute to a very patient Georgie.

"This is my revenge for Georgie threatening my vacation," Clemency said, caressing his hand where it rested on her thigh.

"You're a cruel woman," Peter said. "I am going to take pity on her eventually and change seats. I'm just not ready to let you go yet."

"You're certain you trust me with your daughter for the weekend?" Clemency asked.

"My only fear is your inability to say no to her," he replied. "I saw the list of bookstores she wants to hit. You still have the credit card I gave you?"

When Clemency had drifted off, her head resting against the window, Peter watched her thinking how different this flight was from the one they had shared four months earlier. Reluctantly, he finally gestured to a grateful Georgie to switch seats and tried to convince an over excited Gracie to also get some rest.

Clemency woke to the sound of Gracie's squeals of excitement. They were descending and the girl had gotten her first glimpse of the city in the distance. Clemency was nervous. Everything had fallen into place so easily this week. It was like kismet. Surely that had to come to an end soon.

They landed and quickly made their way to the train that would take them into the city. Checking her watch, Clemency saw that they had plenty of time until Lucy was scheduled to arrive. She saw a flicker of sadness cross Peter's face as he, too, checked the time. Soon they would be parting...

"Everything will be fine," he murmured in her ear, his arms wrapped around her as they waited in the crowded Penn Station terminal.

But everything wasn't fine, Clemency realized as her daughter came running up the stairs and into her arms.

"I tried to stop him, but he wouldn't listen," Lucy said breathlessly as she hugged her mother.

"Tried to stop who--" Clemency began before spying Elliott in the middle of the throng of people climbing the steps from the track below. She let out a quiet expletive before turning her back on her husband and pulling Lucy over to meet the others where they stood waiting.

"Luce, you remember Georgie, of course. And this is Peter and Gracie," as Clemency performed the introductions, she felt Elliott come up behind her. She stifled a grin as her daughter launched herself into Peter's arms.

"I'm so glad to finally meet you," the young girl gushed. "You've made my Mom so happy!"

Meeting Georgie's eye, Clemency saw her friend trying to hold back laughter as they witnessed the drama queen at play in her daughter. Georgie gave her a surreptitious wink before moving to shepherd the girls out of earshot while Clemency turned to face her husband.

"What are you doing here, Elliott?" she asked.

"You expected me to just put my child on a train to the city by herself?" he asked, not bothering to mask the anger behind his words.

"That's exactly what I expected, what's more, that is what we had planned," Clemency replied, grateful to feel Peter's hand resting at the small of her back for support.

"Well... I... I thought you would want this," he sputtered,

thrusting an envelope at her. "It's the divorce petition. All it needs is your signature and it can be submitted to the courts."

"Thank you," Clemency said, clutching the envelope to her chest and watching as Elliott eyed Peter warily. "Elliott, this is Peter Bennett. Peter, Elliott Oliver."

"I thought you looked familiar," Elliott said as he shook Peter's hand. "I'm a big fan of your work."

"I'm a big fan of your wife," Peter replied and Clemency choked back a laugh.

"Yes," Elliott agreed soberly. "Cee Cee is something special. Don't let her get away."

"I don't plan to," Peter said, an edge of steel creeping into his voice.

Clemency stepped between the two men. "So, will we be meeting you back here next week to take Lucy home?"

"Oh, no," Elliott replied, "Let's just adhere to the original plan. Put her on a train and I'll meet her."

She felt her husband's eyes on her as they turned to make their way back to the others. Peter's hand rested possessively around her waist. When her daughter bound into her arms, she gently told her to go say goodbye to her father.

"He wants you back," Peter murmured in her ear as he pulled her into his arms.

"Too bad," Clemency replied rising to brush her lips across his. "I'm taken."

Her words should have reassured him but meeting her husband had put him in a foul mood. It was taking all his self-control not to brand her as his then and there.

"I love you," he said, resting his forehead against hers.

"I love you, too," Clemency said. "And I'll see you in two days." Feeling her daughter's curious gaze watching her, she settled for a chaste peck. It was going to be a long weekend...

Peter stood watching Clemency and the girls disappear into the crowd before turning to his friend.

"You look like you're plotting," Georgie observed.

"The prick wants her back," he replied darkly.

"I guess you'll have to make sure she isn't tempted," Georgie threw over her shoulder as she joined the crowd heading toward the tracks below.

"How do I do that?" Peter said, scurrying to keep up with her.

Georgie stopped to face him, ignoring the expletives thrown in their direction. "I can recommend several jewelry stores in the city..." she hinted. "Are you ready to take that leap?"

"Are you?" Peter threw the question right back at her. He knew that Donovan had tried to convince Georgie to remarry him on more than one occasion.

"My situation is different," Georgie argued. "Donovan cheated on me. I need time to rebuild trust."

"Bullshit," Peter declared. "Our situations are identical. Vanessa cheated on me the entire time we were married. The difference between you and I, my friend, is I'm not going to waste the next twenty some odd years wallowing about it. I'm going to take a chance on love."

"Good, I guess that means we'll be ring shopping this weekend," Georgie said, turning to follow the few stragglers heading down the stairs. "Oh, and I may stew and plot, but I *never* wallow," she called back over her shoulder.

In typical New York City fashion, it took ages to go the few blocks from the station to their hotel. It was only eight in the evening and Lucy was bouncing off the walls wanting to get out and show Gracie all her favorite sites. Gracie, however, yawned at the sight of the Empire State Building.

"Clemmie, I'm tired," the young girl whined as she leaned against her in the elevator to their room.

Clemency soothed her with the thought of a comfy bed awaiting them.

"We're not going out?" Lucy asked.

"Grace and I are still on London time, sweetness," Clemency explained with an apologetic smile to the bellhop. "Let us get a good night sleep and we can start fresh tomorrow. We have an entire week to explore the city."

Clemency had upgraded her room to a one-bedroom suite and was extremely glad she had done so. The girls settled quickly in the front room. Grace was asleep before her head hit the pillow and Lucy curled up with a book. After giving her daughter one more hug, Clemency adjourned to her room and a much-needed shower.

Exiting the steam filled bathroom, Clemency grabbed her phone and called Peter, wanting to hear his voice again before turning in. He answered on the first ring.

She curled up on the bed as they chatted about their respective plans for the following day. Toward the end of the call, Clemency was distracted by a light tap on the door.

"Have fun and send me pictures," Peter said as she rose to answer it. "I love you."

"I love you, too," Clemency said, opening the door to find Lucy on the other side.

"Can I sleep with you?" her daughter asked tentatively, before smiling broadly when Clemency held the door open for her. "Was that Peter on the phone?"

Clemency nodded, setting the alarm and plugging her phone in to charge before climbing into bed.

"You two love one another?" Lucy asked.

"Yes, very much," Clemency answered with a yawn.

"And you love Grace?" her daughter prodded.

"Mmmm Hmmm," Clemency said into the darkness. "Are they replacing Daddy and me?" Lucy asked after a long pause.

Clemency's eyes shot open. "God, no! Lucy, why would you think that?"

"Well, seeing you with them and all," her daughter began. "I didn't know that you loved them, and you're so close with Grace and all..."

"I have become close with Grace, sweetie, but that doesn't mean she's replacing you," Clemency argued, sitting up. "For one thing, you're irreplaceable. Peter and Grace may have become my family, but you are my blood. My heart. Understand?"

Lucy nodded, tears in her eyes. "Are you going to marry Peter?"

"I don't know, sweetie. All of this has happened so quickly. Besides, I'm technically still married to your father," Clemency replied.

"But you love him?" Lucy persisted.

"Yes, I do," Clemency repeated.

"And he loves you?" she asked. Clemency nodded, wondering where her daughter was going with this questioning. "Do you think he could love me too?" Lucy whispered.

"Of course, sweetness," Clemency exclaimed. "Where is all this coming from?"

"It's just that... with the divorce and all, I don't know what's going to happen to me," Lucy confessed. "I heard Whitney telling Daddy that she had better not get roped into having to help raise me..."

Clemency felt her blood pressure rise. "Your father hasn't talked to you about this?" she asked only to be met by Lucy shaking her head vehemently. Once again, the prick was avoiding confrontation. "Sweetie, your father and I have agreed that you are old enough to decide for yourself who you want to live with."

"But you live in London," Lucy said.

"Yes, I do. The plan is for you to spend time with me over the summer. Why don't we set the deadline of your birthday at the end of July for you to decide if you want to remain with me in England or return to New York and your father."

"Grandma told Daddy that if he knew what was best, he'd make sure I stayed with him," Lucy said with a yawn as she snuggled down under the comforter.

Clemency ground her teeth at the thought of her soon to be former mother-in-law sticking her nose in where it wasn't wanted. "Well it's a good thing this is your decision to make. No one else."

"I love you, Mommy," Lucy said sleepily.

"I love you, too, Sweetness."

CHAPTER TWENTY-SIX

Clemency woke to find herself sandwiched between Lucy and Grace, who had joined them sometime in the night. Reaching for her phone, she found a picture of Peter waiting for her. It featured him looking longingly at an empty pillow with the caption 'me, missing you.' Her laughter roused the girls who, upon realizing where they were, bolted out of bed to get ready for the day. Clemency barely had a chance to reply to Peter before the girls began hounding her to get up so they could begin exploring the city.

So began a whirlwind two days that took them from the top of the Statue of Liberty to Coney Island. Stumbling back into their hotel room late Saturday evening after introducing Gracie to the bright lights of Broadway, Clemency realized that she had barely communicated with Peter all weekend. She dashed off a quick message, wanting to touch base with him regarding his arrival the next day, but fell asleep before her phone dinged, signaling his reply.

Sunday morning found Clemency fighting a losing battle trying to convince the girls to spend a quiet morning relaxing at the hotel. She was on the verge of giving into their pleas when they were interrupted by a knock at the door.

Grace bound over to open it and greeted her father with a quick hug before once again launching into her pleas for freedom. Peter gave Lucy's shoulders a quick squeeze before turning to pull Clemency into his arms.

"Long weekend, love?" he asked, his forehead resting on hers after a lingering kiss.

"There's so much more energy when there's two of them," Clemency replied, sliding her hands over his chest before winding them around his neck and pulling him down for another kiss.

They broke apart, grinning at the girls groans about public displays of affection. Peter tried his hand at negotiating their demands while Clemency opened the door to let Georgie in.

"We want to go shopping," the girls chorused.

"Book shopping," Grace declared.

"Clothes shopping," countered Lucy.

"Looks like I arrived just in time," Georgie stated, tossing her bag onto a nearby sofa. "Did someone say shopping? I have one afternoon in the city and that's my absolute favorite thing to do."

Georgie handed Clemency a card as the girls turned on her.

"Shopping with Georgianna Sutton? My friends are going to be so jealous!" Lucy cried.

"What's this?" Clemency asked, examining the card.

"The key to the room across the hall. Girls, you agree that your parents deserve a break, right? How about you spend the day with Auntie Georgie. We'll go shopping... see a show..." Lucy and Grace were already hanging on the older woman's arms, ready to drag her off.

"Are you sure?" Clemency asked, but Peter just gave his friend a quick kiss on the cheek before dragging Clemency from the room. Before she could utter a single word, he had yanked the card from her hand, swiped it and had her in the room and up against the door, his mouth hungrily devouring hers.

"Peter?" Clemency moaned as his lips nibbled a trail across her jaw up to her ear.

"Yes, my love?" he murmured, pulling her up to wrap her legs around his waist.

"I just... Oh!" she exclaimed as he pulled her shirt over her head and buried his face in the crevice of her cleavage. "Peter!"

"What is it, love?" he repeated.

"It's just that... Oh God... I just wanted to... there's a bed... no more than five feet behind you..." Clemency panted as his deft fingers made short work of her bra. "We don't always have to do this up against a wall."

Peter set her down on her feet and they turned to face the bed in question. Clemency let out a giddy laugh at the sight. Their friend had somehow worked magic on the room in the short time since her arrival. Rose petals were strewn across the bedspread and next to it stood a bucket full of ice and a bottle of champagne.

Beside her, Peter let out a quiet expletive. His friend didn't just want him to take a leap. She was pushing him off the damn cliff.

"Is everything okay," Clemency asked, her voice suddenly tinged with uncertainty.

Peter looked down at her and realized that with her in his arms, he was more than willing to jump, knowing that together they would soar. "Everything is perfect," he replied, kissing her tenderly as his hand moved to gently cup the swell of her breast. "Ever make love on a bed of rose petals?"

Much later, as the afternoon sunbeams crossed the room, Peter lay with Clemency in his arms, her hand in his.

"We have the whole evening to ourselves, is there anything you want to do?" Clemency asked, watching their fingers entwine.

"I want you to take me to your favorite place in the city," Peter replied.

"My favorite place?" Clemency asked, frowning.

"Hmmm... I've been here before, many times. I want to see it through your eyes," he replied, the wheels in his head spinning as he began concocting a plan.

"Are you hungry?" Clemency asked, rising to begin gathering her discarded clothes.

"Always," Peter said with a grin from where he lay propped up on one elbow watching her.

They dressed and checked on the room across the hall, finding it empty. As they exited the hotel, Clemency shot off a message to Georgie. She received a quick reply with instructions to stop worrying and have fun, so grasping Peter's hand she turned and began walking down the street.

"Your favorite place is nearby?" Peter asked.

Clemency shook her head. "No, but it's just a short subway ride," she replied as she led him down the stairs of the nearest station. They emerged a short time later into the twilight of the West Village. "This is where I had planned on living," she explained. "I was going to rent one of these tiny basement flats and find a job working in publishing."

"This place is certainly... colorful," Peter said as they passed a fairly husky individual decked out in sequins and feathers. "Was there anything else to this particular dream that I should know about?"

Clemency threw back her head and laughed. "Nope, that's your dream... or at least according to Georgie, that's every man's top fantasy."

"My top fantasy is you in my bed every night," Peter muttered as she pulled him down the steps into a cramped and crowded restaurant.

"You've got that already," Clemency shouted over the loud din as she wormed her way through the throng of people to the counter. "This place makes the best poutine in the city."

Peter could barely make out what she said over the noise. Something about poo? He smiled and nodded before tilting his head to peruse the menu scrawled across the wall. Apparently, all they served was chips. That hardly seemed very filling...

"That doesn't look like much food for two people," he observed when they finally made their way back out into the night.

"This is just a starter," Clemency explained. "New York is a wonderland of food options. One of my favorite things to do is eat my way across the city."

She had led him to a park full of people. As they sat down at a small rot iron table, he sat back and took in his surroundings. A man with a bucket of soapy water was making large bubbles to the delight of a gaggle of children, while another man had broken out an old keyboard and was serenading the crowd, many of which had stopped to dance along. He found this place absolutely charming and could see why she loved it so much. She smiled back at him when she saw the look of appreciation on his face and handed him a fork.

"Poutine," she declared, indicating the brown glob of food she had uncovered.

Well he had gotten the poo part right... it certainly looked interesting. He frowned as he took a tentative bite before his face broke out in a grin. "What on earth is this?" he asked, digging in with his fork for a larger bite.

"French fries with bacon, cheese curds, and gravy," Clemency explained. "It's traditionally a Canadian dish, but it's been making its way south of the border."

"So, tell me about this place," Peter said, indicating his surroundings with a wave of his fork. "Why is it your favorite place in the city?"

"It's really an example of my favorite places. Lucy loves the bright lights and crowds of Times Square, while I prefer the serenity of the parks. Madison Square, The Bowery and Bryant Park are also nice, but this one has a lot of history behind it. The beat generation made their home here. Protests were born here before sweeping across the nation. And unlike Central Park, you can come here and feel like you belong to the city. You're not just a tourist visiting it."

After cleaning up the remnants of their shared meal, Peter clasped her hand in his as they turned to walk toward the arch that loomed at the north entrance of the park.

"You're very impassioned about your love of this place. Is it still your dream to live here?"

"No," she admitted as they came to stand under the arch. "I realized the other morning when I woke up with both Lucy and Grace in bed with me that I was living my dream."

That was exactly what he had wanted to hear, Peter thought

as he dipped his head to kiss her. "Marry me," he breathed against her lips.

"What?" Clemency pulled back, startled.

"You heard me," he replied. "Marry me. Let's live our dream together. Marry me and sleep beside me every night. Let's raise our girls together... grow old together..."

She wasn't saying yes. Why wasn't she saying yes? Peter's heart was racing as he watched her step away from him. She didn't look upset, but she also didn't appear happy. If anything, she looked scared.

"Peter, I..." Clemency stammered. Oh, God, was this really happening? She looked up to see the fear in his eyes. She couldn't say yes, but she didn't want to say no either. She reached up to cup her hand against his cheek, drawing him down for a tender kiss. "Ask me again when I'm free to answer."

He drew away, looking confused. "What are you saying?"

"I'm not saying no, but I'm still married, Peter," she explained. "I can't say yes until I'm free of Elliott. Do you understand?"

He did and was cursing himself for being so stupid. What the fuck was he thinking? He nodded, reaching out a hand to her and breathing a sigh of relief when she stepped back into his embrace.

"I love you," he murmured.

"I love you, too," she replied.

Breakfast the following morning was a quiet affair. Peter and Clemency had made love again that night, but the shadow of his proposal had loomed over them like an uninvited voyeur. He was still kicking himself when they joined Georgie and the girls in the hotel restaurant. Grace and Lucy took turns yawning, still worn out from their adventures the previous day. Meeting Georgie's eye for a brief moment, Peter gave a curt shake of his head before turning to the approaching waitress and requesting a cup of coffee. Midway through the meal, Georgie rose to her feet.

"Well I hate to cut this lively party short, but I need to go if I want to make my flight," she announced. "Clemmie, walk me out. I want to run a casting idea I had by you."

"Georgie..." Peter gave a warning growl which caused Clemency to pause and look at the two of them.

"Did I miss something?" she asked.

Georgie shook her head. "Peter, I really do need to talk shop with Clemency. You're welcome to join us if you wish."

Peter merely turned his attention back to his eggs. "Are you going straight back home?"

"To London? Yes," Georgie replied. "But I thought I'd head up to Edinburgh for a few days. Any messages you wish me to relay to your family?"

Peter met her eye for a moment before again shaking his head.

"Seriously... what's going on with you two?" Clemency asked as she followed her friend through the hotel lobby.

"Peter and I had a long heart to heart while in Boston. I'm going to tell Donovan that I'm ready to take another chance on us," Georgie explained to Clemency's delight. She was wondering exactly what else the heart to heart entailed when Georgie continued. "Regarding *Tempest,* I have an idea I want you to consider. Don't answer right away... discuss it with Peter and even Elliott if you must... The only part we haven't cast yet is Mila, and that's because it requires multiple actresses to play the various ages. What do you think about Lucy in the role?"

"Lucy? My Lucy?" Clemency asked.

Georgie grinned and nodded. "You've often described her as a drama queen, but I've seen her in action now and she definitely has a flair for the dramatic. Like I said, think about it and get back to me. Now, quick before my car gets here, do you want to tell me what happened between you and Peter last night?"

"I... Clemency began before shaking her head, not sure how to explain it all in such a short time.

Georgie pulled her into an embrace and Clemency felt her

eyes well up with tears. "Did he ask?" Georgie whispered in her ear. "And you said no?"

Clemency pulled away. "I didn't say no, but I couldn't say yes. Not yet, anyways."

"But you want to... eventually?" Georgie asked, hoisting her bag onto her shoulder as a car pulled up. Seeing Clemency's tentative nod, she smiled before sliding into the backseat. "Good, we can begin planning two weddings then."

Clemency found herself smiling at the thought as she watched her friend depart. She returned to the restaurant to find Peter sitting alone. He looked so sad and she hated that she was responsible for that. He had said that he understood and was fine with her decision, but it was as though a wall had come up between them.

"Where are the girls?" she asked, picking up a slice of toast as she sat down across from him. She put it back down just as quickly, finding that she wasn't very hungry.

"They ran up to get some notes they took on places they wanted to see," Peter replied. "What did Georgie want to discuss?" Clemency explained Georgie's idea of casting Lucy in the movie. "Is that something you think she'd want to do? Because it's brilliant. Not only is she perfect for the part, but she would be working with Frankie and I and we could make sure her first acting experience was a positive one."

"I'd need to talk it over with Elliott before broaching the subject with Lucy," Clemency replied as the girls entered the restaurant. "What do you two have in store for us today?"

"Daddy wants a museum day," Gracie replied over Lucy's groan of dismay.

"I take it you don't like museums, Luce?" Peter asked.

"They're just so boring. My dad always insists on seeing *every-thing*," she replied dramatically.

"They're fun," Grace argued. "Daddy and I can teach you the game we play."

"Mom and I have a game too," Lucy exclaimed, suddenly recalling the game they had once played much to the annoyance of her father.

Clemency sat up as she caught the amused gleam in her daughter's eye. "No, Lucy."

"But..." her daughter began to argue before the look on Clemency's face made her stop.

Peter looked on curiously. "What should we hit first? History? Art? Science?"

"Art," Lucy insisted and Clemency sighed at her daughter's rebellious demeanor.

They exited the hotel onto the crowded avenue, the girls walking ahead of them, their heads close together. When Grace looked back at her, eyes as big as saucers, Clemency knew that her daughter was explaining the rules to the game she had created to keep Lucy entertained at an art museum they had visited the year before.

"I'm sorry," she muttered to Peter.

"I told you last night that there was nothing to apologize for--" Peter began, he was beginning to find it difficult to hide his disappointment and frustration.

"Not for that," Clemency interrupted. "For my daughter. She's being a bad influence on Gracie," at Peter's incredulous look, she rushed on. "She's teaching her the game we play when we get bored at museums."

"You get bored?" Peter began. "And what exactly is this game?"

"Not bored exactly. It just always fell to me to keep Lucy entertained," Clemency explained. "As for the game..." Peter watched a blush begin to cover her cheeks and seeing that the girls had stopped to examine a window display, he pulled Clemency aside and waited patiently for her to continue. "It's called Penis' vs. Boobies..."

Peter let out a bark of laughter and before she could continue, he had pulled her into his arms. He was so going to marry this crazy, remarkable woman, he thought as he deepened the kiss. Clemency relaxed into his embrace and it didn't take long before she felt the shiver of pleasure run down her spine straight to her core. When she finally pulled away, it was to gaze into his eyes. They were good. The only thing that had changed was they now knew what they were working toward.

Moving to join the girls who had entered the queue for the Museum of Modern Art, Peter clasped his hands together. "Okay, which of you is Team Boobies? I want on that team," he said to the horror of both girls.

"Daddy!" Grace exclaimed, looking like she wanted the sidewalk to open and swallow her.

"You can't be Team Boobies," Lucy argued. "You're a boy."

"So?" Peter replied.

"So, you should be team… you know… because you, like, have one and all…" Clemency laughed as her daughter tried to argue her position.

Before Peter could begin his counter argument, Grace brushed past him and threw herself into Clemency's arms. "Clemmie, please make them stop!"

"I think we should choose a game that we can all comfortably play, don't you agree?" she asked her daughter.

Lucy reluctantly agreed and they entered the first gallery.

"One point," Peter whispered in her ear as they came upon a painting featuring a rather Rubenesque woman lounging on a sofa. "But they're nowhere as nice as yours." They giggled like a pair of teenagers, much to the disgust of their daughters who moved to get as far away from them as they dared.

Just like that, things had returned to normal. The awkwardness from the previous evening's proposal had dissipated and so began a fun filled week as the four of them explored the city.

On Thursday, Clemency spent the day ensconced in meetings with her agent. When she finally emerged, Peter suggested they walk across the bridge to Brooklyn. There they had a late dinner before taking a leisurely stroll through the park situated under the Brooklyn Bridge.

"This is how our dream will play out," Peter murmured in Clemency's ear. They had stopped to let the girls take a spin on the old carousel and he had wrapped his arms around her, pulling her back against his chest. "We will watch our daughters grow and flourish, and then once they have flown the coop, you and I will make trips here together. Here, Paris, Sydney, Barcelona, anywhere your heart desires."

Clemency turned to kiss him. The dream sounded amazing. She couldn't wait until she could tell him they could make it a reality.

The girls were exhausted by the time they made their way back to the hotel.

"I don't ever want to leave," Grace declared sleepily as she leaned against Clemency.

"Me either," Lucy mumbled from Peter's arms.

They made short work of getting them to bed.

"I love you, Gracie," Peter said as he tucked the blanket under his daughter's chin. "I love you too, Lucy," he added.

Clemency watched as her daughter's eyes shot open and she sat up to wrap her arms around Peter's neck. "Really? I love you too, Peter!"

"Thank you for that," Clemency said as they closed the door to their room. "She was concerned about how you would feel about her. Apparently, Whitney is less than thrilled to have a tween as part of the Elliott package."

"Your daughter is as easy to love as you are," Peter replied, dropping a kiss on her cheek before moving to the bathroom for a shower.

Clemency reluctantly picked up her phone, realizing that she still had to touch base with her husband, about Lucy's travel arrangements as well as Georgie's proposal.

Peter exited the shower to the sound of a raised voice from the adjoining room. Peeking around the door, he saw Clemency on the phone.

"No, I haven't asked her yet, but I'm pretty damn sure she'd jump at the chance," Clemency said. "It's a good opportunity, I think... I don't care what your mother says, Elliott... Yes, Peter is also in the movie... He plays one of Mila's fathers... Yes, I said one of. If you had read the fucking book, you'd understand what I'm talking about... Fine..."

"Problems?" Peter asked, running a towel through his hair. One look at Clemency's face made him turn back to the bathroom, returning a moment later. "There's a hot bath running for you, love."

"I love you," she said, tossing her phone onto the bed and heading for the bathroom. When she emerged half an hour later, she found Peter ending a call on her phone.

"Please don't get upset, but I thought I'd try to convince that idiot husband of yours myself that this was an excellent opportunity for Lucy," Peter replied sheepishly to her questioning look.

"Did it work?" she asked, accepting her phone just as a message popped up.

Ask Lucy if she wants to do it. If so, she has my blessing.

Clemency launched herself into Peter's arms and they tumbled back onto the bed. "Lucy's going to be so excited."

"Forget Lucy, I'm pretty excited myself," Peter said with a suggestive wiggle of his eyebrows.

"You're always excited," Clemency said, twisting to flick off the bedside lamp. She turned to find that Peter had moved to sit with his back against the headboard.

"Only when you're around, love," he replied as he drew her to him, his hands sneaking inside the folds of her bathrobe. Clemency straddled his lap as he pushed the fabric off her shoulders and ran his hands over her still damp skin. He leaned into nuzzle her neck, only to quickly draw back. "You smell like vanilla."

"Hotel bath salts," she reminded him as she leaned in to capture his lips.

"I like the orange blossom better," he complained, causing her to smile into his neck.

His hands settled on her hips, drawing her closer. "Tomorrow," she moaned as she brushed up against his hard prick. "We'll be back home to our own shower and shampoo."

He lifter her so she was positioned to take him into her, watching the pleasure play over the features of her face as she slowly slid down onto him. "I love that you already consider my place home. Shall we make it official? Let the studio foist your flat onto someone else?" He groaned as her movements faltered. "Please give me this. Let's live together as a family this summer."

Clemency gasped and nodded. In the back of her mind she was already thinking that perhaps this was just the thing to convince Lucy to remain with her when the time came. She leaned down to kiss him and began to move more urgently, only breaking away to throw her head back and cry out as the climax washed over her.

Coming down from his own release, Peter held her close. "I'm definitely going to miss watching you come with the city lights in the background illuminating you."

CHAPTER TWENTY-SEVEN

They explained the idea of auditioning for *Tempest* over breakfast, and Lucy agreed before they could even finish. They listened to the girl excitedly chatter on about it all the way to the train station before Clemency finally cautioned her that the project was still hush hush so she wouldn't be able to discuss it with her friends.

"Of course, you conveniently neglected to tell her that it would be several years before she would be old enough to watch the film itself," Peter pointed out as they watched Lucy's train disappear.

Despite sleeping during the majority of the flight home, Clemency stifled a yawn the following morning as they pulled up to Peter's house. Georgie had spied their arrival and was on her front stoop to welcome them back. She gave out a whoop of delight at the news that Lucy would be auditioning and tripped down the stairs to help them haul their bags into the house.

Clemency froze as she crossed the threshold.

"Oh, wow," Grace breathed as she came up alongside her.

The once all white decor had been redesigned in their absence. The foyer was now a light beige that turned into a rich chocolate brown in the living room. The bookshelves that had once displayed cold, glass knickknacks now lay bare.

"I figured we could find something better to fill them with. Perhaps that Shakespeare set I spied in a box at your flat," Peter said coming up behind her to wrap his arms around her.

At Grace's questioning look, Peter explained that he had asked Clemency to officially move in with them. The cry of joy from Peter's daughter let Clemency know that the young girl held no objections.

"Good timing," Georgie said from the doorway. "Colin Fletcher recently approached me, asking if the studio had anything available."

"I thought he had a swanky penthouse in the city," Peter said.

Georgie just shrugged as she turned to Clemency. "The best part is upstairs," she said with a wink before departing.

Clemency followed an excited Grace up the stairs to the room that had once been her mothers. Inside, the room had been transformed into an office. The walls, a light buttery yellow that was Clemency's favorite color. A couch along one wall was framed by bookcases and a large desk sat prominently under the window that overlooked the back garden.

"This is for me?" Clemency asked. "But--"

"No buts," Peter said silencing her with a kiss. "I planned this long before New York and... well, you know... I figured it would cut down on our arguments over you writing long into the night. Do you like it?"

"I love it. And I love you... both of you," Clemency said, pulling Grace into their embrace. "And no worries about long nights of writing for the foreseeable future. According to Georgie, I'll be too busy at the studio."

Just as her friend had predicted, work on the project began to accelerate now that they had returned from their break. It all began Monday morning with the table read. Having nearly everyone together in one place at the same time finally made everything seem real, and the applause she received when she introduced herself brought tears to her eyes.

The next two weeks were spent with the hair, makeup, and costume departments finalizing the characters appearances.

Clemency relished finally getting Peter into the stylist's chair and commanding the woman to chop off his hair.

"I worked hard growing it out," he complained.

"You look like Beethoven," Clemency pointed out.

"I like Beethoven," Peter stated.

"Ugh," Clemency uttered, throwing her hands up in defeat. "We can't even agree on classical music. Rachmaninoff... so much better."

"Tasteless wench," Peter argued good naturedly to the delight of the hairdresser.

"I had good enough taste to fall in love with you," Clemency pointed out, taking a seat across from him, determined to stick around to watch the entire transformation.

Afterward, she couldn't keep her hands out of his close-cropped curls, relishing the feel of his silky hair running through her fingers as she pulled his head down to hers. Once they got through costuming and Peter, dressed all in black had completed his transformation into Kennett Shariq, Clemency couldn't help herself. Grabbing his hand, she dragged Peter back to his office and finally made his couch fantasy a reality.

As April began to transition into May, Clemency's input was needed less frequently, while Peter began working later and later. If he wasn't running lines, he was working with Georgie on how to block each scene. Clemency found it interesting to watch the two actor-turned-directors debate vision. Georgie would listen patiently to Peter's suggestions and often take them to heart, but in the end she made it clear that this was her project.

As planned, they began filming the first week of May and suddenly Clemency found her work was done. She would double check the sets and cast before filming began, but until Georgie was ready for her to start going over footage, she found that the days were her own. She took this opportunity to pick up where she had left off on her new book and most evenings she could be found writing long into the night.

On one such night, Peter reached out for Clemency in his

sleep, only to find her side of the bed cold and empty. It startled him awake. It was three in the morning and he heard the faint sound of typing from the neighboring room.

Rising, he donned his robe and padded through the shared closet, pushing open the door to the room on the other side. It was dark except for the faint light from the screen which illuminated Clemency's face. He stood silently watching her. She would type, then stop and read a sentence or two, frowning at the screen in concentration. She wore glasses, something he hadn't seen before. He loved them on her. She shifted in her seat and he smiled to see that, in her haste, she had slipped on one of his shirts. It was only halfway buttoned, and he sighed when he spied the curve of her breast as the shirt parted.

"Do you plan on just standing there and staring as I work?" Clemency asked smiling and looking up as he stepped into the room.

"Oh gosh, he's gorgeous," Sybella said with a sigh.

"Did I wake you?" Clemency asked, giving her head a subtle shake to silence the voices of her characters.

"Your absence woke me," Peter replied. "Am I interrupting?"

"No. I'm done for the night," Clemency replied. "I had a lightning bolt of inspiration and had to jot it down before it vanished."

"A sex scene?" he asked as he moved closer and saw her flushed skin.

"Oh, yeah," Jessamyn replied.

"Maybe," Clemency said with a grin. She moved to take off her glasses, only to have Peter grasp her wrist.

"Leave them on," he instructed. "They're sexy."

Clemency snorted in reply, then let out a yelp as Peter dropped to his knees in front of her. She watched wide-eyed as he ran his hands over her thighs. He wasted no time, reaching for the waistband of her panties, he instructed her to raise her hips before sliding them off and tossing them over his shoulder.

"Did your characters come in this scene?" Peter asked, his breath a whisper on her skin.

Clemency closed her eyes and saw Jessamyn sitting up on the bed, nonchalantly examining her fingernails. The dark-haired girl shrugged and nodded.

"Twice," Sybella added with a giggle as her head popped up behind Jessamyn's shoulder.

"Yes," Clemency breathed as she recalled the details of the scene she had just written.

"Do you want to come, my love?" Peter asked, running his hands up her calves, pulling her to the edge of the seat and parting her legs so he could kneel comfortably between them.

"Yes, but--" she began, feeling her muscles tense.

"No buts, my love," Peter interrupted. "We can do this. You know how you come when I kiss you..."

Clemency froze. "You know about that?"

Peter nodded. "Since day one. I live for that shuddering cry you give. It's like music to my ears. Now, I want you to relax. This is just me kissing you."

Clemency leaned back and squeezed her eyes shut, waiting.

"No, my love. Open your eyes and watch me," Peter instructed, his jaw nuzzling her inner thigh. He hadn't shaved since the previous morning and his stubble tickled and made her squirm. He took advantage of her movement to grasp her hips and adjust the angle so she was opened up to him.

"When we kiss, I like to begin softly... gently..." he said as his mouth lightly brushed against her outer lips. "Sometimes... if I'm feeling playful, I may nibble a little," he continued as he turned his head to nip at her inner thigh.

"Peter," she gasped, trying to move, only to discover that he had a tight hold on her.

"Mostly... I like to build up to the tasting," he said as he ran his tongue up her. "I love the way you taste. You may smell of orange blossoms, but your flavor is pure nectar."

He glanced up to see her head tilted back and eyes closed. Sitting back on his heels, he waited patiently until she opened her eyes to look down at him.

"Didn't I tell you to watch me? Now I have to start all over," he gently chastised before his mouth once again began applying soft kisses, this time focusing on the hooded bud of her clitoris. "Gentle kisses," he murmured, his breath hot between her thighs. "Then a little nibble," Clemency gasped as he captured the engorged pebble between his lips. "Followed by tasting," he said before sliding his tongue into her.

"Oh fuck," Clemency cried as his tongue moved to swirl around the head of her clit and Peter watched as she shuddered, and her eyes glazed over.

Rising, he pulled her with him as he backed up to sit on the couch. She straddled him as he pushed the folds of his robe aside to reveal his cock, hard and ready. Clemency cried out again as she impaled herself on him, spasming all around as she took him into her depths. He was already close. He could feel his balls tightening as he watched her rock back and forth on him. She was so focused, staring at his mouth, licking her lips.

"What is it, love? What do you want?" he demanded.

"I want to kiss you," Clemency breathed. "I want to taste myself on your lips."

Peter groaned as he pulled her head down to him. He erupted into her as her tongue delved into his mouth, searching... tasting... and given her moans of pleasure, savoring.

She was already half asleep when he finally felt his heart rate return to normal. She was limp as he gathered her into his arms and carried her back to bed.

CHAPTER TWENTY-EIGHT

By mid-May the production had settled into a routine and was smoothly moving forward. It was Friday afternoon and they had wrapped for the week. Clemency had joined Georgie in her office to review the following weeks schedule before heading home.

"I think it's time for you to start going over some of the raw footage," Georgie said, tapping the calendar with her pencil. "You can begin Monday. It will get you away from the set for a while."

"Don't forget, Lucy graduate's this week. I'll be flying out on Wednesday morning," Clemency reminded her friend. "But she'll be returning with me, so if you still expect her to pass the audition, we can look to pencil in the London location shots soon."

"I actually wanted to talk to you about that," Peter's voice came from the doorway. "Last night, Lucy asked if I could also attend her ceremony. Any chance I can skip out for a few days too?"

Clemency frowned as Georgie studied the schedule. What was her daughter up to?

"We can rearrange a few of the scenes, just don't make this a habit, Peter," Georgie replied.

"I'm aware that I'm being a pain in the ass, Georgie," Peter said with a grin. "Now at the risk of being even more obnoxious, may I please steal this lovely woman away? This is the last weekend that we'll have the house to ourselves. I want to have my way with her while she can comfortably scream her head off without traumatizing our children."

Georgie laughed while Clemency rose and swatted at Peter. Still, she loved the way 'our children' sounded coming from his lips. She truly hoped that this would be the week that Elliott would tell her she was finally free.

Wednesday dawned grey and cloudy, and the weather once they landed in New York wasn't much better. Clemency opted to rent a car this time, wanting to show Peter some of her favorite childhood haunts. Peter hoped he lived to see these places. He held tightly onto the door handle as Clemency muttered a curse and swerved around the car in front of her. He vowed then and there that she would never touch his beloved sports car.

He breathed a sigh of relief when she finally crossed multiple lanes to reach the highway exit. He tried to relax and look about as they entered the small town that had been her home for most of her life. It was early evening and lightning illuminated the sky when they pulled up to the hotel. Clemency had messaged Lucy and they had made plans to meet for dinner. However, there was no sign of her daughter as she exited the car. Her gaze swept across the area and she let out a groan of dismay as she spied a woman hustling in her direction.

"Cee Cee Oliver! As I live and breathe, we all thought you had up and disappeared off the face of the earth," the woman exclaimed as she pulled Clemency into her arms.

Peter, standing silently by suddenly realized why Clemency had been so distracted this past week. Ever since he had announced that Lucy had invited him to her graduation, Clemency had changed. She had become quiet and preoccupied. When he asked if she would prefer that he remain at home, she was quick to say no. Now he understood that she had been stressing about how to juggle her two identities. Now he watched her stiffen at the woman's touch before extricating herself as the woman talked a mile a minute.

"Where have you been? The PTA needed you... parties were not organized... the school carnival had been a disaster... When are you going to return?" Peter wondered if the woman would ever stop for breath.

Clemency obviously was accustomed to the woman's no-stop prattle and knew just when to jump in, explaining that she wouldn't be returning and had moved to London.

"London? But that's not possible!" the woman exclaimed. "We all just figured you were holed up in the house. I mean... we all knew you had embraced this new writing hobby of yours... But we were beginning to worry. Especially when we began seeing Elliott around town with that young floozy hanging all over him."

"While your concern is appreciated, Elliott is welcome to all the young floozies he desires," Clemency replied with a forced smile. "We're in the process of divorcing."

With that said, Clemency turned on her heels and grasped Peter's hand, practically dragging him into the hotel lobby.

"You're much more subtle, my love, but it is quite evident where Lucy gets her flair for the dramatic," he whispered against her ear as they approached the reception desk.

Clemency's laugh was cut short by Lucy calling out their names. They turned as she flew into their arms and Clemency saw Elliott standing just inside the door, Whitney visible through the window standing outside.

"Elliott," Clemency said, approaching her husband.

"I didn't know that he was coming too," Elliott said in greeting.

"Last minute decision. Lucy invited him," Clemency replied, relishing the look of surprise on his face as he glanced over to where Peter stood with his arm around Lucy's shoulder.

"They seem to get on well," Elliott said.

Clemency nodded as she watched Peter listening intently to something Lucy was saying. "Shall we drop Lucy off at home after dinner?"

"Yeah, that should work," Elliott answered. "The ceremony is at eleven tomorrow morning. Mother has a celebratory dinner planned in the evening. You and, uh... Peter are welcome to attend."

"We'll see. I wanted to go through my belongings and send some more back home," Clemency replied noncommittally.

"I thought you had a tiny apartment..." Elliott began, breaking off as Peter and Lucy approached.

"She lives with me now," Peter stated. Clemency suppressed a grin. On one side of her, Peter was clearly staking his claim, while Elliott couldn't help but look dejected.

"I should let you get to dinner," Elliott said, his shoulders slumped as he turned to the door and the impatiently waiting Whitney. "Don't stay out too late, Luce. Big day tomorrow," he threw over his shoulder as he departed.

Clemency and Lucy spent a leisurely evening catching up while showing Peter the sites of the small town. As promised, they returned Lucy home early, before returning to the hotel for some much-needed rest.

Clemency had just entered the shower when she was surprised by Peter joining her. Before she realized what was happening, he was pushed up against her back as he ran his sudsy hands down the front of her. She groaned as he cupped her breasts and placed her hands on the shower wall to brace herself.

"You're mine," he growled as he pushed into her and Clemency gasped at his urgency. She struggled to relax, hoping to let him ride out this sudden need to possess her. Peter, however, was not going to accept passivity. He pulled her back to him, nipping at her shoulder as his hand glided down to the juncture of her thighs. "You're mine, and you're going to come, damn it," he demanded as he drove into her.

Clemency fought to break free from him, turning and sputtering as the shower spray doused her. "You're scaring me, Peter. Where is this coming from?"

Peter stepped back, ashamed. "He wants you back," Peter

said, running his hands over his face and through his hair. "I can see it when he looks at you. He sees the you that I see. The strong, beautiful wom--"

"I don't give a fuck what he wants," Clemency cried taking a step toward Peter and pulling him into her arms. "I love *you*. I want to be with *you*."

"I know," he whispered, kissing the spot on her shoulder where his teeth marks were still imprinted. "I'm sorry."

""Make it up to me," she demanded causing him to lift his gaze to meet her eyes. "I'm all for a quick shower fuck, but only if you're feeling passionate... not angry... not possessive," she said, her hand trailing down to grasp him. "Are you feeling passionate, Peter?"

He claimed her lips and she could feel him harden as she slid her fingers slowly up and down his shaft. He pulled her up into his arms and she wrapped her legs around his waist as he, once again, slid into her. This time he made no demands. Instead, his lips brushed against hers causing her to cry out as she climaxed. As she came down from her high, he eased out of her and set her back on her feet.

"What about you?" she asked, reaching out to stroke his still hard cock.

Peter stepped out of reach and grabbed a towel. "I changed my mind," he said, moving to dry her off. "I'm not in the mood for a quick shower fuck. I want to make love to you. All night long."

They were among the last to arrive at the elementary school the following morning and entered the auditorium just ahead of the sixth-grade class. Lucy gave them an enthusiastic wave as she marched down the aisle with her classmates. Even sitting at the very back of the room, Clemency felt more than a few curious gazes turn in her direction throughout the ceremony. At one point she felt a shiver run up her spine and caught Mother Oliver's icy gaze upon her.

Lucy received many accolades for both academics and involvement. As the ceremony drew to a close, Peter handed Clemency a handkerchief.

"I'm proud of you, love," he murmured in her ear. "You raised an exceptional girl there."

As the crowd began to disperse, many eyes were on Lucy as she flew down the aisle toward Clemency and Peter. Clemency's tears began again as she hugged her daughter.

"Mom, you're embarrassing me," Lucy cried as she extricated herself from Clemency and turned to Peter. "What did you think?"

"I think you're absolutely brilliant, and I'm proud of you," he said as the girl's father joined them followed closely by two women who appeared as different as night and day.

"Lucy, bid your farewells so we can get you home to your party," the older, angry woman barked.

"Mom... Peter... you're coming, right?" Lucy turned to them, the hope in her eyes dimming as Clemency shook her head.

"I'm afraid not, sweetie. We have plans for the afternoon," she explained. "But we'll see you bright and early tomorrow. Are you all packed?"

Lucy brightened at the prospect, and they moved as one toward the entrance before Elliott broke away muttering that he would go fetch the car. Whitney followed, her nose glued to her phone, oblivious to those around her, while Lucy got pulled away by a gaggle of her friends. Clemency, Peter's hand in hers, had taken two steps toward the door when a chilling voice caused her to stop.

"You will not be taking my granddaughter away from me," Mrs. Oliver stated quite emphatically.

"You have no say in the matter, so don't even think about sticking your nose in where it doesn't belong," Clemency' replied. "It's Lucy's decision to make."

"My granddaughter will not be subjected to a mother who is living in sin," the woman haughtily exclaimed making Clemency laugh out loud.

"Living in sin? I'll tell you something old lady..." Clemency began before the touch of Peter's hand on her shoulder alerted her to Lucy's presence and calmed her down. "I love Peter and he trusts me with raising his daughter every bit as much as I trust him with Lucy. If that is living in sin, then yes, we're sinning. But only until your son releases me from this farce of a marriage."

She paused only to give Lucy a quick squeeze before she dragged Peter out of the school and away from her infuriating, soon to be ex-mother-in-law. They had walked several blocks and were nearing the downtown, their hotel in sight when Clemency finally slowed down. Glancing over she saw Peter grinning.

"What?" she asked, still steaming over the encounter.

"You're mine," he answered simply, gathering her into his arms.

"You already knew that," she said grumpily.

"Yes, but now you declared it before half the town," he said, leaning down to kiss her. "So, what are these plans we have for the afternoon?" Clemency merely smiled and pressed closer, pulling him down for a more thorough kiss. "Is that your way of telling me you didn't get enough last night?" Peter asked nuzzling her neck.

"I don't think I'll ever get enough of you," Clemency replied. She pulled back in time to see her husband's car pass, the old woman's angry gaze shooting daggers in her direction from the passenger seat.

In the end, Peter played the age card, declaring that at age fifty, it was inconceivable to expect him to be able to pleasure her all night *and* all day. Besides, he was curious to see what all she had stored away.

"Is this it?" he asked when she threw open the door to her unit. "This is everything you own?"

"It's everything I decided to keep," Clemency admitted, looking at the stack of boxes. "I just need to find a box or two to send back home."

"No, you don't," Peter said with a ferocity that startled her. He turned to pop the trunk of the car before beginning to load boxes into it.

"Peter, I can't take it all," she argued as she watched him.

"Why not?" he countered without stopping.

"Well, for one thing, the cost. It would take a small fortune to ship all of this to London," Clemency said, trying to wrestle a box from his grip. "Plus, where am I going to put it all?"

"Damn it, love, we have gone over this. My home is your home now. If you run out of room there, I have a house in Cardiff with plenty of space. Did I mention the vacation home in Scotland? No? Well there's plenty of room there as well. If I haven't made it clear yet, you have a home with me. There is no need to downsize your life. Grace told me about how you disposed of all of your family's belongings, losing all of that history. I don't want you to do the same now just because your marriage died. I know you wish to bury Cee Cee Oliver, but it wouldn't be fair to Lucy."

Clemency swiped away the tears as Peter concluded his impassioned speech. He released his hold on the box to gently brush them away and she turned to kiss the palm of his hand before turning and placing the box in the trunk of the car. It took two trips and more money than she wanted to think about, but by mid-afternoon the unit was clear and the last of her belongings were on their way to England.

Elliott greeted them early the next morning. He was standing on the porch next to Lucy who was sitting on one of her suitcases, clearly struggling to remain awake despite her obvious excitement. Clemency saw the sadness in his eyes as he bid their daughter goodbye and recalled being in his shoes. She knew how hard it was being apart from her daughter. However, when he turned to address her, Elliott was immediately on the defensive.

"The divorce hasn't been finalized yet Cee. I will let you know when it has," he snapped.

"Thank you, E," Clemency replied calmly. "I was curious

about that, but I also wanted to let you know that I'm giving Lucy her own cell phone as a graduation gift. That way it will be easier for you to remain in contact with her."

She noted the look of relief on his face as she turned to leave, but his voice stopped her.

"Mother says if I don't fight for Lucy, she's going to petition the court for custody herself," he blurted out and she saw fear in his eyes as he awaited her response.

Clemency counted to ten as she felt Peter's presence behind her. "She won't win, Elliott," she said. "Even if she tries, I will fight it. Peter and I have a stable and happy home. No judge would hesitate to award us custody."

"Us?" came Elliott's strangled reply. "Are you planning on marrying him?"

"Yes. Yes, I am," Clemency said with a sudden burst of confidence. She turned to the car, ignoring Peter's silly grin as he followed.

Several miles passed and Peter couldn't keep the smile off his face as he watched Clemency's hands steer the car toward the city. Glancing back to make sure that Lucy was soundly sleeping, he cleared his throat. "That wasn't by chance an acceptance to my proposal, was it?"

"No, it wasn't," Clemency said, her hands squeezing the steering wheel tight. "You're still required to get down on one knee and ask me again, old man. Once I'm free and available to answer."

Peter laughed and lay his hand on her thigh before spending the remainder of the drive to the airport envisioning exactly how he would eventually make that happen.

CHAPTER TWENTY-NINE

It was as though London had gone out of its way to look its best to welcome Lucy. There wasn't a cloud in the sky as Peter directed the hired car to Grace's school to pick her up before taking them all home. The girls greeted one another like long lost friends, and as they pulled up to Peter's bright blue door, Clemency felt herself relax for the first time in days. They were home...

"You'll be sharing a room with me, but I still have a bit more school left so enjoy it while you can," Grace was telling Lucy as Clemency and Peter followed them up the stairs.

"Actually, there's been a slight change," Peter announced, stopping to open the door that once led to the attic. Clemency led the way to the space that had been redesigned into two small bedrooms with a shared bath separating them.

"It's so grown up," Grace cried, tears in her eyes as she took in the much more modern and mature decor Clemency had chosen.

"I love it," Lucy cried popping her head out of her room.

"You can thank your mum for it," Peter explained with a smile on his face. "It was her idea to update your bedroom, Gracie, and when we realized we needed more room for Lucy as well, it became obvious that we should use this space.

Both girls threw themselves into Clemency's arms before Grace turned to the stairway. "Lucy, help me start moving my stuff up here!"

"I'll go start hauling up the luggage," Peter said, turning to follow his daughter.

Lucy, however, turned to her mother. "Does this mean I'm staying here? Are you going to marry Peter?"

Clemency drew her daughter into her new room. "Nothing is set in stone, sweetness. It is still your decision to make. If you choose to remain here, this would be your home. Sometime this week, we'll take you to Gracie's school so you can see what it is like," she explained. "Regardless of where you choose to live, you should always know that you have a home with me."

"You didn't answer my question. Are you and Peter getting married?" Lucy persisted.

"Maybe. Someday," Clemency replied with a sigh. "Let's take it day by day. See what it's like living together as a family before we go making permanent decisions, okay?"

The girls spent the afternoon unpacking and decorating their rooms while Peter and Clemency relaxed, curled up on the sofa together, reading and listening to the easy banter between their daughters.

"This is what I always wanted," Peter declared at one point as he massaged Clemency's feet. "A house full of girls chattering away."

Moments later when the chatter transitioned into their first argument and shouts of 'Mom!' and 'Clemmie!' echoed down the stairs, Clemency got to remind a panicked Peter that it would only be seven years until the girls moved out to college. Over the raised voices of their children they traded ideas of how they would spend that peaceful time.

"Secluded cabin on the Isle of Man," Clemency suggested.

"A villa in Tuscany," Peter countered.

"How do you feel about Disney World?" Clemency asked, capturing the girl's attention.

"We want to go to Disney World!" they exclaimed; their argument forgotten as they ganged up on their parents.

"Maybe another day," Peter declared, rising from the sofa. "For now, dinner."

Early the next morning, Peter drove off in his precious sports car and returned in a more sensible SUV. They spent the afternoon touring the city before dropping Grace back off at her school.

"I'd be living here?" Lucy asked, her voice tinged with both awe and fear as she eyed the imposing ivy-covered buildings.

"Actually, Daddy, I would prefer to stay at home more next term," Grace said.

"That's the great thing about Crestwood Academy," Peter explained. "You can choose to board by the term or by the week. If you girls wanted to remain at home, that is fine. However, should your mother and I have a busy schedule that takes us away from the city, or you have a project that you want to work on with friends, you have the option of staying on campus."

Clemency could see the wheels turning in her daughter's head as they bid Grace goodbye with the promise that she would be packed and ready to return home mid-week. Any questions Lucy may have had, however, flew out of her head as they returned home to find Georgie waiting for them. She handed Lucy a pared down version of the script and informed her that her audition was scheduled for the following morning.

"Oh my God! I have to kiss a boy!" came the girls excited screech from the living room a few minutes later. Peter laughed as he watched the blood drain from Clemency's face.

Just as Georgie had predicted, Lucy excelled in her audition. Clemency wished she could have seen it, but she discovered that she was a very nervous stage mother. Instead, she spent the morning locked in the bathroom heaving her guts. She emerged in time to discover Peter on the phone with his agent arranging to get Lucy added to her list of clients and Georgie barking orders to her assistant. Suddenly everyone had something to do except her. It was like standing in the center of a hurricane, and the effect was dizzying.

The production plowed ahead. Clemency entrusted her daughter to Peter and Frankie as her days were now spent checking over daily footage. It was a far cry from the all-nighters she had been working just a few months earlier. Before she knew it, it was mid-June and the crew was beginning to pack up. The London scenes had been completed; they were heading to Wales at the end of the week.

"There's one thing, Georgie wants to try to do before we leave," Peter announced during a rare afternoon break together. "She thinks that the cast has developed a sufficient camaraderie... I mean, she thinks we've become close enough..."

"Are you trying to say that Georgie wants to film some of the more intimate scenes?" Clemency asked, hiding her grin behind her mug of coffee.

"Yeah," Peter exhaled. "She's scheduled a skeleton crew for tonight and tomorrow. You weren't uh... planning on being on set, were you?"

Clemency closed her eyes and shook her head. Once upon a time she dreamed of seeing the love scenes she had written for Kennett, Benjamin and Tempest brought to life. Now, with Peter involved, the idea made her feel nauseous. She excused herself and darted to the bathroom. Peter was waiting for her when she exited, concern written all over his face.

"I'm fine," Clemency insisted before he could say anything. "It's probably some bug that has been going around."

She let him put her in a cab home with the promise that he would call to check up on her when he got a chance. However, once at home, she went straight to bed and didn't awaken until the following morning.

"Good morning sleeping beauty. Feel better?" Peter asked, emerging from the bathroom with a towel hanging low around his waist.

Clemency nodded and instinctively licked her lips as she imagined the towel slipping and falling to the floor. Unfortunately, before that could happen, Peter disappeared into the closet.

"How'd it go last night?" she asked and was rewarded with a muffled reply. His inability to meet her eye when he returned didn't give her much hope.

Georgie didn't offer any additional details, claiming that

things went 'okay' when asked, before flat out refusing to let Clemency review the footage. Seeking out Peter that afternoon to say goodbye, Clemency was startled to find herself pulled into his office, the door slamming shut behind her.

"Fantasy or reality?" he whispered when his lips finally traveled from her lips to nibble on her earlobe. Clemency looked up at him questioningly, trying to play it coy and ignore his arousal that was pressing into her. "The threesome scenes... are they a reality or a fantasy," he clarified.

"Fantasy. Pure fantasy," Clemency gasped as his hand moved under her shirt.

"Thank God," he said, resting his forehead against hers before he moved to flick the lock on the door and draw her back toward his couch. "Help me take care of this before I end up scaring poor Frankie to death with it," he said indicating the bulge in his pants.

"With pleasure," Clemency muttered as she knelt on the floor between his knees. Gently easing down the zipper, she let out a moan of pleasure as he sprung from the open folds.

Peter groaned as she took him between her lips, her tongue swirling around. He threw back his head, relishing the feel of her mouth. He wasn't certain that this would help, but he had to try something, or risk thinking about her all evening and ruin another night of filming. She had paused in her ministrations and he looked down to find her gazing up at him as her hand slowly stroked him.

"Watch me," she commanded, and he recalled the time he demanded the same of her. He kept his eyes on her as she drew him into her mouth to the back of her throat. Her moan of pleasure reverberated through him and he felt his balls tighten. He was already so close, but when he gently tugged on her hair to let her know, she somehow managed to take him deeper.

Clemency sat back on her heels, watching him as he tried to collect himself. "God, I love you," he groaned as he zipped up his trousers. "And I'll definitely be making that up to you later."

"I'll hold you to that," she said, brushing a quick kiss across his lips as a knock came at the door. It was time for him to head for the set.

Peter made it home much earlier than anticipated, but this time because the night was much more successful. He found his girls curled up on the couch watching a movie and while Gracie and Lucy were quick to rise and greet him before heading off to bed, Clemency was dead to the world. She never stirred when he carried her up to their bed. Instead, her eyes fluttered open the next morning in time to watch Peter dress for the day.

"Georgie said to tell you to take the day off," he informed her as she sat up and stretched. "If you and the girls can get everything packed and ready, we can go out for dinner and call it an early night before heading out tomorrow."

It was a struggle to find the energy to do so, but by mid-afternoon Clemency had everything done and had fallen back onto the bed with the intention of catching a few minutes rest. She was prodded awake by Peter and was shocked to discover that she had slept for several hours.

She reassured him that she was fine several times throughout the evening, but Peter could see that Clemency was fighting total exhaustion. That night, once the girls were in bed, he left her to take a shower, only to return to find her asleep, face down on the bed, still partially dressed. Concern warred with arousal at the sight of her naked ass in the air as he moved to lie down beside her. She opened her eyes and smiled at him when he brushed aside a lock of hair.

"Are you sure you're okay, my love?" he asked, his lips moving to lay tiny kisses across her shoulder to the back of her neck.

She sighed and nodded when he moved to straddle her hips, gently massaging her shoulders before moving to unhook the clasp of her bra.

"That feels good," she murmured into her pillow as his fingers continued to play across her skin.

"I can think of ways to make you feel even better," he whispered. "Are you up for it?"

"With you, always," she sighed.

"Don't move," he ordered as he leapt from the bed and crossed the room. Clemency turned on her side to watch him, her head resting in the palm of her hand. "I thought I told you not to move," he said crossly when he turned to find her staring at him and the packages he had moved to retrieve.

"Sorry. I didn't realize you were going into Kennett mode," she said, turning back to lie face down on the bed.

"How else can I make your fantasies a reality," he replied, moving to straddle her thighs. His hands moved to caress her ass cheeks and he felt himself harden at the sight of her wetness glistening in the lamplight.

"What fantasy are we addressing tonight?" she asked, allowing him to raise her to her knees and slide a pillow under her hips.

"That's a surprise," he replied as he eased into her, relishing the sound of her gasp. He thrust once, but then held her tight against him, struggling to keep control of his urges. Wanting this to be about her pleasure. Reaching for the first package, he uncorked the small bottle of oil and let it drizzle between her cheeks. She pushed back against him as he teased her rosebud with his finger. Pulling his cock out of her, he added a second finger to her ass, holding still while she moaned and writhed against his hand.

Quietly, he reached for the second package and removed the toy he had purchased expressly for fulfilling this fantasy. She let out a small cry as his fingers exited her, then pushed back as he ran the toy against her, coating it with oil before pressing it against her tight opening. He felt himself getting impossibly harder as he watched it slide into her.

"Fuck, Peter, you feel so good," she moaned, tilting her hips higher. He took the opportunity to move off the bed and he stood watching as her hips continued to thrust and gyrate. "Please... Peter.... Why aren't you moving?" she cried out in frustration.

"Because I'm not inside of you," he said with a smirk. "Yet."

He didn't give her a chance to recover from the shocking

discovery that he had inserted a toy up her ass. He lay on the bed and pulled her onto him, relishing the look of dazed pleasure that played across her features as she impaled herself on him. She was impossibly tight. He could feel every ripple on the toy through the thin membrane that separated it from him. The serene look of wonder on her face as she rode him was quickly replaced with frantic ecstasy when his fingers groped for the button that caused the toy to begin vibrating deep within her.

"Fuck, Peter," she cried as the first climax rippled through her. She dropped onto his chest and he took the opportunity to flip them over. The vibrations running across the underside of his cock as he thrust into her were nearly his undoing, but he was determined to make her come again. He paused, holding himself up on his elbows watching her as she came down from her high. When her eyes finally focused on him, he leaned down to capture her lips.

"Come for me again, love," he whispered as he began to move against her. Clemency didn't think it was possible, but then he deepened the kiss and the coil deep inside of her began to lash out and the spasming deep inside began anew. Peter cried out, feeling her tighten around him again as he poured himself into her.

Eventually his heart rate began to settle. Clemency continuing to writhe and whimper beneath him didn't help, but he eventually realized her cries were due to the toy still vibrating inside of her. Turning it off, he eased it out and she cried out as she came for a third time before becoming quite limp.

"That's the closest you will ever come to a threesome," Peter said as he pulled the covers up over them. "At least with me."

"It was more than enough," Clemency replied, snuggling closer to him and letting sleep claim her once again.

CHAPTER THIRTY

They left for Cardiff early the next morning. The phone calls from Elliott began the following day. It had been lovely, sun shining bright in the sky as Peter drove Clemency and the girls around the city, showing them the sights. Now they were back home, he could hear the girl's music thumping upstairs as they worked to unpack and put their mark on the bedrooms they had claimed. He spied Clemency dozing out in the garden and frowned. Despite the warmth of the sunshine, she still appeared pale. He poked the last pepper onto the skewer he was prepping, hoping that some good food would help perk her up when he saw the screen of her phone light up. His heart skipped a beat when he saw the identity of the incoming call. Grabbing it and the tray of food, he quickly moved to the patio.

"Your soon to be ex-husband is calling, my love," he announced, jostling Clemency awake. He tried to remain calm as he arranged the food on the grill. Tonight could possibly be the night... but no, he wanted to make this special. He couldn't just rush in and propose. Especially when she already expected it. "Is everything okay?" he asked when she set her phone down a few minutes later.

Clemency's reply was ambiguous as it was lost amid a yawn as she stretched and sat up. "He was calling Lucy for their weekly talk and dialed me by mistake," she said, moving to examine Peter's culinary efforts. "Smells good."

"I hope it tastes good too," he said. "You didn't eat much today."

"Good thing too since what I did eat didn't stay with me too long," Clemency replied with a shudder as she remembered the bout of sickness that had plagued her earlier in the day.

"Are you sure you shouldn't see a doct--" Peter began only to have his concern waved aside as Clemency moved toward the house.

"It was just carsickness," she said dismissively.

Elliott called again a few days later. The production had broke for lunch and Clemency had joined Peter and Georgie for an impromptu meeting when her phone buzzed. She excused herself, hoping that her husband was finally calling to tell her their divorce was final. But no... instead, the usually reserved Elliott was just in the mood to chat. He said he was calling to thank her for some pictures she had sent him of Lucy on the set, but then he quickly launched into talking about work before segueing into small town gossip. Before she knew it, her lunch break was over, and she could only shrug her shoulders at Peter's questioning look.

The reason for Elliott's chattiness became clear a week later when Clemency blindly answered the phone, croaking hello from where she hung over the toilet. Hearing her husband's voice come over the phone's speaker that morning, it took all her effort not to heave into the toilet yet again.

"Cee, Whitney's pregnant," Elliott said, sounding despondent as Clemency struggled to her feet.

"Well, bloody congratu-fucking-lations," she muttered in reply as she wiped a cold, wet cloth over her face.

"What was that, Cee? I can't hear you," Elliott said.

"I said congratulations, E. I hope you two will be happy," Clemency said through gritted teeth.

"We won't be," Elliott said in defeat. "I won't ever be happy again unless you're in my life."

Clemency glanced up to see Peter's reflection in the doorway. The look on his face made it clear that he had heard every word. Picking up the phone, she turned off the speaker. "I'm sorry, E. That's no longer an option," she said before ending the call.

"I told you," Peter said. His voice, while quiet and calm, held an edge of steel as he moved alongside her and began prepping for his morning shave.

"And you heard me soundly reject him," Clemency snapped as she grabbed her toothbrush and began to vigorously attack her teeth. "Fuck," she muttered as the taste of the toothpaste made her gag and she moved back to the toilet.

"Will you please go see a doctor?" Peter asked yet again while he held back her hair and placed a wet towel on the back of her neck.

Clemency brushed him aside and flushed the toilet before reaching for a glass of water to rinse out her mouth.

"I'm fine," she muttered as she stormed out of the room, leaving Peter to finish his shaving. Her hope was that if she repeated that mantra enough, she would begin to believe it. She had seen the underlying fear in Peter's eyes. She knew he was thinking of his first wife and her bout with cancer. Unfortunately, that fear wasn't enough of a catalyst to spur her to seek out medical advice. She had nearly died at the hands of a doctor once, and the same man had robbed her of her dream of having a home full of children. The mere sight of a white coat caused her to panic.

Thankfully, over the following week, Clemency found that her mantra seemed to work. The queasiness disappeared and her energy level returned to normal. If anything, she began feeling ravenously hungry.

Friday afternoon found her grazing at the craft services table in between scenes when she felt the vibration of an incoming call. When she saw the caller's identity, her eyes automatically darted across the room to find Peter already watching her intently.

"Hello Elliott," she said in greeting.

"Cee," Elliott replied, sounding weary. "I just wanted to let you know that it's over. The papers came today. We're officially divorced."

While she managed to refrain from giving a loud whoop of joy, Clemency did grin and flash Peter a thumbs up sign. His broad smile in return let her know that they would definitely be celebrating later that night.

"I'm sorry, I didn't catch that last bit, E," Clemency said, turning her attention back to the call.

"I just said that mother is still pressuring me to fight for Lucy," Elliott repeated. "I'm trying to hold her off... It's just that Lucy sounds so happy when I talk to her... I don't have much hope of winning, do I?"

"It's not a competition, E," Clemency said softly. "Our daughter is happy. That is what is important. She still has until the end of the month to make her decision."

"And if she chooses to stay there?" he asked.

"We've already looked into schools. Her schedule would give her a week break every other month as well as two weeks at Christmas and a summer holiday," Clemency explained. "You would still get to see her a great deal more than I would if she were to return to the States."

She could hear Elliott breathing on the other end of the line, but there was silence for several minutes and she realized that he was crying. "I want her to stay with you, Cee," he finally whispered. "I need to get out of here... Away from my family and figure out what to do with my life."

Clemency sighed. She had been waiting years to hear him say that. "Tell you what, E. Why don't you start by coming here at the end of the month? Surprise our daughter for her birthday and discuss things with her face to face."

Elliott seemed to perk up at the suggestion and they chatted a few more minutes making potential plans. It felt good to be on friendly terms with the man who had once shared so much of her life. She was on the verge of ending the call when Elliott said that there was one more thing he had to tell her. Something he had wanted to say for a long time but could never quite figure out how. Clemency felt the blood drain from her face as she listened to her ex-husband's final confession.

Her phone clattered as it hit the floor and Clemency grasped the edge of the table to keep the room from spinning. She turned, stumbling for the door. Somehow Georgie was suddenly by her side, directing her toward the bathroom across the hall, catching her before she could fall. Spying the toilet, Clemency pushed her friend aside before pitching forward and losing her lunch.

When she finally exited the stall, she found her friend sitting on the edge of the sink.

"So, what brought this on?" Georgie asked, handing over a wet towel.

"That was Elliott," Clemency replied, leaning back against the wall. Finding that her knees were still shaking, she slid to the floor and looked up at her friend. "The divorce is final."

"Ah yes, the post-divorce celebratory up-chuck. I somehow missed out on those," Georgie said. "Talk to me, Clemency. Something else happened..."

"He had a vasectomy," Clemency whispered, watching her fingers as they shredded the paper towel.

"Elliott had a vasectomy?" Georgie asked. "Okay... good for him? Why does this have you so upset, sweetie?"

Clemency gazed up at Georgie, tears in her eyes. "He had the vasectomy nine years ago after I had a bad miscarriage. He never told me. He let me think that my failure to conceive was my fault. I thought I was infertile."

Clemency saw understanding begin to dawn in her friend's eyes. "That fucking asshole," Georgie began to rant. "You are so much better without that prick. Big picture, sweetie... you have Peter now--" Georgie stopped as Clemency suddenly burst into tears. "What is it, love? I know it's not Peter. The look on his face when you gave him the thumbs up... I'm not going to get another ounce of work out of him today, he's too preoccupied imagining the celebratory shag he has planned for tonight."

Clemency pushed Georgie away and darted back toward the stall where she began heaving all over again. This time when she exited, it was to find Georgie examining her closely. She avoided her friend's eye and moved to wash her face.

"You thought you were sterile all these years?" Georgie asked. Clemency nodded and accepted the towel handed to her. "You and Peter haven't been using protection."

It was a statement, not a question, but Clemency shook her head, nevertheless. "I can't be pregnant," she whispered, the word sounding foreign to her ears.

Georgie leapt into action. Before she realized what was happening, Clemency was bustled out of the studio and into the back of the familiar SUV. At Georgie's townhouse Clemency found herself settled onto the sofa with a glass of water and a box of tissue as Georgie paced the floor issuing orders into her headset. When the doorbell rang, Clemency rose to answer it and accepted the bag Roger handed her with a consoling smile. Georgie appeared at her side and, rubbing her back, she directed her through the house to the bathroom. There Clemency peeked inside the bag to find a home pregnancy test.

"Everything okay, love?" Georgie's voice startled Clemency ten minutes later as she poked her head around the door.

Clemency let out a laugh that sounded borderline hysterical. "I swear it turned positive the moment I touched it," she replied, holding up the stick for Georgie to see.

"How are you feeling?" Georgie asked.

"Happy... I mean... it's a baby. I always wanted more children... and it's Peter's... the thought of holding his child... oh God, Georgie, it's too much," Clemency began to tear up again. "But then... it's Peter. We have all these plans for what we want to do once the girls are grown... He's not going to want to start all over again."

Georgie pulled the test from her friend's hand and tossed it into a nearby trash can before placing her hands in Clemency's and giving them a squeeze. "There's one thing you have absolutely right there, love. It's Peter. He loves you and nothing is going to change that. And he's going to love this child. Now, let's get something to eat and discuss how you plan on telling him."

Clemency perched herself on a barstool at the kitchen counter watching Georgie bustle around the room. When her friend paused to turn to her, she hurriedly dashed away the tears that continued to fall. "I'm sorry. I'm just thinking about... well, tonight was supposed to be the night that I was finally free to accept Peter's proposal..."

"I think you and Peter need to discuss what's happening before he pops the question again, don't you?" Georgie said. "Do you want me to take the girls tonight?"

Clemency shook her head. Tonight was too soon. She barely had enough time to digest the news herself. "I don't want to do anything that will affect Peter and his work," she quickly improvised as an excuse. "We break next week and are going to Scotland. I'll tell him then."

The look of disapproval on Georgie's face was evident, but Clemency turned away and moved to the living room before anything could be said.

They shared a quiet meal, Clemency's thoughts obviously elsewhere. Midway through lunch she began giggling and once she began found it impossible to stop.

"It's karma," she finally gasped to a perplexed looking Georgie. "Elliott... he called a week ago to tell me that Whitney was pregnant. Now I realize why he sounded so miserable..."

"It couldn't happen to a more deserving man," Georgie claimed with a grin.

CHAPTER THIRTY-ONE

Peter found himself examining Clemency closely when Georgie dropped her off later that evening. Her eyes were red, and her smile was forced as she accepted his kiss before quickly alighting the stairs to greet the girls as if she hadn't seen them in ages. Was she regretting the divorce?

"It's not what you think," Georgie's voice said from behind him. "She loves you Peter. With all her heart. Just be patient with her."

His friend gave his arm a squeeze and he turned to enter his home, a smile tugging on the corner of his mouth as he heard the shouts of laughter coming from his girls. Patience... well, seeing as he obviously wasn't hosting a romantic dinner and getting down on one knee this evening, he had no other choice than to be patient.

Patience, however, was not an easy trait to come by. Leaning against the door frame to their bedroom several nights later, Peter let out a soft curse. This was not turning out to be the summer he had envisioned. For one thing, their schedules just never seemed to align. If he finished filming early, she had to stay late watching the footage and conferring with Georgie. If she had a free day, he was stuck shooting extra scenes. If he was awake, she was asleep. Like now... he watched the gentle rise and fall of her chest. They had been in Cardiff for three weeks now, and it felt as though they were drifting apart. Even more so since she had gotten word that her divorce was final. The thought of losing her made his chest physically ache.

Kicking off his shoes, he moved to lay beside her, pulling her against his chest. She murmured his name in her sleep as her hand moved to clasp his, moving it to settle over her abdomen. He relaxed. Banishing all thoughts of losing her, and they slept.

The late summer sunset created a beam of light that nearly blinded him when his eyes fluttered open. He had no clue how long they had dozed, but he was happy to find her still in his arms and shifting to face him. He dipped his head to meet her lips, smiling when he felt the shudder of pleasure his kisses still created.

"Hi there," he whispered, relishing the moan of pleasure elicited from his hand sliding under her shirt and brushing over her nipples. "You're quite responsive today, love," he muttered as his lips trailed lower and he moved to unbutton her shirt. Her hands however stilled his fingers. Glancing down, he saw a myriad of emotions play across her face. Patience, he reminded himself as he pulled his hands away from her. "Just tell me what you need, love?"

He sat up as she shook her head and rose from the bed. He watched silently as she crossed the room to the door where she paused before reaching out to flip the lock. The smile on her face was tentative as she turned back to face him. Her shirt was unbuttoned and fluttered to the floor as she took a step in his direction.

"I need you," she whispered. "I need you to love me."

Peter's patience was beginning to wear thin. It was their final days of filming in Wales and the days were spent on location by the sea. Clemency's work was done, she was spending the time basking in the sun along with Gracie.

"Daddy, do you know what's wrong with Clemmie?" his daughter asked one evening after dinner. Peter had his back to her rinsing dishes, and he suppressed a sigh. This was the final straw. If his daughter noticed something was wrong...

"I don't sweetie, but I'm going to find out," he said with determination as he turned to grab his phone and car keys from the counter. "Take over for me here. I'll be back in a while."

He placed the call en route to his favorite hole in the wall pub and fifteen minutes later he was joined by Georgie in a corner booth.

"Tell me what's going on," he demanded without preamble.

"Peter, have I told you how much newfound respect I have for you lately?" Georgie asked, nodding to a passing waitress who recognized them and darted off to fetch their usual drinks.

"What the hell does that mean?" he ground out.

"Well, suddenly I find myself in your shoes... the friend in the middle," Georgie explained. You were there for me and Frankie right after she was born... I think you changed more diapers than Donovan did. It was because you knew all along, didn't you?" Peter stared at the bowl of pretzels refusing to answer. "You knew that Donovan was screwing around on me, but as his friend you kept his secret while trying to comfort and assist me any way you could."

"Are you trying to tell me that Clemency is cheating on me?" Peter croaked, suddenly finding it hard to speak.

"God, no," Georgie exclaimed. "She loves you Peter and would never do anything to hurt you. What I'm saying is that I understand what it's like to be in the middle... to know one friends secret while trying to comfort the other."

"Just tell me," Peter implored, meeting Georgie's eye.

"I can't. It's not my secret to tell," Georgie replied firmly. "You just need to be--"

"Patient," Peter growled, slamming his palm on the table and startling the waitress who had appeared with their drinks. He mumbled an apology as she placed his beer in front of him.

"I can tell you that this is not the sort of secret that one can keep forever," Georgie said cryptically over her wineglass.

"Does it have something to do with that bastard of an ex-husband then?" Peter asked, noting the slight hesitation from his friend before she answered.

"Directly? No," she replied. "But you nailed the description of the man. He is truly a bastard."

"Did he do something to hurt her?" Peter asked and was again met with a pause.

"It's not my place..." Georgie began. "Tell me... are you stopping in Edinburgh next week?" Thinking that she was trying to change the subject, Peter shook his head and took another swig from his mug. "Maybe you should. I'm flying up tomorrow after we wrap. I'll be spending some time with Donovan. You should bring Clemency to see him. It will give you a chance to introduce her to your fam--"

Georgie flinched as Peter's hand forcefully met the table once again. She opened her mouth to continue, but he shook his head before rising to storm out of the pub. He would be damned if he was going to introduce Clemency to his parents now when there was so much uncertainty to their future. Slamming the car door, he smacked the steering wheel. And why was Georgie suggesting he bring Clemency to see Donovan, he wondered as he pulled into traffic.

It hit him halfway through the short drive home. Donovan was a doctor. Georgie was suggesting he bring Clemency to see her ex-husband in his professional capacity. He slammed to a halt in front of the house and flew up the stairs only to find Clemency sleeping soundly in their bed. The pieces were beginning to fall into place. Hell, even Gracie had been aware of it. He was such a fool.

Watching the gentle rise and fall of Clemency's chest, counting each breath, he wondered how many more did she have left. Was she truly dying or was this something they could fight together? Quietly moving to the solitude of the bathroom, he let the tears fall. In the shower he let the hot water pound his body as he pounded the tiles with his fist.

The final day of filming dawned grey and rainy. That didn't

stop Clemency from leaping from bed, she was certain that it was going to be a good day. She was feeling more and more positive with each passing day. Her back to Peter as she dressed, she let her hands drift down to settle on her abdomen. There was a slight bulge now, and as her fingers splayed over it, she murmured reassurances to the life taking shape beneath it. This was happening.

"Did you say something, love?" Peter said. She turned to find him sitting up in bed his eyes perusing her body.

"Just that today is going to be a good day," she said brightly, quickly pulling a shirt on to cover herself. She gave him a reassuring smile before moving to the bathroom.

It was going to be a good day, she repeated to herself. It had been a week since she had discovered her pregnancy, and all was well. Okay, there had been one final bout of morning sickness that Gracie had unfortunately been witness to. But other than that, she was beginning to feel like her old self. She was regaining her energy and best of all, she was beginning to believe that this was really going to happen. Yes, she had yet to inform Peter about their impending parenthood, but she had faith that they could make it work. They loved one another. She had come to realize that her initial fears were about the pregnancy itself, not necessarily Peter's reaction to it. She had spent the past week focused on her body, waiting for any sign that indicated that she was going to miscarry again. Instead, her body blossomed. Almost before her eyes she witnessed her curves rounding, her breasts becoming fuller, and every inch of her body becoming so sensitive she swore she could feel Peter's eyes on her from across the room.

She knew that it was time. They just needed to get through this last day on set before heading off on holiday. Then she would tell Peter the news that would change their lives forever.

The mood on set was celebratory as they wrapped up by mid-afternoon. Clemency wrinkled her nose at the sip of champagne she had taken before Peter drew the flute from her fingers.

"These wrap parties can get quite rowdy and last long into

the night," he said. "Let's get you home to rest. We have a busy day tomorrow."

Deaf to her protest, he eased her through the crowd of well-wishers. At home, he sent the girls off to pack while he popped her onto the bed with the instruction not to move while he dragged their suitcases out of the closet. So much for a good day, she thought with a pout as she settled back against the pillows and promptly dozed off.

She should have considered herself lucky, Clemency thought the next morning. The previous day had indeed been good... free of morning sickness. Today, not so much. The car was packed with Peter and the girls waiting for her while she occupied herself with losing her breakfast. Still, she plastered a smile on her face and told herself it was just nerves as she climbed into the passenger seat. She tried to ignore the look of concern on Peter's face, turning to check with the girls to make sure they had everything that they needed.

"Seven-hour drive," Peter said, his voice sounding forced. "Shall we begin with some Zeppelin?"

"Ugh," Clemency replied. "How about The Who?"

"Clapton?" Peter countered.

Clemency shook her head. "The Clash?"

"Guys, if you're going to sit there fighting over music, we'll never get out of Wales," Gracie pointed out from the back seat.

"I have an idea. How about we listen to our playlist," Lucy suggested.

Clemency met Peter's eye. "One Direction and Ed Sheeran?" she said, causing them both to shudder.

"Random shuffle?" Peter asked and Clemency readily agreed as the girls grumbled about their old-fashioned music taste and popped in their earbuds.

Settling back into her seat, Clemency closed her eyes and let out a soft sigh when Peter's hand slipped into hers. She hadn't meant to fall asleep, but the next thing she knew she was jolted awake by her daughter's voice shouting at her.

"Lucy! Remove your earbuds and stop yelling," Peter demanded, glaring at her in the rear-view mirror. He gave Clemency's hand a squeeze as she sat up and glanced at the clock on the dashboard. It was nearly noon. How could she have slept so long? She turned to face her daughter who was muttering apologies.

"Mom, Daddy just messaged asking me if you have made the arrangements for his visit yet," Lucy said. "What is he talking about? Is he coming here?"

Clemency felt Peter's hand slip from her own. Shit, she had totally forgotten about suggesting that Elliott come talk to their daughter in person. Apparently, the dumb ass thought that was still an option after the bombshell he had dropped on her. Not only that, but he clearly expected her to make all the arrangements.

"Your father mentioned the idea of surprising you for your birthday, sweetness," Clemency said slowly, watching Peter out of the corner of her eye. "Tell him we'll be back in town by the end of the month and to make his own arrangements."

They drove on in silence. Clemency noted how Peter was fighting against grinding his teeth while his hands were practically strangling the steering wheel in their grip. Half an hour later the girls began piping up from the back seat, demanding a bathroom break. It had begun to rain as Peter pulled off the motorway and into the parking lot of a small restaurant. The girls quickly darted around puddles toward the building, leaving their parents behind.

Peter remained seated with his hands on the wheel watching the view of the world outside the windshield become obscured. "Your husband is coming here?" he finally asked.

"Ex-husband," Clemency quickly corrected and immediately regretted doing so as Peter turned to face her. His normally bright blue eyes had darkened, and she realized that she had never seen him so angry before. "When he called to say the divorce was final, he said he wanted Lucy to remain here," she rushed to explain. "He said he wanted to make a new start and I suggested he come here to tell Lucy himself, but that was before..." she trailed off.

"Before what?" Peter demanded.

"The girls are waiting," Clemency said, turning to open her door before his tight grip on her arm stopped her.

"Before what?" he repeated.

"You're hurting me," she whispered, and he immediately released his hold.

Fuck. Patience, he reminded himself as he muttered an apology and moved to exit the car. Inside the restaurant they found the girls already seated at a table excitedly discussing their holiday plans. Peter joined the discussion, keeping a close eye on Clemency and frowning at how little of her lunch she managed to eat.

"Do you girls think you can fit a day or two layover in Edinburgh into your itinerary?" he asked suddenly, causing Clemency to look up from pushing her eggs across her plate.

"We're going to see grandma and grandpa?" Grace asked excitedly.

Peter hesitated. His plan had originally been to introduce Clemency to his family on this trip. But his parents were not young, and they had already had to endure Vanessa's death the previous year, did he really want to risk inflicting more loss? He gave a vague reply, mentioning that Donovan and Georgie would also be in the city as he paid the bill and bustled them all off to the car.

Clemency watched Peter's profile as they headed back to the motorway. She wondered what had prompted this sudden change in plans. She pressed a hand to her gurgling stomach, willing it to settle down as she turned to blindly watch the passing scenery.

"Pull over," she finally said in a strangled whisper as she groped for the release button to her seatbelt.

"What?" Peter asked, lost in his own thoughts and not hearing her at first. He slammed on the breaks as she repeated herself louder and began struggling with the handle to her door.

"Daddy," Gracie cried as they watched Clemency stagger behind a nearby bush. Peter glanced back to see that his daughters' eyes were as big as saucers. "Is she sick like mom was? Is Clemmie dying?"

Lucy had removed her earbuds in time to hear Grace's questions and Peter watched the blood drain from her face.

"You girls wait here," he commanded. "Your mother is fine. Just a little carsick."

By the time Peter exited the car, Clemency had moved. Her back was to him as she rested her hands against the wooden fence separating the motorway from the green fields beyond it. As he approached her, he noticed the slight tremble of her shoulders and it broke his heart to see her in such pain. Fighting back his own tears, knowing that he needed to be strong for her, he slid his arms around her. Pulling her back against him, he held her tight.

"Whatever this is, we're going to fight it, love. Together," he murmured in her ear. "I'm not going to lose you."

Clemency struggled to turn in his arms. "What?" she asked, gazing up at him.

"Just tell me... is it cancer?" Peter asked.

Clemency suddenly realized the damage her silence had wrought. In Peter's eyes she saw a mix of pain and fear, but underneath it all was love. She shook her head, reaching up to caress his face. If he was already imagining the worst, surely the truth wouldn't be so bad to bear.

"I'm not dying," Clemency said, struggling to smile through the watery tears forming in her eyes. "I'm pregnant."

Peter stepped back; shock evident on his face as he gazed down at her. Suddenly all the puzzle pieces scattered and began to fall into place once again. Her exhaustion... the frequent sickness... his eyes perused her body, taking in the fullness of her breasts... When his eyes returned to her face, he saw for the first time the fear and uncertainty in her eyes. Stepping forward, he placed a hand on the swell of her abdomen and pulled her back into his arms.

"A baby?" he murmured as the tears began to fall. "How?"

She pulled back and quirked an eyebrow up at him causing him to grin. The smile quickly slid from his face, however, as he listened to her explain about her last conversation with Elliott. He felt his heart give a nervous flutter at the mention of her miscarriage.

"Everything is okay now though, right? You've seen a doctor?" he asked, knowing the answer as the words passed his lips. Of course, she hadn't seen a doctor. It was clear she was terrified at the thought.

Clemency watched as Peter whipped his phone out and listened wide eyed to his end of the conversation as he took charge. "It's me... yeah, two rooms... and Donov-- okay, nine o'clock... we'll see you then."

"What was that all about?" Clemency asked, perplexed.

"That was Georgie. She's already expecting us and had booked us rooms for the night," Peter explained.

"And nine o'clock?" Clemency prompted.

"We're meeting Donovan tomorrow morning. He'll give you a checkup," Peter explained. Seeing the fear creep back into her eyes, he pulled her into his arms. "I will be with you the entire time and Donovan is an excellent doctor. He also knows I would kill him if any harm should come to you or our child."

"You're not disappointed?" Clemency asked, the words 'our child' still echoing in her ears.

"Why on earth would I be disappointed?" Peter asked.

"We had plans... all those adventures we were going to take once the girls were grown," Clemency explained.

"Love, raising a child with you is better than any adventure the world has to offer," Peter said, his lips brushing hers.

CHAPTER THIRTY-TWO

Returning to the car, they reassured the girls that all was well. Clemency saw the concern in her daughter's eyes, but suddenly found it much easier to smile brightly and say that everything would be okay. She found herself believing the words as Peter's hand rested on her thigh, his pinkie finger lightly brushing over her stomach from time to time. Feeling as though the weight of the world had lifted from her shoulders, she peacefully drifted off to sleep.

Peter, on the other hand, struggled not to put his foot down on the gas. He was tempted to take a page out of Clemency's driving book, but the cargo he was transporting had suddenly become infinitely more precious. Thankfully, the miles flew by as his thoughts focused on the amazing woman beside him and the future that awaited them. By the time he pulled up to the hotel he was feeling exhausted. The last hundred miles his thoughts had been plagued by 'what ifs.' What if something was wrong with the baby? What if something happened to Clemency? Then there was the realization of his age. Could he really start all over again?

He felt completely ragged as he exited the car. Clemency, in contrast, looked as fresh as a daisy after several hours rest. Georgie and Donovan were there to greet them, and the girls rushed to give them quick hugs before disappearing into the hotel clutching the room key Georgie had slipped to them. Peter found his friends eyes on him as they approached and reached for Clemency's hand.

"You're okay with this? You're happy?" Georgie asked when they stopped before her. Her concerned gaze darted from his face to Clemency's and back again.

"I'd be singing it from the rooftops if she'd let me," Peter reassured her with a grin and he watched her visibly relax.

"See, I told you," Georgie chided, turning to Clemency and drawing her into an embrace. "How are you feeling?"

"Relieved," Clemency replied. "Scared," she added, looking over her friend's shoulder to where Donovan stood. "I'm nervous about tomorrow. I don't trust doctors, Georgie. I know Donovan is your... whatever he is... I just..."

"There's nothing to fear. I will do everything in my power to take care of you and the wee one," Donovan said, stepping forward. "Peter will be with you the whole time, Georgie too, if you want."

"I want," Clemency whispered over the lump forming in her throat.

After a leisurely dinner with Georgie and Donovan, they called it an early night and Clemency woke the next morning to find the suite empty. A note from Peter informed her that he had taken the girls to his parents and would return shortly for their appointment.

Dr. Donovan McDougal was far more professional looking than the handsome devil that persistently tried to win the hand of her best friend, Clemency thought when he greeted them at the door of his clinic. He was immaculately attired in a suit and tie underneath a pristine white lab coat, a stethoscope slung around his neck. Clemency felt her breath catch in her chest and her vision clouded as her anxiety returned. Peter sensed her reluctance to move and placed a gentle hand on her shoulder.

"I'm right here," he reassured her, and she took a tentative step forward. She focused on his soothing voice as he directed her toward the exam room, but she was still hyperventilating by the time they got her perched on the edge of the table.

Peter watched over her in silence despite the pain of her fingernails digging into the palm of his hand. Donovan began by taking her blood pressure and when Georgie's eyes widened at the numbers he jotted down on the chart, Peter knew there was cause for concern.

"Give me a moment, love," he said to Clemency, giving her hand a reassuring squeeze before handing her over to Georgie's care. He pulled Donovan from the room. "Lose the coat," he demanded as the door closed behind them.

Donovan looked down at his attire with a frown before realizing what Peter was saying. He excused himself with a nod and when he returned to the exam room a few minutes later he was dressed more casually in jeans and a polo shirt.

Taking his seat again, he began chatting with Georgie and Clemency. They discussed what sites to see while visiting the city, the weather, the movie, everything except why they were there. After several minutes of this, Donovan moved closer to Clemency, taking her hand gently in his as they continued to talk. They had moved on to the topic of Georgie's little annoying habits, much to the woman's chagrin. Clemency didn't even seem to notice the blood pressure cuff slipping around her arm as she and Donovan laughed about the horrendous sounds that emanated from Georgie when she was sick.

"Velociraptor in its death throes is the perfect description," Donovan said as he happily noted the now much lower numbers on the chart. "Speaking of being sick, how often would you say you've experienced morning sickness, and how long has it been occurring?"

Peter held back an expletive when Clemency explained that she had been feeling ill for the past two months. Had he really been that negligent to have not noticed for that long? She gave him an apologetic look and explained that she had been trying to keep it hidden so he wouldn't worry.

"Well, I think it's time we get to know this wee one a little better and see if we can figure out when he or she will be joining us," Donovan said with a smile. "When you're ready, just lie back and we'll begin by listening to the heartbeat."

Taking a deep breath, Clemency gave Peter a tentative smile

as he assisted her in reclining on the table. Once she was settled, she felt Georgie give her other hand a squeeze as she stepped to her side. Feeling safe and confident, surrounded by those she loved, Clemency gave Donovan a nod to let him know she was ready. She let out a small gasp at the coldness of the gel on her abdomen and in the next instant she and Peter were frowning at one another as they tried to discern a heartbeat from the whoosh whoosh sounds filling the room. They were so lost in one another, sharing this moment, that they missed the look of concern Donovan gave Georgie as he removed the wand.

"Donovan?" Peter asked as the room fell silent. Clemency, hearing the note of concern in his voice struggled to sit up, only to have Donovan's hand rest on her shoulder.

"It's okay," their friend reassured them before turning to pull another piece of equipment forward. "I'm going to switch to the sonogram now. I think you may be further along than I anticipated."

Donovan prepped the machine and soon the room was once again filled with the sound of Clemency's uterus. She focused on the little screen trying to make sense of the image she was seeing. Peter, however, kept his focus on Donovan this time. He had sensed the concern in his friend's voice. He hadn't realized that he was holding his breath until Donovan looked up at him, a grin on his face.

"I thought things sounded a little off," he said with a laugh. "Peter, how many of your siblings are twins?"

"Two sets, plus my mother was a twin," he said, feeling the blood drain from his face as he fell back onto the stool, his eyes glued to the monitor.

"Clemency, you had twin brothers, right?" Georgie asked, her own face splitting into a grin as she looked down at her friend.

Clemency silently nodded, her gaze still fixated on the screen where she was finally able to discern what Donovan was seeing. Two heads were visible facing one another and just below she could see the beating of two strong hearts. She was mesmerized by what she was seeing and barely noticed Donovan working to take measurements and jot down notes on her chart. Once the machine had been shut down, she turned to see Peter still sitting silently stunned beside her.

"Are you okay?" she asked, breaking him from his reverie.

"Never better," he croaked. "This is... it's wonderful... Donovan, how does everything look?"

"Like you said - wonderful," his friend replied. "As I thought, you're further along than expected. The wee ones are... well, wee at the moment. But you should begin to feel less peckish in the coming days. I think we'll have something to celebrate come the new year. Do you want to know the gender?"

Georgie let out a squeal of excitement at the announcement before Donovan led her from the room, instructing Peter and Clemency to take their time. When Clemency moved to get up, Peter swiveled the stool he was sitting on to block her. Laying his head on her thigh, he caressed the swell of her abdomen and began talking to their children. Clemency threaded her fingers lightly through his curls as he spoke such tender words. Her heart swelled with so much love for him.

"Peter?" she said, and after a moment he looked up at her. Her fingers were tentative as they traced the lines of his face.

"What is it, love?" he asked, rising to his feet.

In reply she pulled his head down to her, her lips brushing against his. He deepened the kiss, smiling when he felt her shudder. She pulled back slightly, still feeling dazed with pleasure.

"Marry me," she whispered, watching his eyes widen in surprise.

EPILOGUE

Keep calm... You've got this... the voice in Clemency's head soothed as she ran her hand over her rippling abdomen. She opened her eyes to see Georgie's concerned gaze reflected beside her own in the mirror.

"You good?" her friend asked. Clemency smiled in reply marveling, not for the first time, at how much her life had changed. A year ago her characters, mere voices in her head, gave her the support and comfort she needed to take a leap into the unknown. She gazed over Georgie's shoulder to where Lucy and Gracie were fussing over their hair with the aid of Frankie and Sam. No, she no longer needed the support of imaginary characters, but on this day, she was happy to hear Carraig's voice, nonetheless. "You've got this," Georgie echoed, giving her hand a squeeze. "I'm going to go check up on Peter."

Peter... her Kennett... her dark magician... her everything. He had been her rock during the past several months. After promptly accepting her proposal and slipping the ring he had been carrying around with him on her finger, he had whisked her off to meet his family and tell any and all who would listen their wonderful news. That didn't mean that he was any less worried than she was about the situation. She swore they both held their breath until she felt the first flutter of movement from the babies.

By then they had settled back down in London. Elliott had come and gone, expressing surprise at Clemency's condition and making Lucy's decision for her, telling their daughter to remain in England until he got settled in his new home in Phoenix. The girls acclimated quickly to the idea of being older sisters, but Clemency imagined once the reality of the situation hit, Lucy and Gracie would appreciate the opportunity to board at school.

The time flew by. There was just as much, if not more work to be done on the movie postproduction, and Clemency worked as much as Peter and Georgie would allow. There just never seemed to be time enough to fit in a simple wedding. Granted, Georgie and Donovan illustrated how easy it was by slipping away to Las Vegas one weekend in October and eloping. But Peter and Clemency wanted a ceremony that included friends and family, and they wanted it before the babies arrived.

"Mom, are the old ladies okay? You keep rubbing your belly," Lucy asked from across the room.

"I'm fine sweetness," Clemency replied, grumbling yet again at the nickname Lucy and Gracie had attached to their new siblings. Matilda and Agatha were perfectly good names for the babies, she thought as her hand moved to rub the ache that had moved to her back.

Downstairs Peter was pacing. He wasn't nervous. No, he was excited. Today was the day. He clapped his hands and looked expectantly at the doorway when Georgie appeared.

"Our boy's chomping at the bit, love. Please tell me the bride is ready," Donovan said, giving his wife a quick kiss when she joined them.

"I don't know... I think you appeared a bit more eager on our wedding day," Georgie said, as she examined Peter.

"With very good reason," Donovan countered. "You were making me wait until I got a ring on your finger... It's not like Peter here is anticipating an extravagant wedding nigh--"

Georgie silenced her husband with a none too gentle punch on the arm before looking to her friend.

"A week. I made him wait a week," she said in exasperation.

"You got this?"

Peter nodded, glancing again to the door as more guests filed in. He had this. This ceremony was mere formality. He had already given his heart and soul to Clemency and in turn he knew that she belonged to him. No, he was anticipating something far more than a simple exchanging of vows... something his little minx had managed to keep secret up until today...

Then suddenly she was there in the doorway. His mind registered a change in the music as she began to walk, or maybe amble was a more apt description, down the aisle. He smiled at her encouragingly when she suddenly paused mid-stride, her hand grasping her back. She waved him off though when he took a step in her direction and after a moment, she continued shuffling her way toward him. When she reached his side, he couldn't help but gather her close, bending to press his lips to hers. They parted soon after her shudder of delight, when the register cleared his throat. They turned to him, ignoring the tittering audience behind them.

"We are here today to celebrate one of life's finest moments as we join this man and this woman together in vows of marriage," the man began before addressing Peter. "Please repeat after me. I Peter Alistair Bennett, take the," there was a pause and Peter found himself holding his breath as he watched the man's eyes widen before he continued on. "Take the, CalliopeJane Clemency Oliver to be my wife..."

Peter found himself facing the fierce gaze of the woman he loved and forced his features to remain impassive as he took up the challenge he saw in her eyes.

"I Peter Alistair Bennett, take the, Clemency Oliver to be my wife..."

The remainder of the ceremony was a blur. When they were finally declared man and wife, Peter swooped down to claim Clemency's lips once again.

"Callio--" he began once they had parted, halting at the feral growl she launched in his direction.

"You lost the bet. You owe me a hundred pounds," she said

with a gasp and he reached for her as she doubled over. "But for now, get me to the hospital. My water just broke."

AFTERWORD

Clemency's story is fictional. I need to begin by stressing that. However, there are parts of it that are true to life. The *Tempest* novel and it's characters described in *Begin Anew* exist. It was my first novel.

Tempest began as a New Year's Resolution challenge. Write a 50,000 word book in a year. By that March it was complete, the first draft totalling well over 120,000 words.

I loved my creation, but saw no way of taking it further. It had a 'happily ever after' ending and there was no plausible reason for a sequel, let alone a series. That's when the daydreams began...

What if *Tempest* were optioned for a film? What if my life got turned upside down? That's how Clemency's story got started. Again I need to stress that this is where the world of fiction took over. I love my husband, he is nothing like that prick, Elliott.

However, Clemency gave me something *Tempest* could not, an opening to create a series. Actually, I should clarify and say that Georgie offered this opportunity. While a prequel story of her and Donovan's first courtship is still percolating, I'm happy to announce that her daughter, Frankie's story is complete and awaiting editing.

Ever wonder how Frankie handled being thrust into the lead

role of *Tempest*? And what was up with the tension between her and Colin Fletcher? Stay tuned for *Standing on the Precipice*, due out later this year.